MINOR PROPHETS

ALSO BY JIMMY CAJOLEAS

The Good Demon

MINOR PROPHETS

Jimmy Cajoleas

AMULET BOOKS
NEW YORK

Library of Congress Cataloging-in-Publication Data

Names: Cajoleas, Jimmy, author.
Title: Minor prophets / by Jimmy Cajoleas.
Description: New York, NY : Amulet Books, an imprint of Abrams, 2019. | Summary: After their mother's death, Lee and his sister escape their horrible stepfather by fleeing to their grandmother's farm, where Lee hopes to discover the truth behind his haunting visions.
Identifiers: LCCN 2019010422 | ISBN 9781419739040 (hardback)
Subjects: | CYAC: Visions—Fiction. | Cults—Fiction. | Brothers and sisters—Fiction. | Family life—Fiction.
Classification: LCC PZ7.1.C265 Mi 2019 | DDC [Fic]—dc23

Text copyright © 2019 Jimmy Cajoleas
Illustrations copyright © 2019 Jaya Miceli

Book design by Siobhán Gallagher

Printed and bound in U.S.A.
10 9 8 7 6 5 4 3 2 1

Amulet Books are available at special discounts when purchased in quantity for premiums and promotions as well as fundraising or educational use. Special editions can also be created to specification. For details, contact specialsales@abramsbooks.com or the address below.

Amulet Books® is a registered trademark of Harry N. Abrams, Inc.

ABRAMS The Art of Books
195 Broadway, New York, NY 10007
abramsbooks.com

"With Dreams upon my bed thou scarest me &
affrightest me with Visions"
—William Blake

THE NIGHT MOM DIED I HAD A VISION.

I was half drowsing in my bed, my headphones cranked, watching the ceiling fan swirl. It was probably four in the morning, and I couldn't sleep. I could never sleep. I'd read until two thirty, when my eyes had started burning, and I'd shut all the lights off, turned the music up, and prayed for a sleep miracle, but that miracle just wasn't coming. I was in the middle of that kind of gray state between waking and dreaming, and I got this strange feeling like I was being watched, like I wasn't alone in the room anymore.

I looked toward my window.

A man's face was there, grizzled and wild-eyed, staring into my bedroom. It was like I was paralyzed, like I couldn't move at all, not even to scream. Because I knew this man, and I knew he wasn't real, that he only came in my visions. I called him the Hobo, and when I saw him he was always watching me, his eyes bloodshot, his beard ragged, his face pressed against the glass, like any moment he would smash his face through and come for me. He was a bad omen, a promise of awful things to come.

I felt the terror grip my chest, the horrible tingling in my arms and legs and face that meant the rest of the vision was coming, that meant the world was about to split in half and reveal itself to me.

In a flash, I saw it all.

Mom's car swerving through the night. The right front tire rattling weirdly, shaking itself free, rolling off toward the highway median. Mom's car jerking and sparking, yanking itself from the road, slamming into a tree. The car crumpling, now half a car, the hood smashed skyward, tree limbs gouging the windshield. The stillness after the collision. Smoke and the smell of burnt tires.

Mom's bare bloody arm, limp, dangling out the window.

I saw other things too.

A sunset glimmering over a lightning-split tree, two gray clouds like watchful eyes in the distant sky.

A blank gravestone, fireflies floating around it glowing holy in the nighttime.

A red cloud of hummingbirds flitting wild over a field, a whirlwind of color and fire.

A woman who looked like Mom but older, gray-haired with eyes that sparkled like the stars.

An owl, wings spread wide like a crucifix, perched on top of a barn.

Horace's Trans Am in the garage. My sister, Murphy, sad in a black dress searching the trunk as if some kind of secret hid inside.

When I came to, I was screaming.

I flicked my lamp on, and the room was empty. No man was at my window, no hummingbirds anywhere.

I know what you're thinking. I'd just finally fallen asleep and had some kind of nightmare. But I told you already: It wasn't a dream, not some random assemblage of the day's events thrown together haphazardly in the back of my mind, not a weird brain film collage that meant absolutely fucking zilch.

It was a vision.

A warning, a premonition.

I had to hurry. I scrambled out of my bedroom and onto the stairs to find my stepdad, Horace, screaming at Mom in the foyer below.

I saw Mom look back at him, her eyes fierce and burning. She wore jeans and a plaid button-down and combat boots, and her long blond hair was wild and tangled, like she'd been fighting in her sleep.

"Just you goddamn wait a minute," he hollered.

I hated Horace. I hated Horace more than I'd ever hated anyone in my life.

"This ends now," said Mom. "I'm going, and don't you fucking try and stop me."

Mom left, slamming the door shut. I ran down the stairs and outside, but she was already in her car, swerving out of the driveway. I chased her down the street in the hot starlit summer night, waving at her, screaming, begging her not to leave, until her headlights disappeared around a corner.

My sister, Murphy, came walking outside, half awake and worried.

"What's wrong?" she said.

I yanked her out of the way as Horace's Trans Am came roaring past us, cutting over the neighbor's lawn, laying black tread marks all over our street.

Please, I prayed, *please let this one be a false vision. A lie, like so many of the others.* Even though I knew it wasn't. I could feel in my bones that this one was real.

"They're just fighting, Lee," said Murphy. "It's okay. She'll come home in a few hours, same as usual. Right?"

But I couldn't answer her. Because I knew that wasn't true. I knew exactly what was going to happen.

I knew Mom was never coming back.

THINGS HAD BEEN WEIRD WITH MOM THE LAST few months. She just hadn't been herself.

Like the time two weeks before when I went downstairs for a midnight snack and found Mom peeking out the windows and then snapping the blinds shut, like she was watching for someone. Before I could ask what she was doing, Horace swooped in and threw his arm around her, trying to coax her back into bed, them whisper-fighting the whole way.

Or the time when Mom opened our front door one afternoon and screamed. Murphy and I came running up behind her.

"What is it?" I said. Mom only pointed, her hand trembling, her eyes all bleary with tears.

It was a hummingbird, its throat ripped open, its guts splayed across our welcome mat.

"A stray cat probably did it, Mom," said Murphy. "It's just nature."

But Mom turned and ran to her bedroom, slamming the door behind her. I knew hummingbirds were Mom's favorites, but this wasn't like her, not at all. I mean, Mom was the toughest woman I'd ever known. I'd seen her take a machete and chop the head off a cottonmouth that had wandered up the gutters to our house without a second thought. She was never one to be mortified by gore.

Or strangest of all, the morning when I woke up early and found Mom staring up at the living room wall, the furniture moved away and all the photos taken down. A picture was painted on the prim white, a kind of mural, wild slashes of colors like blossoms blooming, all light and energy. It covered the whole wall, maybe six feet tall and four across—a painting of a tree, little flames hovering all around it like birds, a giant gash down the middle of it like a cave you could crawl into. It wasn't exactly a realistic painting, but it felt real, if that makes any sense. It felt real in the way my visions feel real, like you could slip into them and live forever. Realer than real—that's how Mom described her dreams sometimes, and that's what this painting felt like too.

"Mom," I said, "who did this?"

She seemed startled by me and even more so by the mural that had sprung up on our living room wall. Mom looked at her fingers, her clothes, all speckled with paint.

"Why," she said, "I suppose I did."

That tree loomed over us. There was something so famil-iar and strange about it, like maybe it had fallen out of an old memory that I didn't remember having. I realized Mom was shaking.

"We have to cover it up," she said. "Quick, before Horace and Murphy wake up."

"But this is amazing, Mom," I said. "I didn't know you could paint."

"I can't paint," she said. "Not anymore. Now help me."

We took what was left of the white and covered over every-thing as best we could.

I told Murphy about it later, and she could hardly believe me.

"That's insane," she said. "I've never seen her so much as doodle on a napkin before."

"I know," I said. "And Murphy, it was good. I mean really good."

"Why does all this worry me so much?" she said.

"I don't know," I said, "but it worries me too."

See, none of this made any sense if you knew our mother.

Mom was a badass, a chain-smoker who had never attended school a day in her life but could fix a flat and clean a gun with equal precision. She was gruff and rude and a total genius. Mom had homeschooled us since we were kids. She taught us basic self-defense as toddlers, and she trained Murphy in Brazilian jiujitsu until Murphy accidentally broke Mom's arm in the sixth grade while performing a particularly vicious reversal. I have never seen our mother prouder. She even had Murphy sign the cast first in her shaky looping scrawl.

I guess maybe all the weirdness started when Mom married our stepdad, Horace, about a year back. Yeah, that was definitely the first time I started to worry about her.

Because Horace was a hard man. Six-foot-seven, 250 pounds of unsmiling cruelty. I would watch him smoke cigarettes while he did dumbbell lifts in the garage, his mostly bald head shimmering, his one last lock of hair dangling down his forehead in a swoosh. We called it "the unicorn" when he wasn't around. That was because if we had mocked his desperate hairstyle in front of him, he would have thrown us down the stairs. Not that Horace ever actually laid a hand on us. He never needed to.

For example, one night three months before he married Mom, Murphy stayed out well into the night doing god knows what with god knows who, and she did not return until three A.M., exactly six hours after her curfew.

Did Horace scream at her? No.

Did Horace whip her? No.

Did Horace ground her? No.

Did Horace take Murphy's 1967 Fender Telecaster and hurl it through her window, shattering glass onto the driveway, the two-story drop snapping the neck of the twelve-hundred-dollar vintage instrument into pieces?

Yes, that's exactly what Horace did. As our mother watched on, curiously silent.

As if in awe.

So marrying Horace was Mom's first out-of-character act. We never thought she would get married, never even considered it. At first—for six months or so—she was happier than I'd ever seen her before. I mean, Mom positively giggled walking around arm in arm with the asshole, and that was a welcome sight. I don't know if you can understand this, but when you've seen your mom bounce from guy to guy your whole life, always disappointed, always somehow let down that yet another fellow couldn't measure up, it's a real joy to see her with someone she actually likes, someone she seems to respect. And he was good to her—he really was, at first. Things seemed like they were going to be okay. We even sold our janky old bungalow and bought a newer, nicer (but way more boring) two-story borderline McMansion, because that's what Horace wanted, and we all moved in together. But each day, as Mom became less and less recognizable as the strong, brilliant, estimable single mother who had raised us, Murphy and I became more and more worried. Mom blew us off, saying she wasn't feeling well and she had a headache and could we please leave her alone. We pleaded our case to

Horace, who told us—and I quote—to "mind your own fucking goddamn business."

"She's our mother," Murphy said, "so it is our own fucking goddamn business."

At which point Horace merely pointed his finger at her and held it there, one inch from Murphy's face.

I waited for her to bite it. I hoped she would snap it clean off at the knuckle.

But such was Horace's power—the fierce, unblinking stare, the menace of his outstretched pointer finger, the lit cigarette smoking (indoors, a thing that would have been inconceivable in our house before)—that it cowed even Murphy. She shrank from him, trembling.

For the life of me, I could not understand what Mom saw in the guy. And I guessed now I'd never know.

THE DAY OF THE FUNERAL WAS GRAY, THREAT-
ening rain, the sky all rumbles and groans. No one came to the
service except a few kindhearted busybodies and some old lady
named Shondra that nobody knew. None of Murphy's cool
friends showed, and I didn't have any friends. I figured at least
a few of Mom's exes would be there—Mom had more than
enough to pack the place—but turns out jilted ex-boyfriends
don't show up to funerals. Not even our grandmother came—
our mother's own mother. It would have been nice to have met
her for the first time. After all, this was the woman who had paid
for everything in our lives—even down to our old house, the
one we had before we moved in with Horace—through this
bank trust she had set up for us. I had always wondered about
her, begged Mom to let us know her, to go and see her sometime. But Mom just went grim and refused, same as always. I
wondered if Grandma even knew that Mom had died.

Horace kept his distance from us. He hadn't said a word to us all day—not when we ate breakfast together (stale Cheerios in skim milk), not when he drove us to the funeral, not even at the visitation as we stood next to our mother's mannequin-looking body in the casket. I mean, what they had done to her was shameful. She looked fake, like some kind of human Barbie doll, her cheeks caked with this awful makeup, a contented smile on her lips, the sort of placid look I never saw on Mom's face when she was alive.

At the service nobody spoke except the preacher, and he didn't have a clue who Mom was. It was insulting, him droning on about being in a better place, about God forgiving, about all of us meeting again in the hereafter. What fucking hereafter? Mom had never believed in God or the afterlife or anything except the moment, the *right now* of everything. And right now Mom was dead—a corpse, emptied-out and embalmed, a husk. There was nothing left of my mom in that casket or maybe anywhere else. The whole thing felt like a mockery.

I was so grateful for Murphy, that I didn't have to do all this alone. I sat there bawling my eyes out, watching Murphy try not to cry, her back unnaturally straight in that black dress of hers, gripping the pew all white-knuckled, holding everything in. I wished I could get her to just let go for a minute, but that wasn't the kind of thing Murphy did. I was the weepy sibling, something Murphy managed to never give me any hell about. Murphy was good like that.

I couldn't figure out why Horace was acting so weird. I mean, he wasn't ever a warm person, but you could at least expect fury or anger from him, some bit of rage under the surface. But that day he just seemed preoccupied, like something else was on his mind. It was strange, you know?

At the gravesite, which was unbearable, by the way—a gray-grassed plot of nothing, little tombstones with their humped backs slouching around us, Mom's coffin up on this mechanical lowering device, a little blue tarp slung up to keep out the rain—Horace kept looking over his shoulder, scanning the trees for somebody, like he was afraid of being watched. I couldn't figure out what he was doing or what he was looking for.

The time came for us to sprinkle soil on the casket. Horace was supposed to go first, but he wasn't paying attention, and the preacher had to give him a nudge. Then he just walked up to the casket, tossed some dirt on it, and stormed off like he had something better to do.

We found him sitting in the Trans Am, honking at us. Our mother was dead, and the asshole was honking at us. He rolled the window down and stuck his head out of the car.

"Move your asses," he said.

They were the first words he had spoken to us all day.

After the funeral, Murphy and I hung out in the garage, still in our nice black clothes, while Murphy smoked. I was shell-shocked and numb, all cried out. I kept trying to write a funeral poem for Mom the way Auden had written one for Yeats. "Mad Ireland hurt you into poetry" and all that, but nothing was coming, nothing seemed right. I couldn't stop thinking about my vision: Mom's car sliding wheelless over the pavement at a hundred miles per hour. The police told us she hadn't felt anything, that she'd died instantly. I sure hoped so. And what an awful thing to hope, you know? It made no sense that the best thing you could ask for in life was an instant, painless death. I mean, what did that say about the world, about living in it? How easily, how quickly an entire life—the whole universe of a person—could just vanish forever. What was to become of us, the ones left behind? Who was going to take care of us? Horace? Are you kidding me?

Murphy stomped out her cigarette, walked inside the house for a minute, and came back with a pair of keys.

"What are those for?" I said.

"It's time we check out this trunk situation," she said.

"What are you talking about?"

"Well, you saw a bunch of weird shit in your vision, right?" she said. "One of those things was me in this goddamn dress opening Horace's trunk. Since it's going to happen anyway, I figure we might as well get to it."

"You really want to do that?" I said. "I mean, it wasn't a happy vision. And besides, my visions don't always come true. You remember all the times I've been wrong."

Murphy was the only person I still told my visions to, the only person who ever listened and gave a shit. But Murphy knew as well as I did that for each one of my visions that came true—each one that happened more or less how I'd foreseen it—I had another that fell way off the mark or flat-out didn't make sense at all. That was just the way with visions, and it was a tricky business to count on them.

Murphy smiled at me a little sadly.

"Well, you've been right so far this time," she said. "I might as well check."

Murphy walked over to Horace's car. She stuck the keys in the trunk and popped it.

"Please don't," I said. "It's not worth it. Horace will kill us."

"There's something in here," she said. "Look."

I peeked over her shoulder as Murphy rummaged around the lining of the trunk, moving aside a bunch of clutter and a particularly heavy-looking tire iron, then lifted the cover off of a secret compartment. Inside were a bunch of manila file folders and a ziplock bag full of handwritten letters.

"I knew it," she said.

Murphy went for the folders, and I snatched up the ziplock bag. I pulled one letter out of the bag and read.

Please just let me see them, Jenny. Please bring them to me just once. You know I can't bear to leave the Farm. I can't travel. I just want to see my grandchildren once before it's too late.

Holy shit. These letters were from Grandma, and there must have been hundreds of them. Why didn't Mom ever tell us about them? More importantly, why were they in Horace's trunk? Was it because he was afraid we'd go snooping through Mom's things after the funeral and find them? Was he trying to keep us from contacting our grandmother for some reason? I mean, I understood that she and Mom didn't get along, but what did Horace have to do with it?

"Uhh, Lee?" said Murphy. "Look at this."

She held up a stack of pages, and I read over her shoulder. It was a bunch of legal documents, all signed and notarized. Murphy flipped through them. They seemed to be adoption papers.

Our adoption papers.

"What the hell is this?" I said.

They didn't have anything to do with Mom or our birth. They were newer than that, dated not more than a month ago. Murphy flipped to two typed, identical statements, one for each of us, that read, "I hereby consent to my formal, legal adoption by Horace Dunluth Powell III," complete with our signatures. Forged, of course. There was no way in hell either one of us would ever consent to be adopted by that asshole.

"Oh my god," she said. "Horace adopted us."

"Why would he do that?" I said. "He hates us."

"The trust from our grandmother," she said.

The garage got quiet then, eerie. I wondered about all the bugs and spiders hidden in the corners of this place, tucked away in boxes, lingering there, silent and listening, waiting to hear what we would do next. It felt like the moment before one of my visions came, when the world went sharp and strange, when I felt the electricity of the whole earth in my fingertips.

"In your vision, you said Mom's wheel fell off, right?" said Murphy. "Like it had been loosened or something?"

"Yes."

I looked back and forth between the tire iron and the adoption papers. We were both thinking it, but only Murphy was brave enough to ask.

"Does that mean Horace killed our mom?" said Murphy. "So he could have all the money to himself?"

That's when I realized Horace was standing right behind us.

"The fuck do you kids think you're doing?" he snarled.

Murphy whipped Horace's tire iron from the trunk and whacked him across the skull with it. There he lay, facedown on the floor, a red, swelling, dripping welt on his bald head.

"What do we do now?" I said.

Murphy looked up at me, eyes all sad and scared and full of wonder. "Run, I guess."

I know what you're thinking. If you found a folder full of forged adoption documents in your shitty stepfather's trunk, not to mention the tire iron he probably used to sabotage your mom's car, why wouldn't you go straight to the sheriff with it?

Well, I'll tell you: It's hard to report your stepfather to the county sheriff when the county sheriff is your stepfather.

We had no choice. We ran.

WE TOOK HORACE'S TRANS AM, THE ONLY non-government-issue vehicle on the premises. We made it about thirty miles out of town before Murphy finally spoke up.

"Shit," said Murphy. "I forgot my phone. I must have left it back in the garage. And goddammit, I got blood on me."

It was true. It looked thick and scabby against the black of her dress. I handed her a tissue out of my left pocket, and she dabbed at it, but the stain was there for good.

"I hate this dress," she said, her eyes watering. "I hate funerals."

"Me too," I said.

I kept the car steady on the highway, trying not to cry, the sunset like a gaping wound up in the sky.

"Oh god," she said. "What did I do?"

"You did something smart, that's what you did," I said. "You saved both of our hides."

"But what happens now? You have another vision or something? The cosmos tells us where to go next?"

"You remember how I saw Mom in my vision that night, but an older version of her? I think maybe that was Grandma. I think we're supposed to go and find her."

"Are you kidding me? She didn't even come to the funeral."

"But you saw all the letters she wrote, right? Grandma's been trying to talk to us forever. She has to take us in now. We need her."

We'd never been to Grandma's before, of course, but Mom had sometimes talked about the house where she grew up in Benign, Louisiana, this placed called "the Farm." None of the letters I had seen had a return address on them, but I was pretty sure Grandma still lived there.

"I know it isn't the best plan," I said, "but do you have a better one?"

"Will Grandma even want to see us?" said Murphy.

"Judging from those letters, definitely," I said. "Besides, she set up that trust for us, didn't she? We're her family, Murphy, and that means something in this world. At least it should. We'll hole up with her until we figure something out. And we need an adult to protect us from Horace, since for all legal purposes he's our father now."

"Fuck that," said Murphy.

"That's what I was thinking," I said.

"A'ight," said Murphy. "To Grandmother's house we go."

I REMEMBER THE FIRST VISION I EVER HAD. IT'S
maybe my oldest memory.

I was around five years old, sitting on the floor of our old
house, nestled in that deep white carpet, playing with a yellow
Tonka truck. *Vroom-vroom*, squealy breaks, that kind of thing.
Regular kid stuff. When this cat came slinking across the den
floor. Which was a big deal, because Mom was allergic to cats.
Like, majorly allergic. Her eyes would swell shut, and her throat
would close, and she would go around wheezing and snotting
for days. So there was no reason a cat should have been in our
house. It was probably a good idea for me to go chase it out.

But then I realized it wasn't a normal cat. Not even kind of.

See, this cat was rainbow-colored, glowing stripes all up
and down its body. It shimmered like fish scales in the sun. The
cat pawed its way across the room as I laughed and clapped
my hands.

"Mom, look!" I hollered. "Come see!"

I was pointing at it and jumping up and down while the rainbow kitty rubbed and meowed around the room.

"What is it, Lee?" said Mom, running in like the house was on fire.

"Look at the pretty cat!" I yelled, or something equally five-year-old-ish. "Look how pretty!"

"What cat?" said Mom.

"That one," I said, "right there!" I pointed at the rainbow cat.

But Mom wasn't so enthusiastic. Instead she had this strange, lip-bitey look on her face.

"Lee, there's no cat here."

"Yes, there is," I said, and I turned back to look at the cat. Only it wasn't a kitty anymore. It had become a tiger, all rainbow-striped and fierce, at least six feet long. It opened its mouth at me, its fangs glistening white in the fluorescents.

Then it roared.

I fell over backward, screaming, covering my ears, sure I was about to get eaten, sure that this was the end of me already.

Mom ran over and yanked me up into her arms.

"Look, Lee," she said. "Look! There's nothing there."

And there wasn't, not anymore.

"But I saw it," I said, all tears and wailing. "I saw it with my own eyes."

I'll never forget the look she gave me then, this miserable droop in her face.

Mom set me down on the ground and grabbed me by the cheeks and looked into my eyes. "Just because you see something, that doesn't mean it's really there. Never forget that."

"But Mom," I said.

"If you see something that shouldn't be there," she said, "you just ignore it, okay? Don't tell me about it. Don't tell anyone about it. Just close your eyes until it goes away. Got it?"

"The cat was real!"

"Lee," said Mom, "listen to me. You don't want people thinking you're crazy, do you? You know what they do to people who see things that aren't there?"

I didn't.

"They lock them up," she said. "In special hospitals. For the rest of their lives. And no one ever gets to come visit them, and they never see their families again, and they're alone forever. You don't want that to happen to you, do you?"

I shook my head.

"Good," said Mom. "Then we'll keep these little hallucinations to ourselves, won't we?"

I nodded at her.

But it wasn't as easy as all that. It was hard to ignore it when reality broke, when it was like time snapped in half and some new world would wash over me like a flood. Remember, these were visions, not simple hallucinations. They weren't just little images conjured up by my mind or chemicals or drugs or something. They had an extra dimension to them. They had *heft*, is what I'm saying.

A real vision refuses to be ignored.

And in that case, the vision came true. Not a week later an orange tabby cat showed up on our doorstep, mewling something awful. It had just been in a fight, you could tell—it was all mangled and bloody, like a dog had gotten to it—and I was pretty sure it was pregnant. The cat limped around, its back left paw curled up under its body, moaning that horrible sound hurt cats make. I opened the door and let it in, even though I knew Mom would be furious. Because something in me knew that this was the cat from my vision, more or less, and that this cat needed me.

I picked up the bloody, wounded thing, and she went slack and quiet in my arms, which seemed like a miracle to me. And I demanded that Mom take us to the vet. I told her I'd hold the cat the whole way, that she wouldn't even have to touch the thing, just could we please help this poor creature?

Mom agreed, and we went to the vet. The cat lived, and so did all the kittens. Of course Mom wouldn't let me keep any of them. Her eyes were already swelling shut just from having the cat so close to her in the car. We ended up leaving them all at a shelter. I cried and cried, but Mom wouldn't relent.

"But it was supposed to be my cat," I said. "Remember? I saw it last week."

"I thought you said that was a *rainbow* cat," said Mom, smirking at me. "These were just normal little kittens, as far as I could tell. The whole thing was just a coincidence. Besides, it all worked out just fine, so let's drop it, okay?"

But it wasn't so easy for me. The older I got, the more intense the visions became and the fiercer I was punished for telling Mom about them.

Sometimes, though, I *had* to tell her about them. There just wasn't any other choice. I mean, it's one thing to keep quiet about a rainbow cat in your living room. It's something else to ignore your own doomed future flashing before your eyes.

Like once when we were riding in the car and I had a vision of the three of us dead and mangled after our car had struck a deer. I'd seen the whole thing—the deer running in front of us, the Jeep flipping, the death of each and every one of us. Now I was sitting in the passenger seat, Murphy in the back, begging Mom to be careful, that we would all die if she didn't stop the car right then.

"What have I told you about these goddamn daydreams of yours?" said Mom.

"But they aren't daydreams, I swear!" I said.

Mom turned to me and pointed her finger right in my face. "I have just about had it with you."

That's when the deer leapt into the road.

It was a big one, maybe an eight-point, and it raised its head all regally, the antlers like a woodland crown, its eyes gone green in the headlights. It looked like a forest spirit, like some kind of ancient lord of the woods come out to meet us. Fate is what it looked like.

"Mom!" I screamed.

She slammed on the brakes, yanking the wheel hard.

We spun, skidding across the cold, wet road. We clipped the deer, the antlers smashing into the hood of the car. We hit it so hard the car flew the other way, slamming into the metal barrier on the side of the road.

The airbags deployed, breaking Mom's nose. Mine hit me too, but it didn't hurt much.

Murphy got whiplash.

We stood on the side of the road then, huddled together, the three of us, waiting for the ambulance. Shattered glass was all over the highway, reflecting the moonlight like diamonds. The deer's head had been ripped clean off, a long trail of blood and gore slathered on the pavement between the body and head like a grotesque stretched neck. Its antlers were snapped off, gouged into the hood of the car like claws.

I was crying. I said, "I told you, Mom. I told you there was a deer in the road."

Mom looked down at me, her face all busted and bruised.

"What you saw was wrong, Lee," she said. "We didn't die, not Murphy or me or you. Whatever you saw, it wasn't the truth."

"But I saw the deer coming," I said.

Mom's eyes went fierce. "Yeah, you saw the deer," she said. "But everything you saw after that—the car flipping, us dying— all of that was a lie. That's why you can't believe in visions, not yours or anybody else's. They never tell the whole truth."

How could Mom know something like that? But by then the ambulance had arrived, all lights and sirens, and we had questions to answer, and they loaded Murphy and Mom onto stretchers, and we had to go to the hospital.

Three times I asked Mom what she meant that night.

Three times I was punished for it. The last time, Mom locked me in my room for a whole day and night, only letting me out when I had to pee.

So I gave up. And I almost never mentioned my visions to Mom again.

At least not directly.

A FEW HOURS LATER MURPHY AND I STOPPED
at a gas station. I didn't have any idea where Benign, Louisiana,
was, and my phone reception was getting spotty. So while Murphy pumped gas, I went inside to look at a map.

I have this thing where I love gas stations. They're like
shitty airports, you know? All these people from probably-
not-that-far-away places converging to eat junk food and get
gas and use the bathroom. I love watching them file in and
out and wait in line—cops and lawyers and truck drivers and
personal assistants. Everywhere sells the same boring crap, the
same ironic T-shirts, the same Coke Icees and Gatorades and
burnt coffee. Gas stations are some of the only places where we
all belong.

And yet there's something different about each one, something unique. Once in Arkansas I found a gas station with
a boar's head mounted in the bathroom, giant tusks ready to

gore. In another one I saw in Pensacola, they had a functional bait shop, minnows darting around Styrofoam coolers and cages of scritching crickets all over the place.

This one had something special too. In the middle of the dirty tile floor was a foldout table full of pickled eggs. These were home-canned in mason jars, swirling with green liquid like science experiments. I wondered who had made them, if it was all some old lady's handiwork. I could imagine her then, this bent-backed woman with crazy gray hair dropping eggs into the brine like a weird witch casting spells. I could see her beleaguered husband on the couch, the TV blasting COPS while their beautiful daughter smoked cigarettes on the roof, watching the sunset. I could picture this old woman wandering the woods outside her house, snatching up eggs out of nests, praying for her daughter to turn into a bird and fly away, wishing her husband's bones would dissolve and he'd sag into a fleshy pile of guts she could just scoop up and dump in the trash.

I bet all those eggs tasted bitter. I bet they tasted like captivity, like the desire for freedom.

I found Benign on a foldout road map. It was only a few hours away, tucked off in northwest Louisiana. I bet the town was so small it barely merited the dot on the map. We should be there by evening, I figured.

Back in the car, Murphy and I cruised the Trans Am easy, sixty miles per hour on the dot. We weren't about to risk getting pulled over, this being a sort-of-stolen car and all. Outside there was nothing but trees and billboards and the occasional Arby's sprouting ugly out of the landscape, some abandoned wreck of a shop or half-hearted strip mall nearly overtaken by kudzu. I turned on the radio to a classical station that was half-buried in static. It seemed appropriate for the landscape—the best intentions of humanity being swallowed whole.

"Man, I hate classical music," said Murphy. "It's nothing but earhole torture."

So I shut it off.

In the silence I kept thinking about our grandmother, who we were about to meet. I was a little nervous.

Mom had never told us much about her childhood. We knew she had grown up in a place she called "the Farm" in the backwoods of Benign, Louisiana, hunting and fishing and learning all kinds of survivalist shit from her hippie mother. We knew her father wasn't around, that he had run off when she was little. We knew that she and our grandmother had some kind of falling out, a rift that was so bad they never spoke in person again. At least not that we knew of.

Every now and again Mom had tossed out a memory. Like this one time, sitting on our old front porch, Mom sipping a beer and me reading Yeats and Murphy off somewhere exploring, a hummingbird flew right up to our porch swing. Mom didn't hardly move, that big toothy smile sliding across her face, nothing but joy, as the bright red thing flittered and darted around her. I'd never seen one up close like that before. It seemed to like Mom, circling her head and dashing away only to come right back. The bird hovered in front of her ear as if it were trying to tell her a secret. Then it was gone, so fast it seemed to have vanished. Mom fell back against the swing, laughing.

"We used to have them on the Farm," she said, a little dreamily. "I loved them so much. My mother hung feeders on all the trees in the grove, and they'd flock to us."

"How many?" I said.

"Dozens," said Mom. "Hundreds even. They would fly around and bash into each other, trying so hard to get at that nectar. It was almost dangerous to walk out into the middle of them when they were all out there. You'd get smacked or pecked or swarmed every time. Hummingbird season was my favorite time of year."

I used to love to think about that: My mom as a child, standing in the middle of a barrage of bright red flitting things, kind of like the way electrons whirled around atoms in the chemistry book Mom taught us from. I loved to think of them following her around, an impossible entourage of kinetic energy, bright as rose petals.

There was another time, when we took a weekend trip to Pensacola to swim in the ocean. In the hotel afterward, Mom again a few beers in, holding a sleeping Murphy in her lap.

"I used to love swimming," she said.

"Back at the Farm?" I said.

Mom nodded.

"I'd strip off naked—what? I was like twelve, it was fine—and I'd go flop in the lake while Mother laughed at us. We'd snatch cattails out of the ground, get dragonflies to land on our fingers, float with the long-legged frogs bounding around on lily pads, same as in a cartoon."

"Can I see it sometime?" I said. "The lake and everything?"

"Not if I can help it," said Mom.

Just like that, the conversation was over.

Like I said, Mom almost never brought up the Farm. But when she did, all the memories seemed good, impossible and lovely and ideal, as if she'd grown up in some kind of dreamworld fairyland. I wondered what had gone on between her and my grandmother that had ruined everything for her. I had a lot of questions about the Farm.

You could say I was anxious to see it for myself.

It had stopped raining now, and the sun was just beginning to cut through the clouds. We drove on, the sunlight glinting high overhead, the trees catching the light and holding it close, shimmering with it, whispering some kind of promise, or maybe a warning, as we sped closer and closer to the Farm, to whatever it was that awaited us.

THERE WAS BARELY EVEN A SIGN FOR BENIGN, Louisiana. Just a bullet-holed green thing half-dangling from a rusted metal pole. We got lost about twenty times on the way—my phone was basically useless so far out in the country—but finally we found it. Benign was all huge lots with tiny houses on them, most of which looked fallen-in and abandoned. Stray cats lounged everywhere, wise and aloof, glittery eyes watching as we drove slowly by. We stopped at the first nonresidential building we could find, a sort of hybrid gas station, post office, and lunch counter. Two old men sat at picnic tables in the shade, sipping something out of Styrofoam cups. A deep-tanned woman with a poofy gray ponytail sucked a cigarette and glared at me out of the corner of her eye.

"You listen up, Benny," said one of the men, a wild fringe of white hair spilling out from under his cap. "All folks ever do is talk, talk, talk about time. Time this and time that. Times change, ain't it a shame, time don't change fast enough. Dammit, Benny, I'm sick of hearing about time."

"Hi there," said Murphy.

The two men looked up at us as if noticing us for the first time.

"We're trying to find Mena Sanford's place," I said.

"Y'all from Hollywood?" said the guy with the white hair.

"Mississippi," I said. "Why?"

"Because y'all are dressed like some fancy California drug types is all," he said. "Don't be needing that mess in our community. First come the Hollywood folks, then comes the crack cocaine."

"We were at a funeral," said Murphy.

"Les, I tell you, when you're right, you're right," said the other man, who must have been Benny. "Can't trust Hollywood types. Money, money, money, that's all they want. Don't give a hoot for the soul. Never have."

"We were at *our mother's* funeral," said Murphy. "Our mother just died. We're not from Hollywood."

Les looked us up and down, a peculiar squint on his face.

"My condolences," he said. "Never an easy thing, losing a momma, though everybody's got to do it sooner or later." He coughed. "Now what was I saying?"

"You were talking about time, as I recall," said Benny.

"Sure, sure," said Les. "Time. You ready?" He took a big puff of his cigar and blew the smoke out slow, for emphasis. "Time is just a dot."

"A dot?" said Benny.

"Yes, sir," said Les. "A dot. As in, it all already happened."

"All of it?" said Benny.

"Everything. The whole history of the world." He snapped his fingers. "Boom. Over and done with it. It all already happened, and we're just now getting around to it."

Benny snorted.

"That's bullshit," he said. "It ain't a dot, Les. It's a loop."

"A loop, you say?" said Les.

"Yeah, a loop. You know, the same things happening over and over again. Nothing ever really changes."

This was useless. I guessed we'd just have to drive around until we found the Farm ourselves. I turned to head back to the car when the lady with the ponytail called out to me.

"What do you kids want with Mena, anyhow?" she said. "Don't nobody go out to the Farm anymore, not these days."

"She's our grandmother," I said. "We just want to see her."

The woman squinted at us for a minute. Then she flicked her cigarette on the pavement and toed it out, a second cigarette somehow already in her hand. She lit it and took a long deep breath, held the smoke in, and squinted at us again.

"Grandkids, huh?" She shook her head. "Well, that figures, doesn't it."

"What figures?" I said.

"That Jenny's dead."

The way the woman spoke that sentence made it seem final to me somehow. It was like a big black crow of sadness came and perched on my shoulder right then and there.

It was true. Mom was dead, and she always would be. That was the end of it. In that moment, the sun burning down on us, the light tossing shadows everywhere, it felt like I was on the fringe of the world, the very teetering edge.

"Farm's about a mile up yonder," the woman said. "Nothing but dirt roads, I'm sorry to say. They're gonna do a number on that vehicle of yours."

"Who gives a shit?" said Murphy. "It's our stepdad's."

"Well, that I certainly do understand," said the woman. "Hated my stepdads, both of them in their turn. Could have danced at their funerals." She took a long drag of her cigarette. "Good luck, kids. Hope you find what you're looking for."

"You too," I said, and she smiled.

We turned off the pavement and onto a gravel road, bumping and snaking along, the trees growing thicker around us, Spanish moss hanging down, all of nature doing its damnedest to capture the light. We drove down a dirt road to a padlocked metal gate that was rusted and chained, big metal KEEP OUT signs hanging all over it.

"So maybe this isn't a great idea," I said.

"Too late now," said Murphy.

Murphy hopped out of the car and went to work on the gate. Turned out it wasn't locked, the gate just had a rusty metal chain draped over it to look like it was.

"See?" she said. "Grandma's not even trying to keep people out, not really. It's just for show."

The gate swung wide open, and we bounced and bucked down the pockmarked dirt and through the trees. It had been ages since I'd been so far into the country, and I remembered how much I loved it. I'm not really a nature kid, but it's hard to love poetry and not get a rush from all the green light hazing around you, from the flitter and dart of birds, the brown scurrying squirrels, the idea that there's all this life everywhere and you're just a small part of it. I guess what I mean is, being in the woods is kind of like staring up at the stars. You realize you aren't so important, that you're just one of a billion different things out there, and this world wasn't really made for you. At least not you alone. And there's something to that. A whole heap of poems have sprung up from that very idea.

We had dawdled so long trying to find the place that the sun was on its way to setting, and it burned mean and orange over the treetops, a far-off fire casting its glow on us. It felt like we were departing the real world for this sunburnt dream forest that clutched all the light deep in its leaves. I don't know what I'm trying to say except that it felt like we were leaving what we knew and traveling on into something else, something different. I felt a shiver go right through me. Murphy just stared wide-eyed out the window.

The trees broke, and before us stood a house, old and columned with flaky white paint, three stories high, gold-cast from the setting sun—a kind of glimmering angel of a house, each of its windows like the black eyes of cherubim in the Bible, dozens of them, all fixed on us bouncing down the rutted driveway. I felt like how I felt in church the few times Mom ever let me go, when I looked up at the wounded wooden Christ dangling up there, all carved agony and red-paint blood, and it was like He could see me, like those wooden eyes were flesh and that painted blood became real, and all that pain was actual pain, was my pain, and that hunk of wood was Christ alive and watching me. It was just like that, driving up to that house—it seemed alive and watching, each of its black eyes fixed on us, the secrets of death and life and salvation hidden inside.

We pulled to a stop next to a gray Chevy truck that looked like it was from the 1980s, and I cut the engine, and there we were at the Farm. I realized Murphy was holding her breath, same as you do in tunnels or while passing graveyards.

"What are you doing, Murphy?"

She shrugged. "It seemed like something important was happening, something superstitious. I didn't want to jinx us, so I held my breath."

"But you don't believe in luck," I said.

"I know," she said. "But it can't hurt any."

I saw a woman peeking out at us from one of the windows, and then the front door opened and there she stood: a slim, slight lady with long gray hair and a faded yellow dress. It was like seeing a ghost right there, a ghost from our future, one that should have come to haunt us in our own old age. Because there stood our mom. I mean, the exact spitting image of her, only aged twenty years or so—older than Mom would ever be—wringing her hands on the porch, big tears in her eyes, like this was the day she'd been expecting, dreading, for years and years and years. She looked exactly as I'd seen her in my vision.

"Holy shit," said Murphy.

"I know," I said. "It's her. It's Mom too, what she would have looked like." I turned to Murphy. "And it's you. It's you in fifty years, seeing as you look so much like Mom already."

Murphy's mouth hung open, dumb and wide. I didn't blame her any. Must be weird looking right into your future like that.

We stepped out of the car and onto the gravel.

"Grandma?" I said.

The woman nodded. Then she ran down the stairs and over to us and threw her arms around us, pulling us into a hug the likes of which we'd never gotten, a squeeze so tight I thought it would crush me for a minute, until Grandma started crying, and Murphy started crying, and then so did I. I couldn't stop. None of us did for a full minute there. We just knelt down in the gravel, and it was like we were repenting, like we were all saying sorry to each other for never having been around before, and now it was all going to be okay because we were becoming a family in that moment, being fused into one by this great weeping hug from a woman stronger than she looked.

And I liked that. I liked it a whole hell of a lot.

"Come on, kids," said our grandma, wiping the tears from her face. "Come on inside. We have much to talk about. But that can wait until after dinner. It can all wait. Because I have my family back now. My beautiful family has returned to the Farm, and I've never been happier in all the days of my life."

We followed Grandma inside the house, the big front door slamming shut behind me like a closed book.

OVER THE YEARS I FOUND OTHER WAYS TO heed my visions without having to tell Mom about them. I learned to deal with them in my own way, to protect my family as best as I could. God, I wished I knew why I had them. I wished I knew what their purpose was, or, if it was just a curse, why I had been cursed like this.

As I got older, I started researching other people who saw visions, other mystics around the world, people like Julian of Norwich and Margery Kempe and Hildegard von Bingen, Saint John and Ezekiel and Jonah and Daniel, Nostradamus, Aleister Crowley, anybody I could find.

That's part of how I got into poetry. Turned out poetry was a place where it was okay to talk about your visions. If you had visions and wrote poetry, nobody thought you were crazy or horrible—they thought you were a genius.

The first time I read William Blake, it was a revelation. I'll never forget flipping open a big full-color copy of *The Book of*

Urizen I got at the library, gazing upon all those illuminated wild men and women and skeletons and swirling columns of fire, holy books and angels. It was like seeing into my own mind, like somebody had taken my biggest shame and made something beautiful out of it.

I even tried to write my own poems sometimes, same as my heroes had.

Problem was, my poems sucked. I mean, they were total shit.

Every time I took the fury and terror of my visions—the burning gorgeous reality of them, the way they felt and smelled and tasted to me, the electric jolt in my bones before a big one—it all just came out flat and dull on the paper, toothless. William Blake was a prophet, you know? An honest-to-god seer, and he wrote his verses with lightning, scalded them right onto the page. Me? There wasn't an ounce of wildness to my words. I could have made the goddamn apocalypse seem tame. But I kept at it anyway, hoping that someday I'd be able to make sense of all this and that my visions would become a blessing to me and not a curse—or a lie, like Mom always said they were.

The thing is, Mom wasn't totally wrong about them lying. Because sometimes my visions don't come true. It's a real problem.

Take, for example, Murphy's tenth birthday party. We were supposed to go down to the lake for fishing and a cookout with homemade ice cream and possibly canoeing, depending on how many kids showed up (because, you know, unlike me,

Murphy had actual friends). The night before the party I had a vision. I was just lying in my bed, watching the fan whir, trying to write a poem in my head, when the ceiling vanished above me and I saw the whole thing play out like a movie.

Mom and Murphy and me and a whole bunch of kids gathered lakeside, laughing and eating. Clouds blotted out the sun, and the sky took on a yellow hue, that hot, uneasy feeling drifting in the air. Rain began to fall, pelting the party, spoiling the cookout. Canoes flipped, and children were dashed into the churning water. Lightning struck a tree, and sparks went flying. A branch fell and snapped the picnic table in two. Sirens began to wail, that eternal beacon of terror in the hearts of all Southern kids. And far off in the distance fell a spiraling brown bulldog of a tornado, squat on its haunches, ravaging everything in its path as it barreled toward the birthday party. It all happened so fast no one knew what to do. There wasn't enough room in Mom's car for all the kids from the party. It was loud as a railroad train, the screaming column of wind barreling down on us, lifting lake water and yanking up trees, plucking children into the air one by one, sucking them into the swirling void before they could even make a sound.

I sat up screaming. I ran to Murphy because I knew she would listen, because I knew Mom would just ignore me or ground me or worse.

"You have to cancel your birthday party," I said.

"No," she said.

"You have to. Or you'll die. See, I had a vision. A tornado's going to come. We'll all die."

"No."

"*Mom* will die."

Little nine-year-old Murphy sighed. "Fine," she said. "If your vision said so."

"It absolutely 100 percent did," I said. "You can pretend you're sick or something. I'll make it up to you. Thanks, Murphy. You just saved all of our lives."

The next day Murphy faked being sick, and the party was canceled. Murphy sat in her PJs eating chicken broth, watching her favorite movie, *Point Break* (the old one, with Keanu and Swayze).

Thing was, no tornado ever came. The skies were bright blue and beautiful, an even seventy degrees. The most perfect day possible to go to a lakeside birthday party. Murphy just sat on the couch and cried.

"You ruined my birthday," she said.

And she didn't talk to me for a whole week.

So the whole vision thing isn't always completely accurate. I can't tell the difference between an honest-to-god prophecy vision and one that has no shot at coming to pass. I mean, who knows, maybe some kid would have drowned or gotten snakebit at Murphy's party and I wound up saving someone's life anyway. It's pretty much impossible to tell. All I know is that I can't always trust the visions, not completely. But I'm afraid not to. Because when they're right, they're hideously, horrifyingly right.

Only thing is, why didn't I have the vision about Mom in time to save her? Why didn't it come ten minutes earlier, when it actually would have been useful?

Frankly, visions are a pain in the ass, and I wish they happened to somebody else.

In the history of visions, this is not an uncommon position. Almost nobody in the Bible likes being a prophet. Isaiah initially refused his anointing from God, and Moses tried to get out of it by saying he sounded dumb when he talked. Jonah turned tail and bolted, and you know what happened to him. Joan of Arc was burned at the stake. Even William Blake's mom spanked him every time he had a vision of God, and when he grew up, everybody walked around giving him shit, calling him a loony.

I mean, I'm not even sure these visions are from God. (Mom didn't believe in God, and Murphy doesn't either. But I do—always have. It's like I was born with faith, knowing that God was in the world, same as oxygen and gravity. God was just a part of things, and it didn't do any good for me to deny it.) There was a demon-possessed woman in Acts who could tell the future and who Paul exorcised just because she was annoying. What if I just have an annoying demon? Or worse, some mysterious tumor in my brain that no one has bothered to check for yet?

I always wanted there to be some kind of purpose for the visions, you know? I wanted them to be of real use to someone, to have been chosen for all this.

Or what if I'm just fucking crazy, huh? That occurred to you yet?

So I don't know what to do with my visions.

I don't know what to do with myself.

GRANDMA'S HOUSE WAS ALL CREAKING WOOD floors and tall ceilings and antique faded peeling wallpaper. Framed photos were nailed to the wall everywhere—old ones, black-and-white, and nothing in color. I didn't recognize anybody from the photos. They seemed ancient and severe, women in gray dresses and men with big white mustaches in suits. I didn't really know where our family was from, what our heritage was—Mom always said she was born without a past and it suited her fine—but I figured all these strange geriatrics were our ancestors. It was wild to see a hallway full of where you came from, like time was one long consecutive gallery that we were all a part of. There were a few bleary snapshots of a woman who looked kind of like Grandma except thicker, tougher-looking, like she was birthed in hardier times, holding two babies, twins. Nowhere, however, could I find a picture of Mom.

"Get a load of this place," whispered Murphy.

The furniture was of the old chipped-paint kind. A cuckoo clock clicked its pendulum back and forth, and the light from the windows cast golden dusty beams across the floor. A piano sat in the corner, sheet music propped up on it. It looked recently polished, the bench a little crooked, like someone had played it not too long ago. I wondered if it was Grandma. But then I realized how dumb that was. I mean, of course it was Grandma.

Who else would it be?

Grandma led us to the kitchen, where all laid out on a big wooden table was a banquet's worth of food. Biscuits and gravy, collard greens, roast turkey with cranberry sauce, and homemade mac and cheese, with a fruit salad on the side. I mean, it was the whole Thanksgiving treatment complete with napkins folded, knives and plates and forks at the ready.

My mouth hung open all drooling and silly, and I realized just how long it had been since we last ate. We sat down at the table with Grandma at the head and Murphy and me on either side of her.

"I cooked every bit of it for you," said Grandma. "I figured y'all two would be hungry."

"You figured right," said Murphy. "Holy shit."

Grandma's smile flinched a little at the curse, but she didn't say anything.

"How did you know we were coming?" I said.

"I had a premonition," she said. "I get those from time to time."

A premonition? That was like a vision, wasn't it? Did Grandma have visions too?

Grandma seemed to know exactly what I was thinking. She smiled at me and reached her hand out and placed it on my forehead. It shocked me, like when you walk around on carpet barefoot and then touch a door handle. I jerked backward a little, and Grandma frowned.

"Then it's true, isn't it?" said Grandma. "My Jenny's dead."

I didn't know what to say. We all just sat there silent for a moment before Murphy finally spoke.

"Yes," she said. "She died a few days ago."

Grandma sucked in a deep breath and let it out real slow. "How did it happen?"

"A car wreck," I said.

It was like something broke in Grandma then. Her eyelids fluttered, and her head lolled a little to the side, and for a second, I was worried she might keel over. But the moment passed, and Grandma shook her head and smiled at us, dabbing at her eyes with a napkin.

"My goodness," she said. "I've got all this food prepared. We mustn't let it get cold."

I looked at Murphy, and she looked back at me and nodded.

"There's something else we need to tell you," I said, "about Mom's death."

"What is it, children?" said Grandma.

"We think our stepdad, Horace, killed her," said Murphy.

"We think he sabotaged her car," I said, "to get our trust. I mean, the money you set aside for us."

"He adopted us," said Murphy. "Illegally."

"That's our theory, anyhow," I said.

Grandma scrunched up her eyebrows at us.

"Do you have proof of this?" she said. "Or is it all speculation?"

"Yeah, we've got proof," said Murphy. "We've got documents showing the adoption, and we can testify that they were forged."

"Also we heard a fight he and Mom had on the night she crashed," I said. "She drove off hollering about how something was going to end now. She had to mean her marriage to Horace."

"He might be after us," said Murphy. "We left him back in Mississippi, all knocked out. We need to contact the police as soon as possible."

"Well, there's no phone in my house," said Grandma, "and I doubt you'll have any service out here in the country. The nearest phone is at the filling station about twenty miles back. Y'all passed by there, didn't you?"

"Yep," said Murphy.

"I'll tell you what," said Grandma. "We'll head into town first thing in the morning and phone the police. How does that sound?"

"I'd feel a lot better if we did it right now," I said. "You don't know Horace. You don't know how dangerous he is."

"My goodness," said Grandma. "Well, if he's that vicious, we'll just have to dead bolt the front door, won't we?"

"I don't think you quite understand," I said.

"Perhaps not," said Grandma. "But my mind is made up, and your food is getting cold. Why don't you go on and eat now? I know you're hungry. I can see it all over your faces."

She was right. I was hungry. Very hungry. And if Grandma wasn't worried about Horace, then what could we do to change her mind? She seemed stubborn like that, in the same way Mom had been stubborn, in the same way Murphy was stubborn. When they were set in their ways, arguing was useless. Besides, did Horace even know where Grandma lived? How could he be sure we would head here, a place we'd never been before, to stay with a relative we'd never met? For all he knew we were still in Mississippi, hiding anywhere we could. Surely we'd be safe for just a night, wouldn't we?

Regardless, dinner was ready, and it smelled good. Murphy slopped a serving spoon full of mac and cheese on her plate and picked up her fork, ready to dig in.

"Hmmph," said Grandma, a scowl on her face, and Murphy froze.

"It's only proper that we say a blessing," said Grandma. "After all, my children have come home."

"Your children?" I said.

"Grandchildren, I mean. And I am so, so very grateful that you two are here."

She reached her hands out to us. Grandma's fingers were tough and calloused and wrinkly and warm, and her grip was strong.

"Dear wondrous Spirit of these lands," Grandma prayed, her voice high and bright and full of sugar. "We thank thee for thy infinite mercy and perfect judgment. We thank thee for the shining path leading thy servants along the way of righteousness and truth. We beseech thee for wisdom in the face of adversity, kindness in the face of hate, and acceptance in the face of doubt. And we thank thee for bringing an answer long sought after, a confirmation of your divine will, the way all things have been and must be and shall always be. Amen."

I looked at Murphy, and she looked back at me, a little smirk on her face.

"Amen," said Murphy.

"I never heard a prayer like that before," I said.

"I don't like to address the Spirit in gendered terms, you understand?" said Grandma. "Seems a bit gauche. Don't you agree, children?"

"God is for suckers," said Murphy.

"It's a good thing I don't believe in God, then," said Grandma.

"Then what the hell did you just pray to?" said Murphy.

"The Spirit is not god, Murphy. The Spirit isn't some patriarchal deity with a beard, up there on a throne, hurling out judgments. That would be absurd. The Spirit is a living and active presence, not bound up in any holy book or written down in statutes. It's out in the woods, on the land and in the soil, in the flowers and the hummingbirds, anything with life. Most importantly, it's right here." She tapped her chest with her fist. "That's where the Spirit lives, Murphy. It's a power, a strength. And it can live in you too."

"Nah," said Murphy. "I'm good."

Grandma smiled. "I suppose we'll see about that, won't we? Now dig in, lest the food get cold. Lest all my work be for nothing."

So Grandma was a little weird. That was okay. I mean, have you met me and Murphy, much less our mom? Who in their right mind would expect our grandmother to be normal? Besides, the food was incredible. I mean, when was the last time we'd had a feast like that?

Maybe this one time when Horace had cooked a huge meal for Mom's birthday. Believe it or not, Horace was a pretty great chef, and he took all kinds of pride in his cooking. That night he'd served broiled lemonfish with mushrooms, mashed potatoes, and roasted veggies, with fried oysters as an appetizer. It was one of the best meals I'd ever had in my life. Horace had done the dinner table up fancy with candles and cloth napkins and all that. It was like a date night for him and Mom. I couldn't believe he'd allowed us to be there for it.

Things had been going pretty damn pleasantly when Mom out of the blue told Horace that she'd gotten a speeding ticket a few months back and had forgotten to pay it, and now there was a fine and maybe some other stuff. Mom never could remember to pay for things, especially not bills. That was usually my job, had been ever since I was old enough to read. I liked to organize things, stack mail into piles, sort through all the bills, whatever needed to be done. It's the most boring part of my personality, sure, but somebody had to do it.

"You mean, you—the sheriff's wife—were negligent on a speeding ticket?" said Horace.

Mom nodded.

"You know that means there's a warrant out for your arrest, right?" he said, the fork gripped tight in his fist. "You, the wife of the premiere law enforcement officer in this county?"

"I figured you could take care of that for me, honey." Mom gave him her best smile, all dimples and charm. "You will, won't you? I sure would appreciate it."

Horace's mouth was a straight line, and his head shook a little, the veins bulging out of his neck, as if it were about to pop off and explode. He glared at her as he cut a tiny piece of fish and jammed it into his mouth, chewing so hard I heard his teeth grind.

It would be hard to explain to you the terror of that moment. The way anger can billow out of somebody like heat from a furnace, how it can spread silently across the room and wrap you up tight like a smothering blanket.

Horace finished his fish, calmly placed his knife and fork across the plate, and dabbed his mouth with a napkin. He took a sip of his iced tea.

"Another thing, honey," said Mom.

The plastic glass cracked in Horace's hand, splintering into pieces, a mix of blood and sweet tea pouring out over the crisp white tablecloth.

Horace leapt up from the table. "Our bedroom, now!"

They went in there and slammed the door. I heard them fight, hollering and screaming. Then I heard some other sounds coming from in there. Happy sounds, like they were giggling together, laughing. It was hard to imagine Horace giggling, but there it was. Murphy and I could hear it drifting out from under the door.

They didn't come out of the bedroom the rest of the night.

This meal with Grandma was the exact opposite of that night. Even though we didn't talk much, the food and the company seemed to do all the work for us. We were all so happy to be there, so happy to eat and find our bellies full, so happy to feel loved—because that's how Grandma made me feel, loved, appreciated, grateful—that I didn't need conversation, I didn't need to say a word. I just wanted to sit there at the table together like a family.

I can't tell you how good that felt, how good it was to feel safe and at home.

A voice sounded from the back of the house.

"Hello? Mrs. Sanford?"

"Oh, for Pete's sake," said Grandma. She raised her voice and hollered, "In here!"

A girl walked into the kitchen—about my age, maybe a little older. She was tall and skinny with reddish hair down to her shoulders. She wore a cutoff gray T-shirt and black jeans with holes in them. Tattoos covered her arms, the stick and poke kind, homemade. Her hair was greasy, and she looked like she hadn't bathed in a week. But, like, in a *good* way. I don't know how to describe it.

"Hi there," she said. "Sorry to bother you, but Stephens burned our supper for tonight. Do you have anything you could spare us?"

"That boy isn't much of a cook, is he?" said Grandma.

The girl shrugged.

"He's alright," she said. "He just gets distracted."

"Well come on in, make yourself at home. I'll fix you a plate to take back."

Grandma pulled a platter from the cupboard and started piling it high with food. The girl leaned herself against the kitchen counter, her arms crossed over her chest like she was the coolest, least-bothered human in the entire world. For the first time she seemed to notice Murphy and me.

"Who are you two?" she said.

I just stared at her.

"I'm Murphy," said my sister. "This is Lee. We're her grandkids."

"Grandkids, huh?" The girl smiled at me. Her left front tooth was a little crooked.

I liked that.

"I'm Cass," she said.

"Cass," I said.

She laughed a little. "Yep. That's what I said."

Grandma wrapped the heaping platter of food with tinfoil and held it out to Cass. "This should do y'all well," she said. "Now skedaddle. These kids have been through a lot, and they need their rest."

"Thank you so much," said Cass, lugging the food in front of her. As she left the room, she looked back over her shoulder and smiled at us.

"Nice to meet y'all," she said, and then she was gone.

Murphy kicked me under the table.

"Stop it," I said.

"You got a crush," she said.

"Ugh, can you please leave me alone?"

"Nope," she said. "I promise you right now you'll never hear the end of it."

Grandma sat back down with us at the table.

"Who was that, Grandma?" said Murphy.

"Oh, just one of the tenants. They rent the house out back on the edge of the property."

"There's more?" I said, and Murphy laughed.

"In fact, there's four," said Grandma. "Some kind of music group. A couple of local kids, one or two from far off who decided to play hippie. Come here to play music as loud as they want, record their songs, all that. I wish I didn't have to rent the house out, but money's been tight the last few years, and it helps to pay the bills. Sometimes they work with me in the garden, do odd jobs here and there." She paused a minute. "Hope they won't be a nuisance to you."

"Not a chance," I said.

Murphy kicked me again.

After dinner, Grandma gave us a quick tour of the house. On the first floor was the foyer, the kitchen, a small living room, and a huge dining room that looked like nobody had been in it in years. The second floor had the library (all science books, biology, astronomy, religious books, and how-to manuals—no history or literature and certainly no poetry), Grandma's own bedroom (spartan and empty, like how a monk's would be, with one vase of yellow-blooming flowers on her mirrorless dresser), and a sort of storage room stacked to the ceiling with cardboard boxes, which she said contained nothing but junk. The third floor was off-limits, a rickety attic with holes in the floor. If you stepped wrong, Grandma told us, you could fall right through.

"You'll be staying in your mother's old room," said Grandma. "I hope you don't find that too upsetting."

"No," said Murphy. "I would love that."

I agreed.

"Then it's settled." Grandma walked to a shut white-painted door and pushed it open.

The room was dusty, and one of the light bulbs was burnt out. A pair of bunk beds sat in one corner, a mason jar of long-wilted flowers, a row of paint bottles, and dried brushes on a desk. The walls were a marvel, covered with little murals: Blue-throated hummingbirds hovering over red blossoms bright as flames. A cricket balanced perfectly on a spear of grass. A spiderweb of rainbows and light, a slender yellow spider dangling down so real I wanted to pick up my shoe and smash it. I had only seen Mom paint once, that weird bewildering morning, and this was even better.

"Whoa," said Murphy. "Did Mom paint all this?"

"She was quite the artist in her time," said Grandma. "I'm sorry to hear she ever gave it up."

A few books lined a small bookshelf—one on herbalism, an illustrated volume on plants, as well as a sports car catalog from 1995.

"Well, that much at least looks like Mom," said Murphy.

I know it sounds like I'd gone mute, but I pretty much had. The paintings were amazing, and I wished that had been a side of Mom that we had known. But there was something else about that room that felt strange to me. I don't want to drop fancy mystic words like "aura," but there was definitely a feeling to it, a dusty, shadowed thing hiding itself in the corners. Something about the room wanted to be understood, if that makes any sense.

"Everything okay, Lee?" asked Grandma.

I nodded. "Just tired, I guess."

"I can only imagine. Heaven knows all that you endured the past few days." Grandma smiled. "And frankly, the two of you need showers. I would have requested this before dinner, but I saw how famished you were."

"Fuckin' A," said Murphy, and again Grandma winced.

"Bathroom is down the hall," she said. "You'll find fresh towels in the cupboard. Also, I have some old clothes from years back that should fit the two of you, if you have nothing else to change into. I'll lay those by the door."

"You wouldn't happen to have a phone charger, would you?" I said. "My phone's about to die."

"Of course not, dear," she said. "I try to keep the outside world truly outside, if you know what I mean. Perhaps we can pick up one in town sometime soon."

Grandma yawned big, the veins gone sharp in her neck.

"Goodness me, I'm tired. If you don't mind, children, I'm headed to bed. It is sundown, after all, and in this house, we obey the light."

"Thanks, Grandma," I said. "Thanks for everything."

She smiled so big I thought her cheeks would split.

"It's a pleasure, children," she said. "I'm so glad you've come home."

Grandma kissed each of us on the cheek and tottered off to her bedroom, feet making only the tiniest sound on the creaky wood, as if she weighed no more than a mouse.

"Strange lady," said Murphy. "But cool."

"Yeah," I said. I picked up a small ceramic turtle from the dresser, hand-painted, like something from a craft class at summer camp. "So weird being in Mom's old bedroom."

"No shit," said Murphy.

We had a moment then where the room got quiet and we were surrounded by all of Mom's old childhood things, and it was like she was there with us, like she hadn't died at all. I knew Murphy was feeling it too. She reached out and grabbed my hand, and together we stood there in the silence, trying not to cry. I was so glad I had Murphy. I was so glad I wasn't alone.

After a minute Murphy sighed. "I guess this is our life now, huh?"

"Seems like it," I said.

"We're gonna get through this, okay?" she said. "Remember, I got your back no matter what."

"And I got yours."

That felt good. I needed to know that Murphy and I were in this together, same as always.

"Also," she said, "dibs on first shower."

"Go for it," I said. "But I get the top bunk."

"Ugh," she said. "Fine. I don't like top bunks anyway. I always feel like I'm going to fall out of them in the middle of the night."

"Just do me a favor and don't use all the hot water," I said. "If there even is hot water out here."

Murphy left, and I sat down on the bottom bunk and shut my eyes. What was up with that room? What was so strange about it?

I tried to clear my head like Mom used to make us do when we did group meditation. I know I told you Mom wasn't religious, and she absolutely was not, at least not in the usual sense of the word. Mom believed that meditation allowed you to fall deeper into yourself, to tap into what she called "the lizard brain"—all the passed-down memories from our ancestors that piggyback onto our DNA. She believed that all people were basically geniuses somewhere in the back parts of their minds, in the subconscious, only we were cut off from it, like there was a wall between the front of your brain and the back. She thought that with enough practice you could figure out how to sneak information past it. It was like communing with your elders, she said, talking to the back part of your mind. You could learn all about yourself.

So that's what I tried to do. I tried to communicate with whatever bits of Mom sat quiet in my DNA. I tried to feel everything that the room wanted me to feel.

In short, I wanted a vision. I wanted the room to speak.

I sat lotus-style for maybe fifteen minutes, just waiting, until my knees began to ache.

Nothing happened. The house creaked and moaned, Murphy sang off-key in the shower, and Grandma didn't make a peep. The crickets chirped outside, and the tree frogs burped, and the insect world buzzed and scratched, and the moon rose high. But that room remained silent. Whatever secrets were there, they kept themselves tucked away quiet.

Soon Murphy came barging flat-footed down the hall. I swear, every time she comes in a room, it's like an explosion, like she's not so much entering a place as raiding it, like she's a one-girl SWAT team.

I took a quick shower after her—there was almost no hot water left—and when I came back to the room, Murphy was wearing overalls. Like old-school denim ones with a sunflower patch sewed onto them.

"Get a load of these things," she said.

"It's a good look for you," I said. "Like Scout from *To Kill a Mockingbird*."

"Fuck off," she said. "But don't worry, there's a pair for you too."

"You're kidding."

"Nope," she said, tossing me a faded denim bundle and a white T-shirt. "Grandma laid out clothes for the both of us for tomorrow." She held out a pair of men's white briefs, cottony and faded. "Looks like you got yourself some choice BVDs here."

"Give me those," I said, snatching them from her. "God, I wonder how old these are."

"They were probably our grandfather's," she said.

"Great," I said. "I'll be wearing the underwear of a dead guy."

We went quiet then a minute. Because it was kind of clear who those sunflower overalls Murphy was wearing used to belong to.

"Shit," said Murphy.

"Yeah," I said. "Shit indeed."

I went to the bathroom and put on the underwear and the T-shirt. When I got back, Murphy was already in bed. I flicked the lamp off and climbed into my bunk. I lay there for about an hour, but sleep wasn't coming. My brain just wouldn't stop. Because everybody knows that if you want to sleep, you absolutely can't do it, no way. You have to not want to sleep. At the very least you have to be indifferent to sleep. It's like a cat. The more you gesture and beg for sleep to come sit in your lap, the less likely it is to actually do it. A cat, like sleep, needs to be ignored until suddenly it's there, and the next thing you know it's morning. I wasn't good at being indifferent to anything, much less sleep.

That night all I could think about was Mom and why she took up with Horace in the first place. It seemed like a bad fairy tale, except instead of a wicked stepmother calling all the shots, we had some bald-headed asshole named Horace.

Mom always had a pretty active social life, to be honest with you. My earliest memories were of Mom lugging me and my baby sister on dates. To the Iron Horse Tavern, to Bill's Burger House, to the Blue Goose and the Diamond Slipper and just about every other restaurant in the tri-county area. Looking back on things, it kind of made sense. Brand-new woman in town, pretty and mysterious, with two kids in tow. That was prime small-town material. Most folks probably figured she was looking for a new husband, or at least someone to help her take care of those two poor fatherless kids.

And that's the main thing all the old town gossips got wrong.

Mom wasn't after a new husband, someone to pay her bills and help her raise her kids. In fact, she swore to Murphy and me when I was seven years old that she would never, ever get married. She made us shake on it, like it was an agreement between the three of us.

"Look at me, kids," she said, drunk one night, a little slur to her words. "Look me in the eyes and promise me I will never get married. You got that?"

"Yes," said me and Murphy together.

We didn't want a stepfather. What would be the point?

Because life with Mom wasn't so bad. First off, she home-schooled us, and that meant I had a refuge from other kids. This was a good thing, because the ones I'd met around the neighborhood never took much of a liking to me. We had our lessons in the woods, or by the creek, or anywhere else Mom could get sunshine and creatures.

Mom would take us to the library every two weeks with one instruction: "Load up." Murphy always got practical stuff—field guides, nonfiction about explorers, maps of foreign places. I went straight for the poetry. Like I said, poets were the weirdos having visions, the ones taken up to a higher brainspace. I taught myself Allen Ginsberg and Emily Dickinson and John Berryman and Langston Hughes. I taught myself Rimbaud and John Donne and T. S. Eliot. I taught myself Gwendolyn Brooks and Rilke and Walt Whitman and Georg Trakl. I spent an entire year reading Frank O'Hara, wishing I were somebody else. I ordered books mentioned in other books through interlibrary loan, because reading on actual paper from thick ancient hardback volumes was best, preferably outside, even by lamplight.

Mom never quite knew what to do with me, and that hurt, always. I knew Mom would have preferred another Murphy, running around, trying to break boards with jump kicks, instead of me, reading Gérard de Nerval in a field somewhere.

Like the time she took Murphy and me spelunking in Arkansas. I barely spelunked. While Mom and Murphy plunged deeper and deeper into the underground labyrinth, hand in hand, their laughs bouncing around the cave walls disturbing bats, I mostly just sat at the mouth of the cave with my headlamp, imagining things. I watched the darkness, so thick it seemed to swirl, a whirlpool of empty space, and I wondered and wondered.

It was one of the happiest days of my life.

Things went wrong whenever Mom tried to force me to be normal, to get me to make friends or something.

For example, Mom tried to throw me a birthday party when I was ten. Even at that age, everyone seemed to know there was something off about me. I mean, kids hated me. All of them, without fail. I couldn't figure out why. I wasn't mean or anything, and maybe I was even a little smart. They liked Murphy just fine—she always had her pick of friends. But for whatever reason, all the kids on our block hated me, and I knew it. I didn't want Mom to throw a party for me. I knew something horrible was going to happen, that I was going to find a way to embarrass myself. But Mom insisted. She said I needed friends.

And I did need friends. Hell, I wanted friends probably more than anything on this earth. Somehow Mom cajoled the neighbors into sending their children over. Maybe Mom promised them food, cake and ice cream, party favors, I don't know. It was Mom's idea to give me a piñata. She said her mom had given her one for every birthday and that smashing it was better than eating whatever candy fell out. It was a bright pink armadillo, which I thought was cool. Mom slung it up over a tree limb in our front yard, and I donned the blindfold, and all the neighborhood kids crowded around me, watching.

I gripped the baseball bat and was immediately dismayed. That sucker was heavy, an old Louisville Slugger Mom had left over from the '90s. I heaved it up like it was a goddamn prehistoric club, and I reared back and swung as hard as I could.

I missed, of course. I missed so bad I slipped and fell over and busted my nose. It was bleeding, I could tell, the hot wet penny taste of it on my lips. I heard Mom fussing over to me, but I shushed her, I told her I was fine, even though my nose was bleeding everywhere, even though I was crying a little and trying to hide it. I swung again and missed again, tumbling right over.

I heard a snicker or two then, the neighborhood boys having a laugh at my expense. That was fine. They'd stop laughing when I busted that armadillo and all that delicious candy fell out of its insides.

So I straightened up. I gritted my teeth. I bowed up to the piñata. I listened closely, like a ninja would, until I was certain I could hear the wind whistle past its paper snout. I swung as hard as I could.

I hit the piñata all right. It just didn't bust. I hit it again and again and again. Nothing doing.

By now everyone was outright laughing at me, and I was full-on crying. I hit it and I hit it, and it simply would not bust.

Murphy couldn't take it anymore, watching me make a fool of myself. So she ran up, jerked the bat out of my hands, and whomped it right open on the first try. The armadillo's guts busted, fifty candy bars fell out, and all the kids swarmed them. My moment of misery was over. Murphy was always taking care of me like that, trying to make things easier for me, her loser brother. And I appreciated it. Like I said before, Murphy was my best friend.

Still, Murphy's act of generosity had sealed the deal. My own baby sister had busted my piñata. She was stronger than me. I was branded a loser forever. I took my blindfold off, and there stood my mom, her arms crossed over her chest, shaking her head at me like I was the biggest failure in all the world.

I never had a birthday party again.

So no, I couldn't ever be the kind of kid that Mom wanted. But she did a good job of loving me and making a place for me, and I would always be grateful for that. It was like she understood that I was different, that I couldn't be like her and Murphy, and even if it disappointed her, she never held it against me.

Back to the point: Our life with Mom wasn't all bad. I loved our strange house in an empty cul-de-sac called Drury Lanes. I loved the hammock in the backyard, miles from any traffic, where I could read and swat mosquitoes until the sun set. I loved my sister, Murphy, how much fun we had together when she wasn't giving me shit or hanging out with cool kids. I liked the fact that I had a mysterious grandmother paying for every-thing for us—our house and Mom's red Jeep Wrangler and our food—for pretty much the entirety of our life in small-town

Mississippi. Minus all the shit with visions and the complete lack of friends, my life could have been worse. There was college to look forward to, anyway.

And then Horace had to show up and ruin it.

I remember being home alone one day when I was fifteen, just sitting on the front porch, reading Hart Crane, when this hotshot police cruiser pulled up. I was thinking, *Aw, crap, what has Murphy done now?* But who should step out of the passenger seat but my own mother, wearing a fucking sundress, while this big lumbering hulk of a sheriff got out and walked around the car like he was going to walk Mom to her door. What's more, Mom was laughing like this guy was the funniest person she'd ever met in her whole life.

I couldn't believe it.

As a family, we had always been distrustful of cops. And not just because Murphy was always getting picked up for one reason or another: trespassing, petty vandalism, driving without a license, that sort of thing. I was used to Murphy coming home in a cop car and Mom having to promise and flirt her way out of trouble. I wasn't used to Mom flashing a genuine smile at a gargantuan bear of a man in uniform.

She waved goodbye to him and made her way up the cobblestones to the porch. The sheriff leaned against his car and watched her, clearly pleased with what he was seeing. I glared at him as if to say, *I see you, motherfucker.* He caught me looking, I made sure of that. But you know what this sheriff—what

Horace, my future stepfather—did? He gave me my stare right back, and he gave it harder, and he gave it more furious than I ever could. I remember our eyes locking and feeling a sense of fear way back in my spine. I remember a chill falling over me that blazing hot day. I remember somewhere deep in my mind thinking, *This man is trouble.*

This man could be the ruin of us all.

I don't know why. It was just a feeling. But when Mom made it to the porch and the sheriff drove away with a wave, I braved up and asked her.

"What the hell was that, Mom?" I said.

"Oh, you know," said Mom, smiling all mysterious-like.

"No, I don't know. When did you start messing around with cops?"

"He's not just a cop," she said. "He's a *sheriff.*" And Mom sauntered into the house, singing to herself.

I didn't like it. Not one fucking bit.

And now we were here—Mom was dead, and Murphy and I were on the run, hiding out at our weird grandmother's house.

Life was pretty horrible like that.

The ceiling fan above me spun lazy and slow, and eventually I managed to fall asleep somehow.

I HAD ONLY ONE RECURRING VISION, AND THAT was of the Hobo, the man who always peeked into my window at night. I'd been seeing him since I was maybe seven years old. I named him the Hobo after I found this book in the library, *The Hobo Code.* It was all about the history of transient workers during the Depression, riding trains, eating scraps, searching desperately for work. He looked just like one of the men in the pictures— gaunt, ragged, with that haunted look in his eyes. I knew that real hobos had a language, a system of symbols they scrawled on the doorposts of buildings to say whether places were hospitable or cruel, whether the owners treated you well or cheated you. I looked everywhere for a code from the Hobo, for some kind of symbol telling me what he was or what he meant. But he never did anything except watch me. It wasn't just at the window that I saw him, but that was usually the place he liked best. He was always on the outside, some distance away from me, like there was something barring him from me, some invisible barrier between us.

The first time I saw the Hobo I was just a kid, and I went screaming into Mom's room about some maniac peeping in on me. Mom ran outside, threw on the porch lights, but no one was there. He was gone as a ghost.

Of course Mom punished me for making up stories, made me do all of Murphy's chores for a week. So I didn't tell her about the next time he was there, about a month later. Or the time after that, when I saw him watching us from the grocery store parking lot. He wore a grimy old coat and wretched clothes, like he had spent the last dozen years wandering, dirty and alone. The Hobo smiled, his teeth all rotten, and he gave me a little wave. It sent chills all over my body. By the time we'd loaded the groceries up, he had vanished.

I'd seen the Hobo a thousand times throughout my life. He'd been a constant, a fear lingering in the back of my mind always. And sometimes he climbed to the front of my eyelids, and there he stood before me. Every time I was terrified.

It wasn't because he looked angry or murderous, because he didn't, not exactly. The older I got, the more I saw him watching me, the more I realized he looked *worried*, concerned, curious even. So many times I'd wanted to grab him by the beard, to shake him, to make him tell me what he meant, what he was doing there, why he kept watching me at night. But I was afraid of what would happen if I tried.

I hated the Hobo. I hated him more than anyone, even Horace. I had nightmares about him when I wasn't having visions of him: That he crawled through the window with knives drawn, his mouth agape. That he sliced my throat and gnawed my fingers off. That he bound me and abducted me. That he tied me down and made me listen to the screams of my mom and sister as he murdered them while I lay there, helpless. That he hid under my bed or in my closet like some kind of boogeyman, and when the lights went off he made himself known. And by then it was too late.

I remember one time during a terrible storm that blew in on an April evening when tornado sirens were wailing and Mom made us go hide in the hallway. The lights were flickering, soon to go out, and the rain stopped, and all went quiet and peaceful. I knew what that meant—that the tornado was coming, that it would be here any moment. For some reason, I don't know why, I jumped up and went running. It seemed like fate, you know, this unavoidable calamity flung down from the sky. I was maybe eleven years old, but I knew I had to see it, I had to see what inescapable doom really looked like. I wanted to stare it in the eyes, menacing as an Old Testament idol, something a thousand pagan priests would rend their cloaks for.

I ran to the window and saw the sky gone green and hazy, the clouds black and billowing like waves, the long mean arc of the tornado swooping down, bent strangely, like an insect leg, mangling the neighborhood. And there in our backyard amidst the chaos stood the Hobo, dancing, waving his arms like he was conducting all the madness, like he was commanding the tornado to come and whisk us all away.

Mom yanked me from the window and dragged me to the hallway, burying us in pillows. The tornado missed our house by half a mile, though it did destroy the Shipley's Donuts where we went every Saturday morning. And yeah, she grounded me again. But I'll never forget the Hobo standing there in the yard, directing fate with his fingers, drawing the destruction toward us.

THE NEXT MORNING I WOKE UP ACHY AND sore, like my body had run miles in my sleep. I could smell bacon frying and coffee on the brew. I climbed off my bunk and left Murphy snoozing, curled up in a little ball, a bit of blanket in her mouth. It was how she always slept.

I crept down every creaking stair all the way to the kitchen, where Grandma stood with her back to me, whipping eggs. I started to sit down at the table, maybe grab a cup of coffee, but then I thought better of it. I wanted to see the backyard in the daylight, get a glimpse of what all was out there.

I walked past the kitchen and to the back door, opening it quiet as I could. Grandma still hummed happily in the kitchen in her little birdsong voice like maybe she hadn't heard me at all. I eased the door shut and walked into the ankle-high grass. A field stretched for maybe a hundred yards with trees on all sides. Just before the tree line in the far right-hand corner of the lot stood an old tall barn. Beyond it was a thin four-wheeler-sized path into the woods, one that looked well traveled. I started to head toward it, but about a third of the way there I got sidetracked.

Because there was a gap in the woods to my left, some kind of orchard with trees all lined up and spaced out evenly and bright red somethings dangling from them. The sunlight cut through the leaves in honey-colored slashes, an impossible sweetness pouring down from the sky. But something was moving in the grove, little flecks of color hovering and dashing in the air.

When I realized what they were, I broke into a run.

Hummingbirds, maybe fifty of them, swarming, a whole foggy haze of them darting between bright red feeders hanging from every tree. They were wild. It was like some kind of strange warfare, the way they bashed into each other, so desperate for the sugar water or whatever it was in those feeders. I went and stood in the middle of them. One smacked into my shoulder, floated around me, wondered at me. I don't even know if I can explain the thrill of it, all of these birds moving swift as a thought, all this energy and power and the tiny beats of their wings all around me. It was just like Mom had described, just like I'd always imagined it.

"Not bad, huh?"

I turned, and there stood Grandma.

"This is our Hummingbird Grove. You caught them just in time for their migration," she said. "A little late this year, if I'm honest with you. It's a bit worrying. Well, the whole world is worrying. That's why I tried to make a new life here for me and my family. Something separate from the world but that had all the greatness of the world in it too. The mysterious beauty of the earth. Like these hummingbirds. They were your mother's favorite, you know?"

"I did know that. She told me about this once, the Hummingbird Grove."

Grandma's eye did a little twitch then, and I wondered if she'd start crying. But she shook it off, and all the light came back into her face.

"Come now, before breakfast gets cold," she said. "We got a busy day ahead of us."

I followed her back to the house and then into the kitchen. Murphy was sitting at the table, her plate heaped full of bacon and biscuits and scrambled eggs. She seemed annoyed.

"Hurry it up," she said. "I'm starved."

"Sorry," I said. "I went exploring."

"And?" she said.

I sighed.

"I'll show you later."

Grandma took her seat at the head of the table. She cleared her throat and reached her hands out to us, and I remembered that it was time to pray. Murphy and I each took one of her hands, and she gripped us tight in her calloused fingers and spoke with that same kind of breathless, confidant enthusiasm she'd had before.

"Oh Spirit," she said, "we thank thee for thy abundance this morning. For an abundance of hummingbirds, for an abundance of joy and blessings running in our each and every vein, and for an abundance of light, both that which shines down from the sun over our heads and that which blossoms in our hearts, thy true and secret gifts. May we all prove worthy of it. Amen."

"Amen," said Murphy, extra loud.

"Now then, children," said Grandma. "The blessing is spoken. Let's eat."

I was on my third helping of scrambled eggs with butter and cheese and hot sauce when Murphy asked the question that should have been on my mind all morning.

"So Grandma," she said, mouth stuffed with biscuits, "when are we going to the cops?"

Grandma sighed and set her utensils back on her plate. I noticed she ate slow and deliberate, in tiny postage-stamp-sized bites, and she chewed each one for an eternity. She hadn't hardly finished one serving of eggs yet.

"Manners, Murphy, darling," she said. "There's nothing so urgent to say that you can't finish chewing first."

Murphy rolled her eyes and gulped her food down.

"Sorry," she said.

"That's better," said Grandma, folding her hands on the table. "Now what was it that you wanted to ask me?"

"I wanted to know when we were going to the cops," said Murphy.

"Goodness, Murphy," said Grandma, "it's eleven in the morning."

"It's eleven?" she said. "You're kidding me. We slept that late?"

"Well, just look at the clock, why don't you?" Grandma pointed at the cuckoo clock in the kitchen. It read 11:05. I realized it was the only clock I'd seen in the house.

"Since you children seemed so tired, I just decided to let y'all sleep right in," said Grandma. "And I went ahead and spoke to them myself."

"Wait, you already talked to the police?" I said. "About Mom and Horace and all that?"

"Why, of course I did," she said. "I was sitting in the parking lot when Sheriff Bearden opened the station. See, I wake up at four A.M. on the dot every morning. I feed the chickens and take my morning constitutional, and I greet the coming day with a hymn of supplication, same as I do every morning, same as I have for forty years now. And as you two sleepyheads were still snoring away at six, I decided to go ahead and take myself to town and report the . . . the murder"—her voice cracked a little—"of my daughter Jenny, as well as the fact that a madman was after my grandchildren."

"And they believed you?" said Murphy.

"Of course they believed me," said Grandma. "Sheriff Bearden is an old friend of mine. A friend of the Farm as well. I told him all about your situation, and he was most helpful. When I mentioned your stepfather, Sheriff Bearden found a photo of the man on his computer. Strange to lay eyes on my daughter's husband for the first time in such a manner, and such a brute of a man, with that ridiculous haircut. But Sheriff Bearden promised me he would put something called an 'all-points bulletin' out about the man. An officer is supposed to come around before too long and ask y'all some questions. I expect him before sundown."

"We really should have gone with you," said Murphy. "I mean, we have evidence. Of Horace's guilt."

"Your grandmother will take care of you, children," she said. "I have lived a long and varied life, and I've gained a not unsubstantial bit of wisdom in my time. I believe I am up to the task, don't you?"

"You still should have told us," said Murphy.

"Life is not lived in *shoulds*," said Grandma. "There is only what has been done and what will be done. I've already spoken to the police, and they're sending an officer here later in the day. You may say to them whatever you want then. Okay?"

"Fine with me," I said.

"I guess," muttered Murphy.

"Murphy," said Grandma, her voice gone sharp. "I asked you if that was okay with you. Look me in the eyes and answer my question. Is this plan okay with you?"

"Yes, ma'am," said Murphy.

"That's better," said Grandma. She clapped her hands together, a crack like a gunshot. "Now then, there are dishes to wash and chores to be done. We are on a farm, you know, and it's been ages since I've had any help around here. We'll keep busy until the police come for questions. Because a busy mind is a healthy mind, and idle hands are, after all, the devil's playthings. Of course, the idea of a devil is utter nonsense, but the sentiment remains true.

"Up, children!" she said, shooing us from the table. "Up and to work! Half the day is already wasted, and on a farm, there's no bigger sin than wasting daylight."

GRANDMA WASN'T KIDDING ABOUT WORK. BY noon she had Murphy up on a John Deere mowing the back lot and me in the garden yanking weeds. The sun was nightmare-hot, and my neck got burned, and my back ached from hunching over the ground. I'm pretty sure I got poison ivy too. Grandma kept walking by, gathering up veggies, watering plants, clipping at things, shouting at me to get down in the soil, to get my hands all good and dirty. I kept chancing glances back at the barn when I could, at that narrow path cut through the woods. I wondered what lay back there.

Every couple of hours Grandma called a "hydration break," where she served us some green homemade goop out of mason jars. It tasted horrible, like chalk and weird spinach. I would have preferred water, or really anything else, but Grandma said it was her secret concoction and that nothing was better on a hot day.

"Believe me," she said. "I've been at this for forty years now."

After the garden was good and weeded and the back lot was mowed, Grandma put me to work feeding the chickens while she went to show Murphy where the paint was, since the porch needed a touch-up. I stood next to the chickens—dumb colorful squawking things strutting around in their wire cage like they didn't know their destiny was to be food—and hated them a little bit, how they didn't rise up and murder us when we came for their eggs. The ultimate suckers, those chickens were. Sure, they got fed and protected, but to what end? A comfortable life serving the ones who will ring your neck one day and eat you and all your children? It was a bad deal no matter how you cut it. I watched the chickens and waited, thinking on all this and other stuff, until Grandma was out of sight, then chucked all the feed that was left and took off across the back lot. I knew I only had a few minutes before Grandma came back, and I needed to hurry.

The barn was about twenty feet tall and maybe sixty long with a whole second floor to it. The barn doors were ten feet tall at least, and they were on rails so they would slide open, wide and grand. The barn was huge, is what I'm saying.

Up close it didn't even look much like a barn. For one, it was painted yellow—faded and chipped and long-neglected, but still yellow, not the normal red you'd imagine. Second, it seemed somehow cozier than a barn should, like it had been constructed for much more than just housing hay and equipment, or whatever it was you stuck in a barn. There were windows too, big ones, but they were all boarded up now. The whole thing was shut tighter than a bank vault. A metal chain thick as my arm was draped over the door handles, fixed by a padlock that looked almost too heavy to lift—a real padlock, not a fake one like on the gate at the end of the drive. The barn had an abandoned look to it—not like it fell gradually out of use but like it had been closed up quick and deliberate, for a reason.

I gave one of the doors a pull, but it hardly even budged. A strange smell drifted out of the barn, a living stink. I wondered what was causing it.

"Barn's been long shut up," said Grandma.

"Jeez, Grandma," I said. "You nearly gave me a heart attack."

"Sorry," she said. "Though I got to be honest, seems hard to sneak up on somebody in a field as big as this one."

"I guess I was preoccupied," I said. "What happened to this place?"

"Well, after your mom left, we had to get rid of the horses. Didn't have half the help we used to, understand? Sold off a lot of the equipment, and then it just wasn't worth it to keep the place open and clean."

"What's in there now?" I said.

Grandma shrugged. "Snakes, probably. Snakes and spiders and rats. Can't think of anything else that would want to be in there." She squinted her eyes at me. "Certainly not grandkids."

"I was just curious," I said.

"Dangerous habit, curiosity," said Grandma. "Though I find it to be easily redirected." She motioned with her hand. "Come along, Lee. I've got something a little special to show you."

She led me to the Hummingbird Grove. The birds were out, flitting around, red-throated flames of them cast all over, bouncing and floating and hovering like gravity didn't even exist, like there were no rules in the universe that couldn't be broken.

"Sit down here," she said. "Go on, right there in the grass. It's a good spot, your momma liked it. It'll do you good to sit there. No, on your knees with your feet folded under you. Right, like that, in supplication. You know that word?"

"I do," I said. "It's a humble prayer, right?"

"Humble is the operative word there, yes," she said. "When you are in a holy place, it's always best to take a knee."

"What's so holy about the Hummingbird Grove?"

"Well, what isn't?" said Grandma. "To be frank, what natural place on this earth isn't holy, so to speak? As in set apart, as in a possible paradise for us? The world doesn't just exist, dear boy. It was created for us to delight in. Don't you know that? Don't you believe it in your heart?"

"That's what Walt Whitman said, more or less. And Emerson and those guys."

"I don't know about all that," said Grandma. "I was never much for poetry. Literature is a bit of a blind spot for me, always has been. But we collect our own holy texts, don't we? The Bible for some folks, sure, but whatever's out there, whatever speaks to you—a good meal, the night sky, the moon, poetry, whatever it is—that's where your heart gathers its truth. That's where the world sets its meaning in you. Do you understand?"

"I think so," I said.

"Good. Smart boy." She smiled at me. "Now Lee, I'm going to be completely honest with you, and I want you to do the same with me. Agreed? Okay. I know you have a gift."

I squinted my eyes at her. "What kind of gift?"

"I know that you see things," she said. "Visions."

She must have noticed the look of panic on my face because she immediately laid a gentle calloused hand on my shoulder.

"No, no, don't worry now," she said. "I'm not angry with you, and you're not in any trouble. My, your mother did a number on you, didn't she?"

"Mom thought the visions were shameful," I said. "Like there was something wrong with me, like my brain didn't work right."

"My dear boy, there's nothing in the world wrong with you," said Grandma. "It almost breaks my heart to think that you believe your gift to be a malfunction of sorts. Nothing could be further from the truth. You're just special is all. Your mind's eye is open to things that most people can't even fathom. I'm the same way, of course, though my gift is much more limited in scope than yours, I assure you."

"How do you know?"

"Lee, honey, I felt it the moment you set foot on my porch," she said. "The power emanating from you, like a halo sparkling right over your head. My father had the same power. He's the one who first bought this land. The Farm was his vision originally, before he passed it along to me. You were born for this, is what I'm saying. It's your talent, it's in your blood. But like all talents, it is worthless unless cultivated. You must practice, Lee, learn to open the doorways in your mind so that the Spirit can flow easily through you. You must control the visions so that the visions do not control you."

I thought I was starting to understand. It had never even occurred to me that this was something I could actually have power over.

"Okay," I said. "I mean, that sounds pretty good, I guess. But how do I do that?"

"You can start with this little exercise, okay? Now shut your eyes and try to picture all the truths of your heart. Make them into little objects, bright and shining things, separate, like tchotchkes on a mantle. Or better yet, relics in a church. Picture the best day of your life like a saint's holy anklebone or your favorite poem like the Shroud of Turin. You got it?"

I tried. I shut my eyes and pictured a museum gallery like the one Mom took me to that time we went to Washington, DC. All the portraits lined up in a row, hanging on the walls— all the best memories I had, all my favorite and most beautiful things in the world. I remembered this old Federico García Lorca poem where he said, "They come to me, my essential things. / They are refrains of refrains." And so they arrived: The moon over Lapham Lake in August, fog gathering at the edge of the water. The clock from that one Georg Trakl poem. Mom's laugh, bright and scattered and alive as a flock of hummingbirds. Murphy's grin after she knocked her front tooth out playing basketball. William Blake's painting of a flea. Rilke's puppet show. The last milky slurp of a Coke float. Anna Karina dancing in *Band of Outsiders*. That one eagle's nest I saw, big as a baby's crib. The stars in the desert when Mom drove us to the Hoover Dam, how it was the first time I understood how many there were, how in all of the universe we are unique and not alone.

"Yes," said Grandma. "That's exactly it."

The light pressing against my eyelids began to change, like a cloud had passed away from the sun and for the first time I was seeing the world undimmed. Before me was the Hummingbird Grove, but it was brighter somehow, wilder and strange-colored. Flowers grew up everywhere, so dazzling they hurt my eyes.

A blond-headed boy stood in the Hummingbird Grove. He wore a little black suit like he was just coming back from a funeral, same as I had worn yesterday. He had the brightest blue eyes, like the clearest sky you ever saw.

"Hello," said the boy.

I snapped awake, sucking in breath like I'd been underwater for minutes. I slumped over in the grass, light-headed, and lay there.

And Grandma watched me, a peculiar smile on her face.

Like she knew.

Grandma rose to her feet and dusted off her jeans.

"Come," she said, extending her hand to me. "Get up now. There's work to do. Always more work to do on a farm."

"I'm exhausted," I said. "I feel all jittery."

"Your mind is tired, yes, but your body still has energy to spend. And Murphy needs your help—all that painting to do. Lots to do on a farm. That's what farms are good for."

Grandma began her walk back toward the house. I stood, a little wobbly, and followed after her.

Hours later, as I bent over the porch, spreading white paint from an old can with a hard, flaky brush, I started to wonder when this cop was showing up. I was sunburnt, achy, and exhausted, and my head felt all fluttery. What had happened to me in the Hummingbird Grove? Had it even been real, or was it all in my head?

Still, I felt so much better just getting to talk about my visions for once and not being ashamed of them. To hear Grandma tell me that I wasn't crazy. For the first time I wasn't the outcast, shunned by everybody for being weird. I was special. I had a gift. And that meant more to me than just about anything ever had in all my life.

I looked over at Murphy, working hard on the other end of the porch. She was tanned deep already—Murphy always tanned where I burned—and she had paint flecks all over her face, her mouth twisted into a bit of a scowl. Her overalls were rolled up, and her tiny arms were all strong with muscle. She looked like a warrior, my little sister did. I thought about how proud Mom would have been of her, how much Mom might have liked seeing us here in the place where she grew up.

I wondered again what had happened between Mom and Grandma that had made her ditch the Farm and never return. I wondered why she never bothered to bring us out here to the beautiful home she had loved. I figured it had something to do with Mom's stubbornness, with the way she never admitted defeat, how she never apologized, only accepted apologies from other people. Mom had been a mighty hard person to live with—I knew that from experience—and I could only imagine it was tough being her mother. So I guessed they had their reasons for fighting like they did.

By the time Murphy and I finished painting, the sun was near setting, the sky big and wide and open. The cop still hadn't come to talk to us, and that worried me. Maybe there'd been an actual crime in Benign or something. I'd have to bug Grandma about it tonight. I hoped Murphy wouldn't get too mad. Dinner was coming soon, but I figured we had a little time to wander the Farm. The barn was off-limits obviously, but everywhere else seemed to be allowed. Murphy was game, so we went for a ramble through the strange and ramshackle grounds.

Much of it was old cultivated land gone to seed. The Farm apparently used to be huge: There was fenced-in space for cattle grazing, a horse pen, and rows upon rows of fields now grown over with scrub grass and wildflowers. The effect was beautiful—nature rebelling against the old order of men, reclaiming its own dominion. That was the thing about nature—it was always coming back from the dead, the constantly resurrecting Christ of the world. I thought about all the strip malls back home that got thrown up and then abandoned within a year, all the businesses closed and the cheap buildings slowly falling down. I thought about plants bursting up through the cracks in the floor. I thought about trees growing through the holes in the roof. Being at the Farm made me want nature to swallow every ugly thing and smother it with the tiny yellow suns of wildflowers. It made me want a better world to walk through, a second Eden, where plastic and concrete were banned forever.

"I can't believe how beautiful this place is," I said.

Murphy squinted at me.

"Since when did you get outdoorsy?" she said. "You can barely go outside without something stinging you and your arm swelling up like an eggplant."

"Not here though," I said. "I bet I'm not allergic to anything on the Farm, and nothing has stung me yet."

It was true. Usually when I went outside I just sat around in a hammock, reading. But I realized I didn't want to read at the Farm. I wanted to explore, see everything there was to see out here, touch and taste and smell all of it. From what I could tell, the entire western half of the Farm was given over to forest that was there long before our great-grandfather bought this land. Grandma had said those trees would never be cleared, because how could anyone commune with nature if they tried to tame all of it? Dense thickets of trees led to wide-open pasture-land, and strange winding paths through the brush suddenly opened up onto wonderful places. It was like a sprawling maze, a haunted house of nature, where every left turn surprised you with something new and wonderful.

Murphy and I cut down a path between tall winding birch trees. It swerved around a small cabin with a chimney, a garden out back, and a whole mess of clothes hanging out to dry. A kid in a straw hat sat on a lawn chair, smoking a pipe, reading a book. Inside someone strummed a guitar.

"I figure that's the tenant house," said Murphy.

"Yeah," I said. "I guess so."

I looked around everywhere for Cass, but I didn't see her. I wondered what she did all day, if they just sat around making music.

"Looking for your girlfriend?" said Murphy.

"Fuck off," I said, and Murphy laughed.

We walked farther down the trail. I wanted to find the lake, the one from Mom's memories, the one she had told me about at the beach. But when we got there, I realized it was really just a small pond, only a couple hundred feet across. Cypresses rippled up from the water, all knock-kneed and strange, Spanish moss dangling down like witches' hair.

"Mom used to talk about this place," I said. "She said she used to swim here."

"I think I remember that," said Murphy.

The sun was low now, and it made the water shimmer like liquid gold. I wanted to throw myself in, to strip down and leap, not worried about how deep it would be, not worried about what might be submerged beneath. I wanted to be in there, baptized into this new world and into my new life on the Farm. I wanted to hold myself under and rise up from the water brandnew, cleansed somehow, a better creation. I wanted it now.

I kicked off my shoes and walked to the water's edge and stuck a toe in.

"It's warm," I said, unclipping my overalls.

"Wait," said Murphy.

"Come on," I said. "It's every bit as perfect as Mom always said it was."

She put a hand on me. "No, dude. Hold up a minute."

And then I saw them. Gliding across the pond came three water moccasins. I'd never seen so many together like that, swimming in perfect formation. Moccasins were supposed to be solitary, lonely creatures. But there they all were, like some kind of evil miracle. I would have thought it was a vision if Murphy hadn't seen them too. They wisped past us with that strange curlicuing gait they have, barely causing a ripple, a family of death slithering across the water.

We heard Grandma hollering far away, clanging some kind of bell.

"Guess that means dinner's ready," said Murphy.

I looked back toward the pond. Clouds drifted over the sun, and the water was gray now, cast in shadow, murky and mysterious, as if it were hiding something. The snakes were gone, disappeared back to wherever they came from.

"Yeah," I said. "I guess we should go."

I clipped my overalls back on and stepped into my shoes, and Murphy and I walked back to the house.

THAT NIGHT WHEN WE SAT DOWN FOR DINNER, Grandma grabbed our hands for the blessing, which was as long and strange as all the other ones. I started to ask her about the cop who hadn't showed up, but she shushed me.

"We'll save the conversation until after dinner, shall we?" she said. "I worked hard on this meal, and I won't have it marred by unpleasantness."

The table was immaculate, with roast pork and potatoes, grilled asparagus with olive oil, corn on the cob doused in butter, Texas toast. It was so much food I couldn't believe it, all hot and steaming there, waiting for us, and I was starved. I ate and ate, and Murphy did too, plate after plate, until we were so full and tired I thought we'd both topple over.

Grandma just sat and watched us, smiling, cutting her tiny bites and eating them slowly, chewing forever.

When we finished I was so tired I had to fight to keep my head off the table. Murphy was literally nodding off over her plate, a slab of banana pudding nearly untouched on it.

"Grandma," I said, "what about that cop?"

"What cop?" said Grandma. "Murphy, dear, finish your dessert. It's wasteful to leave food on your plate."

"But I'm so full," said Murphy.

"Then perhaps you shouldn't have gotten such a big serving," said Grandma. "No, in this house we finish what we start. Always."

"The sheriff," I said. "What was his name? Sheriff Bearden?"

"Yes?" said Grandma. "What about him?

"He never came by today. To talk to us."

"Well, he must have had other things to do."

"But this is really serious, Grandma," I said. "Horace is a murderer, and now he knows we know."

"Maybe they already caught him," said Grandma. "Did you ever think of that? Maybe they caught him and detained him already, and they didn't send a man to come and interview you because they couldn't spare one at the moment."

"Okay," said Murphy, "but surely they would have let us know if something like that happened."

"And how would they do that?" said Grandma. "It's not like I have a telephone. I suggest patience, children. All shall be handled in its own time."

Murphy shoved the last bite of banana pudding in her mouth. I thought for a second she might puke.

"Look, we'll just go tomorrow," I said to Grandma. "We'll wake up super early and take Horace's car. You don't even have to come."

Grandma frowned. "Seems like a dreadful waste of gas," she said. "And I hate being wasteful."

I didn't understand her reluctance about this. I mean, maybe leaving home was hard on her, being a sort of recluse and all, but Horace was a maniac, and she needed to understand that.

"You can't stop us," said Murphy. "And besides, it's not like we'll be wasting your gas anyway."

"Fine, fine," said Grandma. "You can drive all the way to town first thing in the morning, and you may bother the sheriff all you like." She stood up from her chair. "If you'll excuse me, children, I'm headed to bed. You may do the same when you finish the dishes."

I looked over at the sink, where piled high was a whole mess of plates and knives and ramekins and everything else it took to cook a gigantic meal. This would take forever to finish.

"But Grandma . . ."

"Is that a complaint I hear, Lee?" said Grandma, her voice sharp again. "Because I do not suffer murmuring, not in this house. Not on this Farm."

"No, ma'am," I said.

"Very good. Dishes, then, and the police first thing in the morning." Grandma smiled at us, her face gone gentle, serene, candlelight flickering in her eyes. "Sleep well, children, and good night."

Grandma whisked herself out of the room, dress swishing around her ankles. Murphy dropped her head to the table and groaned.

"This is going to take hours, isn't it?" said Murphy.

"Yep," I said. "So let's get to it already."

We washed and scrubbed and dried, Grandma of course not having a dishwasher. It was late by the time we were finished, or at least Farm late—eleven fifteen. We were both exhausted and sore.

I climbed into my bunk bed, and in no time I was asleep.

THAT NIGHT I HAD A VISION.

I was standing beside a campfire. There were three men gathered around it, dressed in rags. They looked sad and crumpled up as old paper sacks, and they sat listless, warming their hands. Above us were the vast and glowing stars, the sky as big as forever.

"Where am I?" I said.

One of the men raised his face to me. His eyes were a searing blue, and they seemed to glow in the firelight.

"There are two worlds," he said. "The daylight and the darkness." He clapped his hands together. "They are the same world."

The second man raised his face to me. He had the most beautiful smile I'd ever seen, and his voice came soft as music.

"When the door is open," he said, "the people come and go. We have kept him apart, just as we promised."

The third man raised his face to me, and in my heart I felt peace, like I knew everything would be okay.

"A secret sleeps," he said, "deep in the woods."

"I'm sorry," I said. "I don't understand.

The first man held a finger to his lips. "Quiet," he said. "He comes."

And in the dark I saw something move.

"LEE! WAKE UP!"

Murphy shook me awake. The room was dark, and for a moment I forgot where I was. I forgot Mom was dead and Horace was still out there and we were at our grandma's house. I forgot everything, and that was the best feeling, that my life had started right back where it had been before this nightmare happened. But then I woke up with my face a foot from the ceiling like this bunk bed was a coffin I was buried in. It terrified me, this trapped feeling, pinned down and boxed in and suffocated, ready to be dropped dead in the dirt forever. I jolted up and smacked my head on the ceiling and lay back down, moaning a little.

"Stop fucking around," said Murphy. "You got to see this."

I climbed down from the top bunk and followed Murphy to the window.

Out in the field beyond the house the night was so dark and starless it didn't seem to be there at all, just a mass of long, stretched-out nothing that you could just as easily fall through as walk upon. But there, a lantern burned in the midst of all that empty like a single shimmering wandering star.

"It's Grandma," said Murphy. "What do you think she's doing?"

"I don't know," I said. "Farm chores?"

"In the middle of the night?"

"Maybe," I said. "I don't know shit about farming."

The wind outside picked up a little, and the old house creaked and groaned around us like the walls and the ceiling were having a conversation. The night outside was loud and crickety, and I felt surrounded suddenly, like there was a whole world of creatures out there hidden in the black. It was like the land outside the house had changed, like while we slept the house had sprouted legs and run us off to a different country, a wilder, stranger place than any we'd ever known before.

We gazed out the window into the night as darkness and the woods swallowed Grandma's lantern.

MORNING BROUGHT THE SMELL OF PANCAKES
and syrup and cooking sausages.

"Shit," said Murphy, the sun shining bright through the
windows. "We slept in."

Murphy walked down the hall to the bathroom, and I
climbed out of my bunk and got dressed. I wondered why
Grandma had let us sleep late. Wasn't she big on rules, on waking up at sunrise, "obeying the light"?

Downstairs the food was ready, hot on the stove. Grandma
wore jeans and a red plaid work shirt, her hair done up in a bun.
She chewed a toothpick and hummed softly while she cooked. I
had about a million questions to ask her, and I didn't even know
where to start.

"Glad you sleepyheads could finally join me," said
Grandma. "Dawn waits for no man—you remember that."

"You could have woken us up," said Murphy. "Today's the
day we're supposed to go to the police."

"The police will be there once you've finished your breakfast," said Grandma. "I still believe this trip to the town is a waste of time. Precious, precious time. Time, children, is all we have in this world, and don't you forget it."

"Great," said Murphy. "And today we'll spend our time talking to the police."

Grandma bent over the table and pointed a fork at Murphy's face. "You, young lady, have a smart mouth." I was startled a little. It was the fiercest gesture Grandma had made toward us.

"Sorry, Grandma," said Murphy, a little shaken. "I'm just nervous."

"That's fine, I know," said Grandma. She sat down at the table. "You kids have been through so much this past week, I can't even imagine. Forgive your old grandmother. I'm not so used to company. Shall we say the blessing? Food's getting cold."

We did, and it was long and strange, almost incantatory, a hint of music to the whole thing, like she was chanting at us.

"Amen," said Grandma. "Now eat up, kids. We got us a whole day ahead."

Two bites into my food I heard the sound of an engine, tires crunching up the gravel driveway. I dropped my fork.

"Horace," I said.

He had found us. We were too late. We should have gone to the police days ago. We should have gone the moment we got to Grandma's house.

I jumped up and ran to the window.

A police cruiser. *Oh shit.*

But no, it wasn't Horace's, it was a different make and model. This one was older, dustier, like something out of a cop movie from the '70s.

"Ah," said Grandma behind me at the window. "That'll be Sheriff Bearden." Any trace of fear or surprise had fallen from her face, and she seemed calm and contented. "Told y'all he would be coming sooner or later. I've known Sheriff Bearden for a long time, and he is a man of his word."

Sheriff Bearden was a lanky guy in his sixties with a beer belly and a leery eye. He climbed out of the car and walked up the drive with the slow, wide-legged strut that comes with years of unchallenged authority. He even wore a fucking cowboy hat.

"Y'all go sit on back down now," said Grandma. "I'll let Sheriff Bearden in."

Murphy and I sat at the table and waited. Soon Sheriff Bearden sauntered into the kitchen, Grandma following close behind.

"Howdy, y'all," he said. "Lee, is it? And Murphy?"

"Yes, sir," I said. We shook hands. He dead-fished me, hand limp and damp. Man, Mom would have broken his hand if he had tried to pull that shit on her.

"Sorry about your momma," said Sheriff Bearden. "Always did like her. Fine-looking girl."

"Thanks," said Murphy, gritting her teeth. "I'm sure she would have loved hearing that from you."

I shot Murphy a look like *Cool it already*. She rolled her eyes at me.

"Hungry, Sheriff?" said Grandma.

"Why, I could take a pancake or two," he said, and winked.

He sat down, took off his hat, and placed it on the table. Grandma set a plate before him, and we waited while Sheriff Bearden ate. And oh man, did he ever eat. That guy drowned everything, even his sausage, in syrup until his plate looked like a stew. And the way he chewed—big gobbing mouthfuls of food, the biggest bites you ever saw. He didn't just eat his breakfast, he massacred it.

"Now, kids," he said, dabbing his mouth with a napkin. "I already heard it from your grandmother over there, but I want to hear the story from y'all. Every bit of it, from the beginning."

So I told him everything that had happened, Murphy hopping in on the details. We started with Mom's weird behavior, the fight, her death, and the adoption papers we found in Horace's car. The whole time Sheriff Bearden stared squint-eyed at me and didn't blink or make a sound or even really move much. It was like talking to a switched-off robot of a man.

When I finished talking, the kitchen was quiet, Grandma standing off by the sink, Murphy silent across the table, all of us waiting for what Sheriff Bearden would say.

After what seemed like forever, Sheriff Bearden sighed.

"That is one hell of a story," he said. "I've heard some tales in my time, but that damn near tops them all."

"You don't believe us," said Murphy.

"On the contrary," he said. "I believe every goddamn word of your story. Who in the hell would make up something like that? Besides, I did a little checking in on that stepdad of yours. Did you know he is currently being investigated for evidence tampering? For physical abuse and intimidation of suspects? Rumors abound concerning this fellow. To my mind he's a disgrace to the uniform."

I could have kissed the man, gross as he was. Somebody believed us. We weren't alone in the world. And now they were going to catch Horace. We didn't have to be afraid anymore.

"We got evidence too," said Murphy.

"Well, I'm sure we've got enough already to bring him in," said Sheriff Bearden. "I'll call up the chain of command, see who I can get on the horn. You ask me, though, your man's gone. Took off. Headed southwest, probably to Mexico. Flown the coop, as it were. That is, if he's got any sense in him."

I looked at Murphy, and Murphy looked back at me.

"I highly doubt that, Sheriff," I said.

"Well, we'll keep a lookout anyhow. Put a couple of cars on patrol, have some people at your gate, if that's okay with you, Mrs. Sanford."

"I'd rather you didn't," she said. "No need to waste the manpower."

"It's not a waste," he said. "Protecting and serving is our job, lest you forget."

"It's appreciated, Sheriff," I said.

"Yeah," said Murphy. "Thanks for believing us."

"I find the truth comes most purely from the mouths of the youth," he said. "Isn't that in the Bible? Shakespeare, maybe? Something about innocence and all that. Hell, isn't everything either from the Bible or Shakespeare?" He picked up his hat and plopped it on his head, tipping the brim at us. "Farewell, ladies and gentleman. It has been a pleasure."

"Thanks again, Sheriff," I said. "You don't know how good it feels to be believed."

"I reckon, young fella, that maybe I do," he said. Sheriff Bearden stood up to go. "Thank you, ma'am. Those pancakes were divine."

"I'll walk you to the door," said Grandma.

"Don't bother," he said. "I know the way. Y'all take care, now."

We heard his boots clomp down the hallway, slow and unhurried, the front door swinging shut behind him.

"Now," said Grandma, smiling, "shall we get to work?"

The rest of the day was much the same as the one before. Grandma had me tending to the garden while Murphy trimmed tree limbs with these giant elongated pruners that stretched out four feet in front of her. They were kind of badass looking, like some weird medieval weapon dug up from a battlefield somewhere.

"Pretty cool," I said.

"Feel free to take over for me anytime," she said.

Around noon Grandma led me to the Hummingbird Grove. I was a little nervous, and excited too. It meant a lot to me that Grandma thought my visions were precious things to be cultivated. But it also scared me, because I didn't know where the visions came from, and I sure as hell didn't know what they meant or what they were for or even if they meant anything at all.

"You look like you have something on your mind, Lee," said Grandma.

"Well, I had this vision," I said, "last night."

"Oh?" said Grandma.

"Yeah," I said. "I was in this dark world with all these stars. And it was scary, you know? It terrified me."

"What is often scariest to us is what we don't understand," she said.

"There were these three guys, and they were dressed in rags..."

"The Gentlemen?" said Grandma, grabbing my hand. "You've seen them?"

"Maybe," I said. "How do you know about them?"

"There isn't much about this land that I do not know," said Grandma.

"There was this other thing there," I said, "something in the darkness."

Grandma shushed me. "Don't speak too much of it. These are your visions and yours alone. You have to solve them yourself. The question is, what are they trying to tell you? Is there a clue to unlock?"

Two worlds. Open doors. A secret in the woods.

"Maybe," I said. "I just don't know yet."

"That's okay. Perhaps our journeys together in the daylight will be more revealing. Come now. Take your place."

We sat on our knees in supplication, the hummingbirds whirring like blood-drop-bright thoughts above us, while Murphy was off fertilizing the garden. I kind of felt bad sitting here in a trance, enjoying the sunshine, when Murphy was doing all the hard work, and I told Grandma as much.

"But this *is* hard work," said Grandma, "and important. Is there anything more difficult than going inside oneself, than opening every last locked door in your heart to welcome the Spirit inside? Fearsome work has been appointed to you, dear boy, and you must be brave to do it."

"I know," I said. "It's just, you know, not backbreaking, like spreading mulch or something, or running a marathon. That seems way harder."

"To each is appointed the task that he can do," said Grandma. "Murphy has her own duties and responsibilities, many of which she is only coming to realize she has. You, dear boy, are the vessel of a higher power, but Murphy must play her part as well. So shut your eyes, Lee, and don't bother concentrating. Let everything go—your mother, your sister, your stepfather, even me. Don't listen to me. Just breathe the meadow in, the forest and the woods. Breathe the air. Let the Hummingbird Grove fill you. Whatever lives in this place, let it also live in you."

I didn't know how I was supposed to not listen to Grandma and follow her instructions at the exact same time, but I figured I might as well try. I imagined my mind as my old bedroom, and all kinds of junk was on the floor—T-shirts, underpants, old fast food bags, crunched Coke cans, Mars bar wrappers, all that. And then I took a big broom and swept it all aside until there was nothing left, until not even my bedroom floor was there. It was only darkness, like the space between stars.

And then I was in the Hummingbird Grove again, but it had gone strange, the colors wild and saturated and off, like in an old movie. Things were hazy but alive, as if everything was realer than it was supposed to be, more solid somehow. Like I was the thing the plants and flowers and birds were dreaming, like I was just a thought in the Hummingbird Grove's mind.

The boy from last time stood before me. He was pale, and his little suit seemed dirty, like he'd been playing in it.

"This is a special place," he said. "Not everyone can come here, you know."

"You mean the Hummingbird Grove?" I said.

"Yes," he said. "The true Hummingbird Grove, the one others can't see. It's always here, tucked away beneath everything, and only certain people may find it."

"So I'm one of the lucky ones, huh?" I said.

"I suppose, yes, you could say that." The boy smiled strangely at me. "Would you like to see a trick?"

"Sure."

The boy gestured toward the whirring birds. A large hummingbird flew right up to his face, hovering an inch from his nose like it wanted to ask him a question.

"Watch," he said.

The boy extended his pointer finger. The hummingbird slowed down. It perched on his finger.

"Now you try."

Slowly I extended my arm and stuck my finger out, and another hummingbird landed on it. I eyed a tiny one darting around a feeder while a bigger bird drank freely. I nodded at the bird, and it flew to me, landing on my arm. Another one came, perching like a pirate's parrot on my shoulder, then two more. I whistled, and they all took off from me at once, flying in a perfect spiral formation.

The boy smiled at me, and it made me feel good, you know? He had the kind of smile that made you trust him, like he was just so happy to see you he could hardly stand it.

"But I am happy to see you, Lee," he said.

"How do you know my name?" I said.

The boy's blue eyes shone with a kind of inward-burning light, like stained glass with the sun streaming through it.

Then something happened. The world went dark for a moment, as if a curtain had been dropped over everything, like the sun itself had been snuffed out. I stood in darkness, deep in a forest with trees all around and no people anywhere. I could feel the woods slithering around me, awake and alive.

In front of me stood a tree, a massive oak as thick as a car, with a huge split in the middle of it, like some giant with an ax had cloven it right through the heart. Its bark seemed to swirl and move, forming a woven cross and a spinning wheel and a lantern and a dagger and the slash and stitch of runes glimmering a moment and then fading, and the leaves above shimmered in the breeze. It was a living tree, a breathing, whispering thing, and it seemed familiar, like I had seen it somewhere before.

I took a step toward it.

In the split of the tree I saw a pair of eyes, bright white against the dark, staring back at me.

"Come closer," whispered a voice. "Don't be afraid."

I leaned my face up to the hole in the tree, and I looked deep into those eyes.

A pale hand reached out of the darkness, grasping at me.

I snapped awake, sucking in breath like I'd been underwater for minutes. I slumped over in the grass, light-headed, and lay there, exhausted. That tree—the one with the split in it—was like the one Mom had painted on our living room wall.

Grandma's eyes were wide, and she had a knowing look on her face. After a minute I caught my breath, my heart beat a little slower, and I sat up and faced her.

"You look like you have a question for me, Lee," she said.

"Grandma," I said, "do you know a tree with a big split in it?"

"What now?"

"A tree, somewhere on the Farm. It's got a gash right in the trunk, like lightning struck it, or maybe an animal hollowed it out. I saw it in my vision."

"Shoot, honey," she said. "There's all kinds of trees like that around here. At least one a year gets struck by lightning."

"But this one is special," I said. "There's something... I dunno, different about it."

I thought I saw the edges of Grandma's lips lift a little, like maybe she was trying not to smile.

"I just don't know anything about that," she said. "If there's a tree out there like what you're saying, I guess you'll have to find it on your own."

LATER THAT DAY I FOUND MURPHY SPRAWLED
out in the grass next to the porch. She tilted her head up at me.

"Yes?"

"I had a vision," I said, "and now I got to find a tree. You want
to come?"

Murphy lay back down and shut her eyes.

"No."

"No?"

"I'm worn out, dude. While you and Grandma were out
there communing with nature, I had to do actual physical
fucking work."

"Sorry about that," I said. "She won't let me help unless I do
the vision stuff first."

"Whatever. I'm too tired to give a shit. Happy tree hunting."

I could tell Murphy was pissed at me, but there wasn't much
I could do about that right now. I had to find that tree. I knew

something important would happen if I found it, that I would be one step closer to understanding my gift.

I shut my eyes and tried to remember my vision. It seemed like the Split Tree was somewhere with dense woods. The only place like that on the Farm was out past the Hummingbird Grove, to the west. I knew the woods there went on for acres and acres. It was a decent enough place to try.

The birds were out whirring, and the garden glowed in the golden light. I couldn't believe this was my life now, that the Farm was my home. As much as I missed Mom, and as scared as I was of Horace, I still felt lucky somehow that I could live in a place like this.

A hummingbird hovered right near my nose, its red head bobbing like a cork in invisible water. In fact, he seemed to be staring right at me, same as the hummingbird had in my vision earlier.

"Hey, buddy," I said. "You got something to show me?"

The hummingbird tilted his head, and in the sunset glare, the light seemed to pass through him, like he was made of dust.

That's when I realized this hummingbird wasn't real—or at least it wasn't real in the physical sense. It was a vision. I knew if I reached my hand out I would swipe through it, clean as empty air.

The hummingbird zipped away from me, taking off in a strange darting trajectory. It was hard to keep up, the way it seemed to change course so quick, to ricochet off nothing at all. I was running full speed, scrambling past tree stumps and molehills down a rough path past the Hummingbird Grove, past the garden, to a part of the Farm I'd never been to before. The trees were taller here, the bark bent and warped, and they stood like sentinels—guardians who had seen windstorms and wars and tornadoes and who had stood strong through all of it. They were wise, these trees, and they had their years scarred into their bark. The hummingbird stopped in front of one tree, bigger than the rest, with a hole right in the middle of the trunk like someone had reached in and removed the tree's heart.

The hummingbird tilted his beak at me and darted off, vanishing into a patch of sunlight.

The tree didn't look exactly like it had in my vision, but it was close enough, and besides, it was here where I'd been led. I felt a chill spiderwebbing up my spine. It felt as if the hole in the tree was staring at me, like any moment eyes would appear in the darkness, same as they had in my vision.

But nothing happened. I stood there and waited. Somewhere far off I heard the sound of wind chimes, the skittering of creatures in the leaves. Was there something I was missing, something I had forgotten?

In the vision, the pale hand had reached out to me. But then, real life wasn't always exactly like my visions. Things changed sometimes, and the details weren't necessarily quite the same.

What if in reality it was supposed to be reversed? Maybe I was supposed to reach into the tree?

I didn't want to. I mean, there could have been spiders or bats or something in there. It's just generally not good policy to stick your hand into a dark place, especially in the woods.

But I was being braver now, wasn't I? The Farm was my place, and I wasn't to fear anything here. And besides, the vision had told me to. At least I thought it had.

I took a deep breath and stuck my arm down into the cleft in the tree. It went in far, past my elbow, like the whole middle of the tree was hollowed out. I grasped around in there and felt something skitter up my arm. But I didn't yank my hand out, not yet. Because I'd found something else in there, something plastic, placed there just for me.

I pulled it out. An old '80s-style tape player. I popped it open. There was a blank cassette inside, a Memorex, with "JEREMIAH 07-18-88" scribbled in black ink on the label. Who the hell was Jeremiah?

I clicked play.

A voice rang out into the forest, bold through the cheap tinny speaker. It was deep and rich and full and lovely and beautiful, more like music than talking. It carried a rhythm in it, a lilting hope and a beauty. I could have listened to it all day.

"Children, have you ever felt alone? Rejected by the world? Cast out, friendless, unfit for the company of others? Do you feel as if you will never find a place of your own, somewhere you can truly belong? If this is so—listen to me now, children—I say you are blessed."

I heard other voices on the tape, people in the room with him during the recording, clapping and hollering along. It was a sermon, some kind of church service. It seemed wild and ecstatic like a Pentecostal church, but also not quite Christian either.

"Blessed, I say. And do you know why? Because I am here to tell you a secret. Would you like to hear that secret? Listen close to me."

Tape hiss, static, more clapping.

"It is not the world that has rejected you, children. No, it is you who have rejected the world. The Spirit has told you that this world is not worthy of you. There is a light inside each and every one of you, and the world is blinded by that light. It drives those born of darkness far away—it repels them. For they want you to deny your own light, to banish the sweetest and most beautiful parts of yourselves. Friends, they want you to become empty, vessels of night, those who live for nothing but their own bellies, their own selfish gain. In short, they want you to become just like them.

"And praise the Spirit, because you are unable to do so. Praise the Spirit, because something in you revolts at the thought of being one of them, your very bones quake at the notion. Praise the Spirit, because you are here now, and you are listening."

The applause was rapturous. People cheering, hollering, going absolutely wild.

"What are you doing?" said a girl's voice.

I pressed stop and whirled around. I also probably made a yelping sound like a tiny terrified little puppy, if you want me to be honest about it.

It was Cass. She wore a brown top and tight blue jeans with patches all over them. Her neck was freckly from the sun, and her hair was all windblown and wild. I was pretty sure I'd never seen a more beautiful human in my entire life.

This, of course, made it very hard for me to talk.

"It's . . . um . . . a tape player," I said. "I found it in this tree."

Cass stared at me, her eyebrows raised.

"And why did you put a tape player in that tree?"

"I didn't put it there."

"Then who did?"

The sun cut through a gap in the clouds, and it got really hot in the woods all of a sudden. I could feel sweat pouring down my neck.

"I honestly don't know," I said.

Cass smiled a little bit at that. It made my stomach go all swirly.

"So, Lee," she said, "how did you know to look in the tree for this tape player?"

"I . . . well . . ."

"Go on."

I don't know why—maybe I was flustered, or maybe I so desperately wanted someone else to know and understand, or maybe I just couldn't think of anything else to say. Whatever the reason, I decided to be honest with her.

"I . . . I have these visions sometimes."

"Hmm," she said. "And a vision told you to look inside a tree for a tape player?"

"Not exactly," I said. "But pretty much."

I wondered what she'd say, if she'd laugh at me or just think I was some kind of creep. I held my breath, and it felt as if the whole forest and even the wind held their breaths with me.

"That's the coolest thing I've ever heard in my life."

I couldn't believe it. There was no way.

"Are you fucking kidding me?" I said.

Cass stared me dead in the eyes. Hers were brown and strange, the color of fall leaves, little specks of light floating in them, the kind of eyes I could spend my life lost inside.

"I am absolutely 100 percent not kidding you," she said.

This was great news. Maybe the best news I'd ever heard in my life.

"So this tree is like magic, huh?" she said. "You have a vision, and then there's something here. Like it's your mailbox from the spirit world. They just drop you messages from time to time, and here is where you pick them up."

"I guess so," I said. "I mean, this is my first time doing this. I don't exactly know if it's going to be a habit or not."

"Worth checking though, huh?"

"I suppose."

"Good to know," she said. Cass smiled her crooked-tooth smile at me. "I'll be seeing you."

And she walked off toward the tenant house.

I waited until she was gone, then hurried back to the house, the tape player in my hands. I snuck it past Grandma in the kitchen, who told me to hurry and wash up, and into the bedroom while Murphy was in the shower. I tucked the tape player under my covers, where nobody could see it.

For now it was my secret.

Mine and Cass's.

REMEMBER HOW I SAID I NEVER HAD ANY friends growing up? I'd like to talk about that now, if it's okay with you. It has more than a little bit to do with my visions. See, I was homeschooled, I didn't play sports, and I didn't go to church hardly ever, all of which pretty much doomed me in the friend department. Besides, our neighbors were mostly old and childless, and if they did happen to breed, the kids were guaranteed to be mean-spirited rednecks. However, I did try to make friends from time to time, even though it never worked, even though it always ended in disaster.

Want to hear about the last time I ever tried making friends?

This was back when I was fourteen or so and going through a phase. The phase was that I only wore black, always, all the time. This was before I'd discovered poetry, when I was still a dork who read *Hellblazer* comics and listened to the Smiths all day. I had a black Punisher shirt, a black Batman shirt, and a black Green Lantern shirt. I wore those shirts in rotation pretty much all the time along with black Converse, black cotton shorts, and black socks. I even wore a blank black baseball cap sometimes, just to complete the look. I know, it was weird, but I liked it. Sometimes when Mom was drinking, she'd laugh and call me her little Johnny Cash, which I thought was badass.

I mean, to my mind I was the coolest person who ever lived. I listened to good music, I read cool comics, and I had mystical visions. Maybe somebody would actually like me now.

So I was really excited when this kid Kent Knoll moved in down the street from us. He was about my age, maybe a year or two older. Word was Kent was rich. He had a giant TV in his bedroom, which was incredible to think of, and a fish tank with all these fancy exotic ocean fish swimming around in it. Even better, Kent had a go-kart that he rode up and down our street at unbelievable speeds. Sometimes other kids would come over and ride his go-kart too. I thought that was amazing. I wanted to ride that go-kart more than I'd ever wanted to do anything in my life. I wanted to meet Kent Knoll and be his friend and have everybody like me just the same as they did him.

One night, as I was getting ready for bed, I felt something strange in my right arm. A kind of crawling, pulsating feeling, like the blood was pumping too hard in my veins, like my blood vessels were about to swell and burst.

I looked down, and I saw a weird bulge in my arm, a kind of bumpy line under the skin, a swollen spot that itched and burned.

And then the spot moved. It crawled, and it burned like fire.

There were other spots, I saw, rippling through my arm. A dozen, then two dozen, then more than I could count. There were hundreds of them crawling under my skin, biting me, burning like all hell was inside of me. The pain was so great I fell to the bathroom floor. I scratched at my arm, slapped it, trying to kill whatever was under my skin, whatever caused me to itch and hurt so. The pain was excruciating. It was unlike anything I had ever felt, as if someone had taken a syringe full of fire and injected it straight into my veins.

The flesh on my arm began to bubble, a blister forming. I watched it boil and throb until finally it popped. Blood erupted onto the tile floor, streaming hot over my arm, the sickly smear of it. And from that wound crawled an ant. A red one—a fire ant. It came out blood-smeared, sticky with it, and I flung it in a smatter on the floor.

They began to stream out of my arm then, a flow of ants thicker than blood, hundreds of them bursting out of the hole in my skin. They were crawling up my chest and onto my neck, biting me, swarming up my nose and onto my tongue and down my throat, ants pouring like blood from my body, covering me, smothering me until I couldn't breathe anymore, until I couldn't see, until I knew I would die.

And then nothing. I was sitting on my bathroom floor, sweaty and out of breath, my throat sore from screaming. Murphy came running in.

"You okay?" she said.

"I had a vision," I said.

She just rolled her eyes at me and left.

The next day I saw Kent and this kid Rob Louis hanging out in front of his house. They were drinking Capri Suns, just lounging like they had nothing better to do, like that go-kart wasn't sitting right there in front of them, ready to ride. I thought maybe that was my chance to let those guys get to know me and see how cool I was. That day I had on my Batman shirt, the one with the yellow logo on the front, which was by far my coolest, most understated shirt of all. It was destiny. I walked myself right over and said hi to them.

"Hi, Kent," I said. "Hi, Rob."

They both looked at me like I was some kind of walking fungus.

"I'm Lee," I said, a little uncomfortable. "I live down the street."

"The homeschool kid?" said Kent. "Yeah, I heard of you."

"You have?" I said.

Kent nodded.

"I heard of you too," said Rob Louis.

I was excited. That meant other kids had been talking about how cool I was. They already knew. Making friends was even easier than I ever thought it would be.

"You guys going to ride the go-kart?" I said.

"Maybe," said Kent. "You want to ride the go-kart?"

"Yes," I said. "That would be awesome."

Kent and Rob looked at each other, then back at me. Kent Knoll smiled a little bit.

"Sure, you can ride the go-kart," he said. "But I got to finish my chores first. You want to help me finish my chores?"

No, I didn't want to help Kent finish his chores. Why didn't Rob Louis help Kent finish his chores? Besides, all they were doing was sitting around slurping Capri Suns and being lazy. But wasn't helping people with their chores the kind of thing a friend would do? I thought probably. And I really wanted to ride that go-kart.

"Okay," I said. "What do I need to do?"

Kent and Rob stood up together and walked down the porch steps and into the yard. I realized how much bigger both of them were than me, taller, and their arms had actual muscles, like they had been lifting weights or something. I didn't know that kids even could lift weights.

"Follow me," said Kent.

He and Rob led me around the house to the back lot. It was about an acre of brown mud with little tufts of grass popping up here and there. It also had the biggest anthills I'd ever seen in my life all over it. They rose up like tiny volcanoes every five feet or so. Some came all the way up to my knees. I'd never seen anything like it.

"Holy crap," I said.

I remembered my vision from the night before. This wasn't good. In fact, this was really, really bad.

"Yeah," said Kent. "It's an infestation."

I knew that I had to turn tail and run, and I had to do it now. The vision had warned me about this place, about this exact moment. But then again, hadn't my visions been wrong before? I had sure as shit been wrong about Murphy's birthday party, which I had totally ruined. Maybe this vision was wrong too. After all, Kent and Rob were both being pretty nice to me, weren't they?

I wasn't going to leave. I was going to make friends. I was going to ride that damn go-kart.

"It's pretty wild," I said. "I never seen so many ants in one place."

Rob Louis stood there with his arms crossed, smirking at me. No one said a word.

"Yeah, so," I said, my voice cracking a little. "What do you guys need me to do?"

They moved together as one, as if they had been planning this for ages, as if it were all practiced and perfectly choreographed. Rob Louis tackled me, pinning down my arms and legs with his body. I fought and struggled, but what was the point? He was bigger than me and stronger than me and meaner than me.

"What's going on?" I asked. "Why are you doing this to me?"

Kent Knoll stood over me, a tiny smile on his face.

"Why are we doing this?" he said. "It's simple. Because we can."

He bent down and in one swift motion scooped up a huge handful of anthill. Then he pulled down the neck of my Batman shirt and dumped the anthill on my chest.

The ants swarmed me, biting, tickling, crawling all over my skin. They bit my chest, they bit my stomach, they bit inside my belly button. They crawled down my pants and into my underwear, gnawing on me. All the while Rob Louis pinned me down, his knees on my thighs, his hands on my wrists. I couldn't fight him off, I couldn't move. All I could do was scream.

So what did Kent Knoll do? He scooped up another handful of anthill and dumped it in my mouth.

I know Kent had to have gotten bitten—Rob Louis too, probably half a dozen times each. But I don't think they cared. I don't think a few ant bites were too high a price to pay to see me suffer.

Rob Louis let me go, and I rolled over and vomited dust and mud and ants. I yanked my Batman shirt off and swatted the ants off my naked chest, which was fat and pink with big swollen mounds all over it. I yanked my black shorts off and even my underwear. I swatted ants off my ass, off every part of me.

Kent Knoll and Rob Louis just stood there and laughed. They thought it was the funniest thing they'd ever seen in their lives.

No one came to help me. Who would have? We were behind the house, with trees and a fence between us and the nearest neighbors. I doubt anyone even heard me screaming. If they did, they probably figured it was a bunch of kids laughing, having fun, doing whatever it was that kids were supposed to do.

I ran out of the backyard, naked and ant-bit all over, my clothes in a ball under my arm. I sprinted nude through the neighborhood, crying the whole way, wailing like some shitty little kid.

Later that day when Murphy found out, she snuck into Kent Knoll's house and dumped a bag of Skittles into his fish tank, killing every last one of those expensive imported pets. Word was Kent was real upset about it.

"I did it for you, brother," she said, and socked me in the arm.

It was a hollow victory. I was feverish, sore, and on Benadryl. I nearly called an ambulance on myself.

You know what Mom did when she came home from wherever she was? It was nightfall when she hopped out of some stranger's car, lit cigarette in one hand, an open Bud Light bottle in the other. Mom was barefoot, her shoes lost to time or some field somewhere, and she stumbled up the porch steps. The door swung open, and Mom burst into the room, laughing.

Then she saw me on the couch, all swollen up and moaning.

"What the hell happened to you?" she said.

I told her. Mom sucked her cigarette and shook, she was so angry.

"I ought to go over and kick those kids' asses right now," she said. "And kick their parents' asses too."

I'd never seen Mom so mad before. I wondered if she actually would go over there and start throwing punches. Yeah, like that would help me make friends.

"It's not their fault," I said. "I had a vision that this would happen, and I went anyway."

Mom whirled around, glaring at me.

"What did you just say?"

I sat there in silence, looking back at her, praying that this time she'd finally believe me.

"You want the real truth, Lee?" said Mom. She got right down in my face, her breath all cigarette-stained and beery, and stared me dead in the eyes. "If you let somebody do something like that to you, then you probably deserved it."

She sauntered off to her room and slammed the door shut.

I gave up trying to make friends after that. I also spent my days afterward taking my visions pretty damn seriously. Even if they didn't come true every time, the kind of misery that happened when I didn't obey them was too much to bear. I still didn't know whether my visions came from God or my own psychotic brain or if there were aliens beaming them directly into my skull.

But I couldn't ignore them anymore.

DINNER PASSED WITHOUT MUCH HAPPENING. We worked, we ate, and we were exhausted. Murphy and I staggered up to bed and slumped down in our bunks.

"This whole thing is weird," said Murphy.

"What do you mean?" I said.

"I mean Grandma. I mean this sheriff guy. Like, where is Horace already? Did he just forget about us? I figured he would have been here by now, trying to get us back for knocking him out and stealing his car."

"Maybe he doesn't want to get caught," I said. "Maybe he's just happy with whatever money he's already gotten from the trust."

"Do you seriously think that?"

"No," I said. "But do you have any better ideas? Maybe Sheriff Bearden is right. Maybe he hightailed it after we escaped."

Murphy snorted.

"Fat chance of that. And I'll tell you another thing, I don't trust that fucking sheriff. Not one bit."

"What is your problem, Murphy?" I said.

"What? I don't have any problem."

"Yes, you do. I mean, it doesn't seem like you like this place much."

"Forgive me for missing our mom and our old life and all our friends," she said. "You know, I haven't even so much as texted another human being since we left. I bet all my friends think I'm dead."

"At least you have friends to miss you," I said. "I don't have anybody."

Murphy softened a little at that.

"You have me," she said. "Always. And I'm sorry I'm being a dick right now. It's just that something feels off about this place. The Farm, I mean. I wish we had decent cell phone reception. I'd google the shit out of it."

"I think it's amazing here," I said. "It's like, holy or something, you know? There's something special about it."

Murphy climbed out of bed, and a few second later I saw the top of her head peeking over the rail of my bunk, her eyes narrowed at me all suspicious-like.

"Why do I feel like you're holding out on me?" she said.

I started to deny it, to lie my ass off and tell my sister that I didn't know any more than she did, but then I saw something in the window.

It was a face, grizzled and wild-eyed, the man who had spied on me in my bedroom ever since I was a child.

It was the Hobo.

I couldn't help it, even if I knew he was just a vision.

I screamed.

Murphy toppled backward, smacking her back hard on the floor.

"What the hell was that?" she said.

"Sorry, Murphy. I saw the Hobo again."

Murphy sat up, rubbing her back, obviously in pain. I felt real bad about it.

"I tell you, I am so fucking sick of that fucking Hobo," she said. "I used to have nightmares about him every night. I used to imagine I saw him all the time in our backyard, hiding in the shadows or whatever. He was the number-one terror of my entire childhood. Christ, a couple of times I even thought I saw him myself. Your visions have really fucked me up, you know that?"

"I know," I said, slumping back in my bed. "And I'm damn sorry about it. I'm sorry I've been such a horrible burden to you and Mom. I'm sorry you're stuck having to deal with me all by yourself."

"Hey," said Murphy, "come on, I didn't mean it like that. I know it's not your fault."

"Good night, Murphy," I said, and I rolled over to face the wall.

Murphy didn't say anything else. I heard her get back in her bunk, and pretty soon she was snoring.

But I couldn't sleep. I could hear the rabble of the cicadas and tree frogs and everything else that makes up the loud southern night. It was just the same as back home with Mom. The moment I shut my eyes, my mind went racing. Who was this Jeremiah person? And who were the other people on the tape, Jeremiah's congregation? Where was his church? I still remembered Jeremiah's voice like a song stuck in my head that would never go away unless I listened to it again.

I took the tape player out from under my covers and turned the volume about as low as it would go. I laid it on my pillow and put my ear against the speaker, and I pressed play. When I heard Jeremiah's voice, it was as if he were whispering secrets right into my ear.

"Humankind was not meant to live alone," he said. "Yes, I know y'all know that, or you wouldn't be here today. No, man was not meant to live alone, nor woman either. We were meant to live together in community."

Clapping, shouting, applause.

"I was granted a vision last night, friends. It came upon me like a whirlwind, a raging of winds and smoke and flames. The sky vanished, and I stood in a dark place, only a campfire to guide me. Three men sat around the campfire, three lonely wretched men. 'What you seek,' the three men said together, 'lies yonder.' And they pointed as one into the darkness."

I couldn't believe it. Jeremiah had a vision of the same people as I had. I felt bonded to him, drawn even closer into his world, into his sermon and voice.

"Treacherous men, they were. I could feel the darkness swirling around them like smoke. But I knew what I must do, what path I must travel. The sky above me was darkened, and the world around me hung in shadow. It was as if I were in a desert, the most desolate place in this world or the next. All I could do was walk. And friends, it was a long way. The road was hard, and I stumbled often in the darkness. Stones cut my feet, and more than once I knew I was lost, that the way was hopeless, that I would never find the path to what I sought.

"It sounds strange, friends, to say that I felt as if I walked for weeks, as if I spent a small eternity in that darkness, but that is the way of visions. It was a wretched journey, and it seemed as if there was no end to the starless black. But when my legs could carry me no farther, when my back ached and my feet bled and my stomach was bloated from hunger, I came across a cave. It rose like an open throat from the ground, a fire burning inside of it like a ruby tucked deep in the darkness. I stepped into the cave, hoping for food and water, hoping for some way out of this world.

"But what I found, friends, was so much more than all that. Inside that cave, in the darkest pit of the earth, I found a garden. Do not ask me how the garden grew, as there was no sunlight and the rock floor of the cave was dry and hard. Yet grow this garden did, and it was magnificent. Cool blue blossoms and burning reds and regal purples all erupted in swirls around me, bluebells glittered like jewels, an entire cosmos of colors blossoming, blooming, flourishing in the dark heart of the earth, in that forsaken, abandoned place. There was no fire here, friends. No, the light came from the garden itself, glowing so bright with its own brilliance that I had to squint to look at it, as if I were gazing straight into the sun. I knew I was in the presence of something holy.

"Friends, I fell on my face in that cave. I was sobbing with all the pain I felt from my long midnight journey, the gratitude that I had come to witness this garden. The sweet fragrance of the blossoms, the colors brighter and wilder than any sunset. I hoped that every night I would dream of that garden, that I would see it flourish every time I closed my eyes. And then I awoke."

A pause. I could hear the quiet of the room, like everyone was holding their breath, scared to utter a sound, waiting in anticipation of what would come next.

"This vision, friends, is not without an interpretation. No, the Spirit does not leave his children mere wanderers in the dark. We are to understand, brothers and sisters. We are to know. And thus the meaning of the vision was revealed to me.

"The garden, friends, is this community. It is the beauty of all of us, all creeds and colors and backgrounds, flourishing in the perfect darkness of this world. The sweet smell it gave off is the fragrance of our love, and its beauty is that of a people working together in freedom and power for the good of the entire world. Our spirits are bound together, sown of different seeds but gathered into one garden, pure and holy, the most beautiful thing in all of creation. That is us, friends. We are goodness, and we are light. For all the world to see."

"Who's there?" muttered Murphy.

I clicked the tape off.

"Huh?" I said.

"Thought I heard a radio or something," said Murphy.

"You must have been dreaming," I said. "Go back to sleep."

I HAD A VISION.

I was back at the campfire, the three Gentleman seated before me. The world was dark and empty except for the stars. On the wind I heard voices, muttering sounds, whispers that I couldn't quite make out.

Something moaned in the darkness as if in pain. I wanted to run, but I didn't know where to run to, if there was only desert all around me, nothing but emptiness for miles and miles.

I heard a shuffling sound from the black, something moving.

A figure stepped into the light. It had no face, no eyes or mouth or hair, just two slits where its nose should be, like a snake. I watched it sniff the air. It was naked, its skin a dull gray. It cried out, the sound stuck in its throat like a mouth had once belonged there, a fierce muffled scream.

Both arms outstretched before it, the monster staggered toward me.

I turned and I ran, whispers whirring on the wind, the stars an eternity off, the monster moaning not far behind. It could follow me by smell, I realized, it could sniff my scent like a bloodhound.

I knew that I would have to run and never stop, that the monster would always chase me, that my only hope was to keep going.

And I fled onward into the darkness.

WE WERE UP AT DAWN, LIKE MURPHY AND I were finally getting this whole "obey the light" thing right. I could tell Grandma was pleased. When she brought our plates to the table, bacon and biscuits and a side of fresh fruit, her eyes were bright and happy. She had her hair down, and she wore makeup and a dress with sunflowers on it. She looked beautiful and so much like Mom—who Mom would have become— that I couldn't help but stare at her.

"So how do I have to bust my ass this morning?" said Murphy. "You want me to mow the grass or hoe some rows or paint the same goddamn thing over and over again?"

"Enough with the vulgarities, Murphy," said Grandma. "I know you are new to this life, but your sarcasm is not appreciated. In fact, you may say it is quite unbecoming on a young lady like yourself. This work has a purpose, even if you're too dense to see that yet."

"Is the purpose to make me miserable?"

"Not nearly, darling," said Grandma. "At least, not ulti-mately." She waved her hand as if dismissing the entire topic. "But no chores, not this morning. We're running low on sup-plies, hence the paltry breakfast before you. No, children, it's time we took a trip into town."

"Wait, really?" said Murphy. "I don't have to do anything?"

"Just smile and be polite and wear a dress."

"Christ almighty," groaned Murphy.

"Watch the blasphemy," said Grandma, pointing her spat-ula right at Murphy's face.

"But you don't even believe in Christ," I said.

"That is quite irrelevant," she said. "What is Christ but a misunderstanding of something true, something higher? We seek the ultimate revelation of the Spirit, and Christ is only a glimpse. As a seer, you should know this."

Murphy rolled her eyes.

"Sorry, Grandma," I said.

"No need to be sorry. Eat up and get dressed and comb your hair. We're going to town, and I'd like to leave within the hour."

And she scurried away, humming to herself.

We piled into Grandma's gray Chevy pickup, all three of us in the front bench seat, because Grandma wouldn't ride in anything that belonged to Horace. The truck was huge and ungainly, at least thirty years old. It bounced and squeaked and popped down the dirt road all the way to Benign. The day was bright and hot, but with the windows down it didn't feel so bad. Grandma found a Merle Haggard song and cranked it, which made Murphy grin a little. Murphy loved the old country guys, especially Merle. Said he was the kind of gentleman who would tip his hat to you and then knock your tooth loose. It's easy to respect a person like that, was what Murphy always said. Me, I wasn't too into tough guys, but I liked Merle. Hell, everybody I knew liked Merle Haggard. Waylon Jennings and Willie Nelson too. It would be hard to be Mom's child and not love all those Outlaw guys. At least the not-racist ones, anyhow.

Grandma drove us past the gas station we had seen when we'd first come through. The old men were still out there in their foldout chairs, Benny and Les, and they stopped their arguing long enough to watch us pass by. The lady with the gray ponytail was there too, and she waved a hand at us, cigarette burning between her fingers.

Murphy and I waved back, and the lady smiled.

Grandma drove us through Benign, every tiny wrecked street of it. Houses worn down, porches sagging, old folks sitting outside and staring at the street. A couple of redheaded kids on bikes rode past, peering at us, suspicious. They followed our truck a few blocks, only to turn back and then show up in front of us again, watching us pass. Several shuttered churches, their clever jokey signs now unreadable for rot and missing letters. The only thriving business was a Sonic, cars lined up in all the spots, folks sitting in their truck beds eating soft ice cream.

"This place is a dump," said Murphy.

"Yes," said Grandma. "It's taken a turn for the worse in the last twenty years."

"What happened?" I said.

"The recession," said Grandma. "Among other things. And here we are."

Grandma pulled into the parking lot of a Piggly Wiggly in desperate need of a paint job. Its big gleaming pig head logo leered down at us with some kind of deranged smirk. The parking lot was potholed and crumbling, and abandoned grocery carts lingered forlorn against the light poles.

"It isn't much," said Grandma, "but it's all we've got. That's why I'm so determined to get the Farm going again. Folks deserve decent vegetables around here, at the very least."

We stepped out of the car and across the trash-strewn parking lot and through the great glass sliding doors of the Piggly Wiggly.

The grocery store was packed. A third of the town had to be in there, and they were all dressed to the nines like they were headed off to church or something. Men wore suits in black and brown and blue, and women wore fancy hats and dresses. It was deeply strange but also kind of cool. I guessed there just wasn't anything else to do in Benign on a Saturday. All through the aisles people stopped to greet us.

"Hi, Mrs. Sanford," said one lady with poofy black hair and a purple dress. "Who's that you got with you?"

"Jenny's kids," she said. "Murphy, and this is Lee."

"Ah, Lee!" said the lady, grasping my hands in her cold wrinkly fingers. "What a pleasure it is to meet you. What an absolute joy."

"Thanks," I said. "Um . . . it's nice to meet you too."

"Oh, what a gentleman he is," she said. "Hope to see you again soon."

It kept going like that as we made our rounds and Grandma filled the grocery cart. Men shook my hand, fierce grabs and squeezes so tight my fingers ached afterward. Ladies curtsied before me, offered their hands for me to kiss. Everyone smiled at us. It was like we were celebrities.

"So sorry to hear about your momma," said one old man, and his wife nudged him. "That is to say, glad you've come to stay with us, despite the circumstances."

"It's okay," I said. "Thanks for saying sorry about my mom."

The man bowed to me. I mean, he just bent over and lowered his head like I was supposed to bless him or something. I thought Murphy's eyes were going to pop out of her head the way she stared at me. I didn't know what to do, so I just bowed back. That seemed to do the trick. His wife smiled at me and yanked him away.

"What a strange man," I whispered as we turned down the canned goods aisle.

"That's old Wilmer Jenkins," said Grandma. "Not a bad fellow, if a bit obsequious. You know what obsequious means?"

"It means he's a kiss-ass," said Murphy. "A right regular brownnoser."

"You are correct, Murphy," said Grandma. "If vulgar as always."

Murphy shrugged. "Mom always said to say it like you mean it and call bullshit wherever you see it."

"Yes," said Grandma, "that certainly does sound like your mother."

"What the hell is going on here?" said Murphy. "I mean, who dresses up to buy groceries?"

"Benign is a quaint town," said Grandma. "Very particular in its ways."

"This is fucking weird."

"Language," said Grandma. "Also, Murphy, can we try to be a little more congenial? These are your neighbors."

A man with a red mustache bustled down the aisle and shook my hand.

"Pleasure to meet you, son, it truly is," he said. "And Mena, how's my boy doing out on the lot?"

"Quite well," said Grandma. "Murphy, Lee, have you all met Stephens yet? Boy who lives out in the tenant house? This is his father, Mr. Brownderville."

"We haven't met any of the tenants except for Cass," I said.

Murphy shot me a look, but I pretended not to notice.

"Well, I'd be honored if you dropped by and introduced yourself," said Mr. Brownderville. "He's a good boy, and faithful. A chip off the old block, I do hope."

"You can be certain of that," said Grandma with a smile.

I had no idea what that meant. It was like Grandma and all the other people in town shared this secret that none of them were going to let Murphy and me in on. But I knew that somehow we were at the center of it.

Another man came walking up to Grandma, all stoop-backed and stammery. His clothes were more raggedy than everybody else's, his tie loose and his suit wrinkled. He had bloodshot eyes, and his hands trembled as he stood there.

"Mena," he said.

Grandma ignored him.

"Are these the children?" he said. "Please, Mena."

Grandma ushered us down the aisle, away from him. I turned to look back, and he stood there miserably, hunched and lonesome and defeated.

"Who was that?" said Murphy.

"You are not to speak to that man," said Grandma. "No matter what."

"Why not?" I said.

"Some people simply cannot be helped," she said. "And one mustn't waste one's time on lost causes."

And she wouldn't say another word about him.

After an hour of shopping and handshakes, we finally had all our groceries, and it was a shit-ton of food, way more than I thought we could eat in a week. The cashier, an old man in a black smock and a bowler hat, just waved us through.

"On the house, Mrs. Sanford," said the man.

"Why, thank you, George," she said.

George reached over the counter and took my hand and clasped it in both of his.

"It's an honor to meet you, son," he said. "It truly is."

"You have no idea," said Grandma. "I'm quite astonished by both of my grandchildren. They will do me proud, I reckon."

Grandma flashed me her biggest smile.

WE HAD A NICE RIDE BACK HOME, THE AFTER-
noon sunlight on the green world around us, Grandma crank-
ing the radio to an oldies station, singing along. She seemed
happy, proud of us, so glad we were there. Even Murphy smiled
a little, until she realized she'd forgotten to buy a phone charger.
Murphy kept demanding Grandma turn around, but Grandma
refused. Besides, there wouldn't be any cell phone service at the
Farm anyhow, so what was the point? To be honest, I'd forgotten
I even had a phone, it had been dead for so long. I hadn't missed
it, not once. That made me pretty happy because it meant that
I had everything I needed—and everyone I loved—right there
with me. Why in the world would I ever need a phone again?
I almost laughed out loud at the thought of it, the freedom I
felt. By the time we neared the Farm, I doubted you could have
found a happier person on the planet.

But when we drove through the gate and down the driveway, Grandma slammed on the brakes.

A family stood in front of us, blocking the road—a grandmother and a mother and two kids, a boy and a girl, who were maybe my age or even older. You could tell they were a family by how similar they looked: The same black hair on all of them, the same wild look, the same scowl on all their faces. Their clothes were grubby and old, hand-me-downs, and everything about them looked ragged and dirty. They stood right at the edge of the driveway, facing us.

Grandma muttered something to herself and hopped out of the car. She stood about ten feet back from them and hollered.

"Y'all can't be here," she said. "You are forbidden to set foot on my property. You know that."

They stood there, dark eyes staring at us, unmoving.

"I said, y'all can't be here. You must leave this place right now."

The older lady spat on the driveway. Then she bent down and traced something in the dirt. I couldn't tell what from where we sat.

"I said *get!*" hollered Grandma, and she stomped off toward them, her hand raised up like she was going to slap the lady.

I was worried for a second because that boy was taller than me, and he looked tough and hardscrabble, and I knew he could whoop my ass if I even tried to fight him. And yet there was Grandma, fearless, charging at them, screaming at the top of her lungs.

"By the Spirit we both serve, I command you to leave!" she shouted. "You are forbidden here. The light always drives out the darkness, and so shall it ever be. Now go!"

The older lady stood up from the ground and straightened her dress. Then she spat again, and one by one they all turned and left, heading down the road. Grandma stood in the driveway until they were gone. Murphy and I climbed out of the truck.

"Who was that?" said Murphy.

"The Urquharts," said Grandma. "Trash. They live right on the property line. Twenty feet over and I'd have the place knocked down."

"What's their problem with you?" said Murphy.

"Nothing I wish to discuss at the moment," she said. "Now get yourselves in that truck. We got work to do, and the day is wasting."

Grandma walked back to the truck in a huff.

I looked at the dirt where the old lady had knelt. She'd drawn a snake on the ground with little star-looking things around it.

"What do you make of that?" I said.

"Just further proof that everybody around here is insane," said Murphy.

"Children!" hollered Grandma out the window. "I did not permit you to dawdle in the road. Get back inside this truck immediately."

Murphy sighed, and we climbed into the truck, and Grandma drove us back to the house, running right over the snake drawn in the dirt.

Grandma put us on cleaning duty that afternoon, vacuuming and sweeping and dusting the whole house. At least all the parts of it that weren't off-limits. She split Murphy and me up, sending me downstairs and Murphy upstairs. It wasn't hard work, just tedious, but I didn't mind. My thoughts were reeling and scattered, so many questions running through my head about what had happened in town, about the Urquharts, about Jeremiah, about everything. By the time night fell, I was happy to be done with my work, hoping maybe Grandma could give me some answers.

But Grandma seemed annoyed and distracted, her whole beaming, glowing mood from earlier in the day vanished and gone. Something about the Urquharts had gotten to her, spoiled her glorious day. I wanted to ask about them, about the symbol that old lady had drawn in the dirt, but Grandma wasn't much in the answering-questions mode. She fretted about the kitchen, ignored our questions, and mumbled to herself like maybe she was praying.

So we had a quiet night. I knew Murphy had about as many questions as I did, but she wasn't saying much, and I didn't push her. I could tell she'd been annoyed with me ever since we'd gotten back from town.

After dinner, Murphy and I washed up and went upstairs. She sat on her bunk and chewed her lip, her face all scrunched up in concentration. I climbed up to my bunk and lay down. After a minute, Murphy spoke up.

"Something's wrong here, Lee," she said.

"You mean about the Urquharts?"

"Yeah, them too," she said. "But I mean all of it. The Farm, Grandma, the town, everything. Are we supposed to go to school here? Or will Grandma just homeschool us like Mom did, keep us trapped on the Farm until we die? I don't even know if I want to go to school in Benign. That whole thing at the grocery store was just too fucking weird."

"I'll be honest," I said. "I kind of enjoyed it. I mean, it was like we were famous or something."

"No," she said, "it was like *you* were famous. You and Grandma. Nobody gave a shit about me."

When I thought about it, that seemed kind of true. Sure, everybody had been nice to Murphy, shaking her hand and all that, but it was me they had been staring at. I wondered why they would ever give me preference over her. Nothing like that had ever happened to me back home. I mean, I was always a loser, the weirdest and worst. It was Murphy who everybody loved. If the people of Benign, Louisiana, took a liking to me, well, I wasn't going to complain.

But I couldn't tell Murphy that. She'd be pissed.

"They seemed like nice people to me," I said.

Murphy laughed.

"Sure, Lee. I bet all the weirdo grocery store people are all just sweethearts."

"Why wouldn't they be?"

"Because nobody is ever that nice to you unless they want something in return," she said. "Trust me, I know."

What did that mean? My sister did have a secret life back home, sneaking out every night, and I'd always had questions, I'd always wondered. But Murphy didn't say anything else, and I wasn't sure how to ask her about it.

Eventually I fell asleep.

MURPHY SHOOK ME AWAKE.

"Lee, get up. She's at it again. Grandma's out in the yard."

I yawned, trying to blink the sleep out of my eyes.

"What time is it?" I said.

"I don't know," she said. "There aren't any clocks in this house, remember? Only that one in the kitchen."

I was so tired I can't even tell you. I would have done anything to stay in bed.

"You're not sleeping through this," Murphy said. "We got to find out what she's up to."

I pulled on a clean pair of overalls and slid into my shoes. Murphy was downstairs and to the back door by the time I caught up with her.

"Hurry it up," she whispered. "She's moving pretty fast tonight. Stay low and stay back."

Out the window I saw Grandma's swaying lantern cutting through the darkness of the field. Murphy and I snuck out the back door, and we made our way quiet through the yard. The clouds ran wild through the night above us, the sky lit alive by the yellow cat's-eye of a moon, all the stars up there like whispered secrets. We walked at a far distance, our feet soundless on the fresh-mown grass, the light like a will-o'-the-wisp guiding us somewhere, past the Hummingbird Grove, past the shuttered barn, down the narrow path toward the trees, into the deep mystery of the forest.

"Holy shit," whispered Murphy. "Look."

An owl was perched on the top of the barn, and it spread its wings wide, like the cross on a church's steeple. I realized I had seen that owl before. It was from my vision, the one I'd had the night Mom died. The owl stayed still like that a moment, as if it were posing in the moonlight. Then it sailed into the wind and night and stars, off hunting, gone from us forever.

I knew it meant something that I'd seen that owl, same as in my vision, like I was supposed to see it, like it was fate. I knew that what was coming next would change me forever and I would not come back from these woods the same.

The farther we walked, the more the tree limbs seemed to close over us like a tunnel through the night. It felt like we were trespassing into something sacred, like we were following Grandma into the darkest dream of her heart. The path was irregular, roots jutting up from the ground like half-resurrected corpse bones, like things frozen in the moment of escape. The tree limbs swayed in the air, a shivering of leaves. I heard the chitter of bats above us, darting through the trees, creatures out on the hunt.

Grandma came to a small clearing, the very end of the trail. We peeked out from behind a massive oak big enough to hide us, watching Grandma. She was staring at something there in the clearing.

It was a headstone, carved from marble and lugged all the way out here, hidden in the woods. Grandma set the lantern down and lowered herself to her knees on the grave. She folded her hands like she was praying, and she began to chant, some strange incantation half like singing, like what the monks did that one time I talked Mom into taking me to a monastery up in Arkansas. I remembered them all, heads lowered, chanting in Latin, all those secret garbled words made more powerful by the fact that I couldn't understand them. Grandma spoke her strange language, words foreign and mysterious, the volume and pitch rising higher until it was as if she would hyperventilate. Her breaths came in gasps, and she began to weep, big heaving sobs that shook her whole body, the kind that seemed painful. Grandma cried and cried, the kind of brokenhearted wretchedness that I hadn't even been able to conjure for Mom at her funeral. I'd never seen grief like that, not before or since, my grandmother's wracking sobs on that grave.

Grandma lifted her head up and screamed, a raw-throated agony let loose like a flock of bats bursting from her throat. She gripped the gravestone in both of her hands and smashed her face into it—once, then twice. I saw a smattering of red across the stone, blood dripping down her forehead, splotching her hair. Grandma lay on the forest floor and pounded the dirt, weeping and screaming. She hugged the earth, she rolled on it, her hair sticky with blood and leaves. Grandma cried and cried until finally her breaths slowed and her sobs grew quieter, gentler. She rose back to her knees, wiping her nose with her forearm. Grandma reached up and felt the wound on her forehead as if it were the first time she'd noticed it. She gasped a little when she saw the blood on her fingers. It was like the whole thing had happened to her in a trance, like she hadn't been aware of any of it at all.

She dusted herself off and stood, staring up at the moon. Then she took up her lantern and began to walk back down the path the way she had come.

We ducked behind a tree trunk as she passed, trying to make ourselves small and invisible. Grandma moved in a daze, slow and rambly as a sleepwalker. Only when she reached the edge of the clearing did she cut her eyes back toward us, to the tree where Murphy and I lay hidden. It was like she knew she was being watched, like she'd grown some strange animal sense and could smell us on the wind. We were dead silent, Murphy and I, while Grandma scanned the woods, the lamp held up to her face, her eyes squinted right at us. For a moment the whole world seemed to stop, I was so scared we'd be caught.

Because I knew we'd looked upon something private, something sacred even, and there were always consequences for spying on the sacred.

But Grandma lowered the lamp, and she turned her eyes back toward the path. She walked quicker now, more sure-footed, through the field and toward the house.

When she was well out of sight, Murphy and I crept out of our hiding spot.

"What the hell was that?" said Murphy.

"I don't know," I said.

I walked over to the headstone, to whatever grave Grandma had been praying over. There was a smear of blood across it, wet and red and dripping. It reminded me of the Bible, how blood was spread over the doorposts before the plague of the first-born. The stone was blank, no name or date.

"Whose grave is this?" I said. "Grandpa's?"

"Maybe," said Murphy. "I thought he ran off, though, right?"

We heard a twig snap in the woods, something hidden scampering away. Murphy and I froze as the moon uncovered itself from the clouds and cast a glow over us bright and clear as a spotlight. I was conscious of a thousand eyes gazing in, of hidden things in the darkness watching over us. I heard another stick crack in the dark, something moving in the trees. We weren't alone, I knew that. I began to hear music from out in the darkness, human voices amongst all the animal sounds. At first I thought I was just imagining it, like maybe it was another vision or something. But then Murphy spoke up.

"Dude, do you hear that?" she said.

"Yeah," I said. "For a minute I was afraid it was just me."

"Definitely not a vision. That shit is real. I wonder where it's coming from."

"Only one way to find out."

We followed the sound down the birch trail. Above us flew the bats and the night birds, the eerie song just a part of the night, same as the starlight. The song led us to the tenant house. A flickering of candlelight shone from the windows, and it cast the forest in a holy glow like in an old cathedral.

"It's just the tenants," said Murphy. "Let's get back to the house already. Grandma's got to be finished with whatever she's doing by now."

Murphy turned to leave, but I stayed.

I wanted a closer look.

I crept up to their cabin, lit up by candles, the windows bright and gold-hued from the light. I heard music, a guitar and fiddle, voices harmonizing. I peeked inside. The tenants were seated in a circle around a fat purple candle, eyes shut, playing a song. It was strange, incantatory and minor-key, a kind of dirge, like an old folk hymn or something. Cass sang lead, her voice deep, gravelly even, not the kind of thing I pictured from her at all, more beautiful than I ever could have thought.

Cass opened her eyes, catching mine in the window.

I ducked down, hiding.

I knew she'd seen me. Now she'd think I was a Peeping Tom or something, and she'd tell the others that I was spying on them. I raised my head to the window again, and she was still staring my way. I caught her eye again, but I didn't turn my head away. Neither did Cass. She stared right at me, her eyes deep and brown, reflecting the candle flame.

Murphy grabbed my arm, puncturing the dream. When I looked back at the window, Cass had her eyes closed, swaying silently to the music.

"Come on," Murphy whispered. "Let's get back to the house before Grandma notices we're gone."

We walked back through the woods. I couldn't shake the feeling that I was being watched and followed somehow. I tried to tell myself it was only my imagination. But from the way Murphy kept looking around, glancing back over her shoulder, I knew she was feeling it too. From the edge of the field the house loomed over us, many-eyed and strange, like some kind of gargoyle sprouting up out of the earth.

There was a light on in the house, a lantern glowing in the attic.

"Grandma told us it was empty," said Murphy, "that there were holes in the floor and we would fall right through. What's she doing up there?"

"I don't know," I said. "Think we can get back to the room without her hearing anything?"

"We can try," said Murphy.

When we reached the kitchen, we took our shoes off and walked soft and careful, the old house creaking no matter how gentle we stepped. Murphy shut the door to our bedroom quiet as she could.

"I think we made it," she whispered.

The floorboards groaned in the hallway. A little shiver of light spread underneath our door. I held my breath. But the lantern passed, and we were alone again in the darkness. We didn't dare speak a word.

I lay awake that night thinking of Grandma bashing her head into that grave. Thinking of the boy I'd seen in the Hummingbird Grove, wondering if that was his grave, and who he even was.

Thinking of Cass, eyes burning, watching me at the window.

WE WOKE UP EARLY, AT SUNRISE, JUST LIKE WE were supposed to. Grandma had a simple breakfast set up for us, fruit with yogurt and honey and buttered toast. She wore a blue bandanna wrapped around her head where she had bashed it into the grave the night before. She seemed distracted, wandering around the kitchen, muttering to herself.

"Grandma?" I said. "You okay?"

"Fine, fine, Lee," she said. "Just have a headache is all."

"Does that mean we get the day off?" said Murphy.

Grandma laughed. "Not on your life. Murphy, you and I are going to clean one of the toolsheds out back by the woods. Been years since I been in there. Too many black widows and all that—like to get my hand bit off. But I figure between the two of us, we can do some damage."

"Great," said Murphy. "Exactly what I wanted to do today."

"I can help," I said.

Grandma shook her head. "You've got your own duties, Lee, and you must attend to them. Murphy and I can manage quite well by ourselves, can't we, honey?"

"Sure," said Murphy. "Why fucking not?"

Grandma glared at Murphy.

"I know, I know," said Murphy. *"Language."*

"You know what the best cure for a bad attitude is?" said Grandma. "Work. Come with me. The sky is threatening rain, and daylight is precious."

I started in the garden, planting and pruning and weeding and watering and all the other crap you do in a garden. To be honest, I was really starting to enjoy it. I liked plunging my hands into the soil, getting all dirty with the earthworms. It felt good, bees buzzing around me, birdsong in the air. It was a hell of a lot better than anything else I'd done so far in my life.

Because Grandma was so busy that day, I would have to do my Hummingbird Grove meditations myself. That was fine with me. I wanted to see what would come to me on my own, without Grandma sitting there.

But when I sat in the Hummingbird Grove and shut my eyes, it didn't quite work. My mind wandered, or I couldn't focus right, or I got anxious and sad. I started to miss Mom a lot, and I got to thinking about how lonely I'd always been, what a fuckup I was. I couldn't stop worrying about Horace, where he was right now, if he would come one night and steal us away from Grandma.

It was hard to focus on something like visions when I had so much banging around in my mind. And in a weird way, it felt like the blond boy I usually saw was hiding from me, like he was peeking out from behind a tree and I just couldn't see him. It made me wonder what else was out there, if the Hobo was watching me too. The whole thing made me sad. I sat in the dirt and wondered about myself, what was happening to me, what any of it meant.

I moped my way back to see if I could help Murphy and Grandma clean out the toolshed. But by the time I got there, Grandma had called a hydration break. I walked over to Murphy, who was slumped down in the shade, sucking on her health juice.

"Get bit by anything?" I said.

"Nope," she said. "But I did murder about six hundred spiders. One of them was the size of my palm, I swear to god."

"Sorry I'm not doing more to help," I said.

"Shit, if I could get out of this, I would." Murphy held the juice up to the sunlight and squinted at it. "Oh god. I think I'm starting to like this crap."

I left Murphy sitting there and stole off for the Split Tree. I wanted to see if there was another tape waiting on me. It was afternoon now, storm clouds blowing up on the horizon. It felt cooler, just a little bit, the wind starting to pick up. I walked under the leaves whispering above me, the crack and groan of limbs in the breeze. As I neared the Split Tree I heard a voice, someone singing, the thrum of a guitar.

It was Cass, eyes shut, sitting on the ground with her back up against the Split Tree. She was singing to herself in that deep voice of hers, a kind of incantatory song, fingerpicked and fluttering. It sounded strange out there, the tree limbs casting long slashing shadows around her.

She didn't notice me watching her. I guess it's creepy that I just stood there listening to her sing. But I didn't dare interrupt her. It was too beautiful—the song, the shadows, Cass herself—and any word from me would spoil the whole thing. So I let her sing, and I stood there happy and silent and in awe.

One of her guitar strings snapped and went plinging into the grass.

"Shit," she said.

That's when she saw me.

Cass gave a gasp, like maybe I'd scared her a little. Dammit, I knew I was being creepy just standing there like the goddamn Hobo in my visions or something. I figured she would hate me now, that after this she would never talk to me again.

But Cass just smiled.

"Howdy there," she said. "Coming to check on your spirit mailbox?"

"I guess," I said. *Come on, Lee. Stop being a fuckup. Say something.* "You sounded pretty. I mean, amazing. Did you write that song?"

"Yeah," she said. Cass stood up and dusted herself off, leaning the guitar up against the Split Tree. "It's still a work in progress though. I don't quite have the lyrics right yet."

"I thought it was perfect."

"Well, I wish you'd tell the rest of the guys that. They think it's too depressing. They always think my songs are too depressing."

We stood there a second in silence.

"So, you going to check?" she said.

"Um, yeah, I guess." I walked over to the tree and stuck my hand in. Nothing there but damp leaves and slug slime. I pulled my hand out all wet and gross.

"No luck, huh?" she said.

"Nope."

Don't let it get awkward again, moron. Say something.

"So how did you wind up here?" I said. "At the Farm, I mean."

Cass bit her lip like she was trying to figure out how to answer that question. I hoped I wasn't being too forward, grilling her like that. But I was curious, and I really did want to know. Mostly I just didn't want her to leave yet.

"To be honest," she said, "it's kind of a long story. The short version is, I was in a bad place in my life. I'd just graduated high school, and I hadn't bothered to apply to college. Just kind of directionless, you know? I was getting pretty fucked up all the time, hanging out with some really sketchy people. But then I heard about the Farm, and I met the other tenant guys, and I thought it might be a pretty good place to try and get my shit together. You know, out in nature and all that." She shrugged. "Hope that wasn't too much information or anything."

"No, not at all," I said. "I'm glad you came here."

"I'm glad you came too," she said. Then it sort of dawned on her why I was there, what had brought me to the Farm in the first place. "Oh shit. I didn't mean it like that. I mean, about your mom."

"It's okay," I said. "It's horrible, and I miss her a lot. But I'm kind of glad I'm here too, in spite of everything."

A beam of sunlight broke through the clouds and cast the Split Tree in gold, and the breeze blew, shivering the leaves.

"Well, I guess I ought to go and fix my string," said Cass.

"Yeah, I got chores. And stuff."

Cass smiled at me. "Be seeing you, Lee."

"Yeah," I said. "Be seeing you."

And I watched her walk off toward the tenant house.

I was about to turn and go when I saw somebody out in the woods, watching me. It was the Urquhart kid, the one who had come with his family the day before. He stood not twenty feet from me, next to a gnarled old oak.

"Was that your girlfriend there?" he said. "She's pretty. I come out and watch her play sometimes. I like to hear her voice."

"You shouldn't be spying on people," I said.

He took a few steps closer to me. His face was unshaven and his teeth yellow, one missing on the left side of his smile. I could tell I'd misjudged his age. He was definitely older than me by at least a few years.

"Weren't any different than what you was doing," he said, "except I'm better at hiding."

"What do you want?" I said.

He chuckled a little bit.

"Calm down now, boss. It's just me, George Urquhart," he said. "What's your Grandma told you about us?"

"Only that you don't belong here," I said. *And that you're trash*, but I kept that to myself.

"That's true enough," he said. "This is your family's property, sure. Wasn't always your family's property though. Used to belong to the Urquharts until your great-grandfather swindled it from mine. The Sanfords were always ones for swindling folks."

"I never swindled a person in my life," I said. "I don't even think I know how to. But I'd rather you not talk shit about my family, if that's all right with you."

"Fair enough, fair enough," he said, and grinned a little. "You're not so bad for a Sanford. Not so impressive either, though."

"Why do y'all hate my family so much? Because of something that happened between our great-grandparents?"

"Nah, that's not the thrust of the argument," he said, "though it don't help matters much. Truth is, I don't have a single problem in the world with you or your family. It's everybody else in my family who hates y'all, my momma and granny and sister. They'd just as soon shoot you as say hello."

That scared me, to tell you the truth. I started figuring if I could outrun him, if I had enough of a head start that I could make it back to the Farm before he caught me.

"Relax, now," said George. "I didn't come to kill you. Don't have any desire to. I just want all this nonsense ended, and I think maybe you could help me out a little bit. See, my daddy disappeared round about twenty-two years ago, right before I was born. Never even met the man. Hard to mourn somebody you never knew in the first place."

"I never knew my dad either," I said. "Don't even know his name."

"Well, I know my dad's name. It's Carl. And my whole family is convinced that your grandma is the reason he's gone."

"Why?" I said. "What would my grandma want with your dad?"

He shrugged. "That ain't for me to answer. You might want to talk to your grandma about it, though, if you feel so inclined. I figure she might know something she'd be willing to share with you but not with us." He turned to leave. "See you later, Sanford. And should you ever bump into my daddy anywhere, please kindly tell him I said hello."

With that, George Urquhart walked back into the woods.

I watched him until he was gone.

I wondered where he lived exactly, what it felt like to be stuck just outside of a place as wonderful as the Farm. To know that it could have been yours if only your great-grandfather hadn't been a sucker. Of course, everything George said might have been a total lie. It probably was a lie, after all.

Grandma did say they were trash.

The rain came soon after that, one of those sudden torrential summer downpours that drowns everything, snapping trees, hurling lightning all over the place, and then vanishes just as quick, like it never happened at all.

By evening Grandma was busy with dinner and Murphy and I had gone upstairs to change.

"How you feeling?" said Murphy. "You seemed pretty down earlier today."

"I was," I said. I thought about Cass and her song. "But I'm better now. Though I did see that Urquhart kid today."

"What did he want?"

I thought about telling her, but something in me felt weird about it. So I just shrugged.

"I don't know," I said. "Just giving me shit."

Murphy gave me a look then, one she'd been giving me a lot lately. It meant she didn't believe me, that she was trying to figure out what I was hiding.

"Anyway," she said, "how would you feel about taking a little trip into town tonight?"

"No way," I said. "Grandma will kill us."

"No, she won't. You're her golden boy, remember? Grandma worships you. I'm the only one she'd actually kill."

"You've got to stop with that crap," I said. "Grandma loves you. She loves us both. You know that."

"I don't know that, Lee. And there's no way I'll believe it until I figure out what in the hell is going on around here. I know Grandma's hiding something. Like what the fuck is that grave in the woods? Why was she bashing her head into it? Lee, the lady is a psychopath. Maybe someone in town can give us answers."

"How? We can't take the car. Grandma will definitely hear that."

"I found some old bikes in the toolshed out back. The tires have to be twenty years old, but I found a pump, and they're holding air okay. We'll be fine for a night."

"You want to ride cracked, mangly old tires on these old roads?" I said. "That's a horrible idea."

"Got a better one?"

"Yeah," I said. "Let's just get back to work and be grateful that we have a nice place to live and forget about all this shit."

"Lee?"

"Yeah?"

"There were three bikes in the shed. Not two. And from the looks of it, the third one belonged to a boy. It was just

Mom and Grandma living here, right? Who was the other bike for?"

Well, damn. Maybe there were some things I needed to find out too. But for myself, not for Murphy. I didn't think she would understand them anyway.

"Fine," I said. "Let's do it."

Murphy smiled big at me, and for a minute it felt great not to let her down. As if there wasn't this ocean of secrets inside of me—the tapes and the prophecies and what George Urquhart had said about my great-grandfather—all of it roiling and churning, a storm roaring in my heart.

Later that night, after dinner and a couple of hours of waiting around, we snuck out of the house and grabbed the bikes from where Murphy had stashed them away. Everything was still wet from the afternoon storm, and the ground glistened jewel-like where the moonlight struck it.

Riding the rickety old bike through the dirt and muck was hard, but it was fun too. The hot night was alive with bugs and night birds and creatures all over. I caught flashes of eyes from the woods on either side, big-antlered deer and scurrying possums, and it was like all of them were our guardian angels, watching over us on the road. And man, what a moon we had, near-full and high and wild, the kind of moon that seems alive with fire, a giant pulsing heartbeat of light.

It was good to be free and off in the night, just a kid with my sister, sneaking out. It was beautiful, really, me taking part in normal teenager stuff.

And then I remembered what we were really doing out there. We weren't on any late-night joyride, nothing fun about it. We were casing a strange town for clues about our dead mother and our weird haunted grandmother and this mysterious preacher child I was seeing in my visions, who I wouldn't tell my sister about. I didn't like having all these secrets from Murphy. I wanted to tell Murphy everything, I truly did, but something in me refused to. Maybe it was the Spirit, or maybe I was just being paranoid, but part of me felt that if I told Murphy all this stuff, it would put her in some kind of danger.

But danger from who? Grandma? There was no way. Grandma loved me more than anyone on this earth ever had. She was the first person ever to make me feel, if not normal, at least beloved for who I was. Mom never did anything like that for me.

Not even Murphy did, not really.

In fact, out of all the times Murphy snuck out at night back home, this was the first time she'd ever invited me along. She only asked me tonight because she needed me, because she was afraid to do it alone. Maybe I was right for not telling Murphy all that I knew. Maybe I couldn't trust Murphy after all. Not with everything, anyway.

Benign was dark, and I mean completely dark. Streetlights were virtually nonexistent, and what light there was came only from the moon and stars, casting a ghostly unreal glow over everything. The streets were completely deserted. I didn't even see a stray cat roaming. Everyone was shut inside, lights off and doors locked. The houses were blank, not even a television light burning through a window. It was like the whole town had vanished in the darkness, like they were all hiding from the night.

We rode past the gas station we'd first seen when we came to town, but it was closed too.

"Shit," said Murphy. "Does this whole town shut down at nine P.M.? What do the kids do for fun around here? Isn't there at least a parking lot they hang out in?"

"We could try that Sonic we saw."

"Good thinking," she said. "At least the loser kids would be hanging out at Sonic on a summer night."

But when we glided by, the Sonic was empty, parking lot abandoned, all the neon shut off and forlorn like a carnival closed for the night.

"This is ridiculous," said Murphy. "Something's got to be open."

"Maybe not," I said. "It's almost midnight. Things close down early in a town this small."

"There has to be somewhere," said Murphy. "Small towns are full of drunks. They have to have a gathering place, like religious folks have church. Let's try the outskirts."

I wished I had my phone. We could just search "bar" and get directions straight to it. But since that wasn't an option, we rode on, hot and sweaty and mosquito-bit, looking for anything open we could find. Eventually we crossed outside the town limits, and as far as I could see it was all woods, county road leading to county road. An eighteen-wheeler roared past us, nearly running us over.

"Come on, Murphy," I said. "Can we please turn back now?"

"Just a little farther," she said.

We wound through trees and down the blacktop, deer watching us from the roadside, their eyes glowing bright in the moonlight. The road felt haunted and endless, like if we rode for days we wouldn't get anywhere and the moment we turned around we'd be right back where we started. It was spooky, the quiet night, the high mournful stars, the moon ducking behind a gray shroud of clouds. I felt a tingling in my bones like a vision was near, like something was about to reveal itself to me.

I heard it first, the rumble of AC units and the buzz of music and human voices above the drone of bugs and far-off highway traffic. A high bright-blue neon moon glowed through the trees, and we headed toward it. The building was small, almost like a concrete bunker hidden in the woods, but it was lit up and bright, cars crammed into the parking lot.

We'd found it, the only open bar in town.

"The Clock Without Hands," I said. "Weird name for a bar."

We walked up to the front door, a big metal windowless thing. I tried the handle. It was locked.

"Read the sign, moron," said Murphy. She pointed to a little white placard on the doorframe that said, "AFTER DARK RING BELL."

I pressed the bell, and the door buzzed. I guessed that meant it was unlocked. I pushed it open, and into the bar we walked.

The Clock Without Hands was one long, slender room full of neon and multicolored all-year Christmas lights. A TV played a black-and-white movie, and the jukebox boomed out soul music, and the whole place was thick and horrible with cigarette smoke. Two older gentlemen wearing suits sat at the bar, commanding it like they were captains on a ship. One wore a fedora over his gray hair and kept popping his knuckles. A few blond women smoked long cigarettes with lipstick marks on them. The bartender was a woman with huge red hair and bright blue eye makeup, and she kept laughing this high weird witchy cackle while she dished out drinks. A bent man in an army jacket slept at one of the coin casino machines in the back. The lights blinked and whirred all around him. A stuffed baby alligator sat on the bar, a pointed party hat stuck to his head. The left half of the bar was all booths, low-lit and easy to slink into. The one farthest to the back seemed empty.

"Let's grab that before anybody spots us," said Murphy.

"Too late," I said. I felt every eye in the bar on us even though no one had spoken a word our way yet. We scuttled to the back booth, our heads hung low, trying our best to blend in.

"So what do we do now?" I said.

"Hush up," said Murphy. "I'm thinking."

I scanned the crowd for anyone who had been at Piggly Wiggly yesterday, but I didn't recognize anyone. The bar was badly lit, and folks didn't look the same in normal clothes as they did in their Sunday best. I mean, they carried themselves differently. Everyone in this bar looked like they had just escaped from somewhere awful they didn't want to talk about. Which is to say, everyone in the bar looked like they had secrets. It was only a matter of time before the bartender discovered us and we got the boot.

Right then the bathroom door swung open, and out strode the squirrely-looking old guy from Piggly Wiggly, the one Grandma wouldn't hardly talk to. He looked even worse tonight. His beard was all scraggly, and his splotchy red tie hung loose around his neck. He seemed to be well drunk and a little wobbly.

"What about that guy?" I said.

"Holy shit, he's perfect," said Murphy. "You can always count on a drunk to tell you everything you aren't supposed to know. Hold up a minute, I'll be right back."

Murphy slid out of the booth and swooped over to the guy like she was a dutiful granddaughter leading her dotty old granddad back from his wandering. She herded him to the booth and sat him down across from us.

"Y'all shouldn't be in here," slurred the man. He leaned in close, his red-rimmed eyes gone big. "If your grandma finds out, I tell you, she will be none too happy about it."

"You know who we are?" said Murphy.

"'Course I know who you are. Every last person in this bar knows exactly who y'all are, even if they don't let on about it."

"What's your name?" I said.

"Herman Cartwright," he said. "And I'm telling y'all to leave. It ain't safe here, not for you two."

"Why?" said Murphy. "What's so dangerous about this place?"

"Because you're Mena Sanford's grandkids," he said. "This used to be an Urquhart place, years and years back. Folks like that aren't too keen on your grandmother or her kin. And the poor woman's been through more than enough without having to worry about you two being here."

"What kinds of things has she been through?" said Murphy.

"Why, the death of her firstborn, of course," said Mr. Cartwright. "Your uncle Jeremiah, cut down in the very prime of his youth. Her sister too, her twin—died when she was a kid, I remember that. Terrible tragedy, that one. And then with your mom passing all these years later, rest her soul, it ain't been easy on the woman. Just tragedy after tragedy after tragedy. I tell you, it's like Death took a special interest in your grandma and he's been haunting her all the days of her life."

I'd wanted it to be true, I realized, but I'd been too scared to believe it. Jeremiah *was* my uncle. I bet he was the one buried out back. But why hadn't Mom ever mentioned him to us?

"I didn't even know we had an uncle," said Murphy. "This is crazy."

Oh Murphy, I thought. *You don't know the half of it.*

"But what about you?" she said to Mr. Cartwright. "You seem to care a whole lot for a woman who won't talk to you in public."

Mr. Cartwright slouched in the booth and shook his head.

"I wasn't always like this," he said. "A drunk. Used to be damn close to the Sanfords, almost like one of the family. But after Jeremiah's death I just couldn't handle it anymore. Took to boozing to calm my nerves, and, well, here I am."

"Why was he so important to you?" said Murphy. "I don't get it. Were you guys friends or something?"

"Friends?" said Mr. Cartwright. He laughed too loud, his face gone red. "Lord, no, we weren't friends. I would never claim a closeness like that. No, that boy was a prophet. Who can claim to be friends with a prophet?"

A prophet? Was that what Uncle Jeremiah was? Were his visions allowed to be called something so grand and beautiful as prophecies? And if Jeremiah was a prophet, what did that say about me?

"I loved him," said Mr. Cartwright. "Your uncle was as close to Jesus as any person I ever met on this earth, and that's the truth of it."

"How did Jeremiah die?" I said.

Mr. Cartwright lifted his eyebrows.

"Don't you know?" he said.

"I want to hear you tell it," I lied. "I always wanted to hear the whole story, but I'm scared to ask Grandma about it."

Mr. Cartwright scratched his head and sighed. "Well, short version is, your uncle was snakebit. It was a moccasin that did it. At least that's what your poor momma told us. Though some folks said he was murdered. That someone had put an end to him. That there was too much light in the world, and so darkness had to come and set a balance to it."

"But why would somebody want to kill our uncle?" said Murphy.

Mr. Cartwright leaned over the table, his teeth all brown and cracked, his breath a waft of booze and cigarettes. He lowered his voice like he was going to tell us a secret.

"There is a great darkness here in Benign," he said. "The woods are very old, and they have a power. But the Spirit has its hand on your grandmother—always has. She is a light-bringer, and once I was too. But there aren't only light-bringers here." Mr. Cartwright turned his head from left to right, his eyes wandering over the room. "Be careful, children, because in this town evil lurks all around you."

That's when I saw him, staring at me from across the bar. He seemed taller than I remembered him, his beard ragged and mangy, his bloodshot eyes gazing right at me.

It was the Hobo.

I started to panic, breathing quicker, hyperventilating.

"What is it?" said Murphy.

He's not real, I thought. *He's just a vision. He's only in your mind.*

"Murphy," I said, "we have to go. Right now."

"Why?" she said. "I still got questions."

The Hobo took a step toward me, his eyes wide like an owl's. I could feel the terror in my heart. He had been chasing me all this time, and now he had me away from my home, where I wasn't safe, where Mom was dead and there was no one left to protect me.

"He's here," I said.

"Horace?" said Murphy.

"No," I said. "It's the Hobo."

"Dude, he's not real. You have to stop."

But he was so close now, he was almost to our table. I grabbed Murphy's hand and yanked her out of the booth and ran. I saw a door in the back, an emergency exit. I flung the door open and stumbled into the night.

Outside the moon and stars lit the woods behind the bar so bright I could see my own shadow cast in front of me, same as daylight. But we weren't alone out here. Off in the woods I heard laughter, cackles in the darkness. People stood in the shadows of the trees, watching us, maybe a dozen of them, their eyes shining in the black like moons.

"Are you seeing this?" I said. "Or am I having a vision?"

"I'm seeing it," said Murphy. "We need to leave. Now."

We ran to the front of the bar and got on our bikes and pedaled the miles back to the Farm.

"I told you," said Murphy once we were back home in our bunk beds, the bikes stashed away. "This whole place sucks. And if your goddamn imaginary Hobo hadn't shown up, we probably would have gotten to the bottom of it."

"I don't know," I said. "I think the Hobo is a sign, a warning. I think he meant for us to leave, that something bad would happen if we stayed."

"Judging by the people staring at us all hungry-like from the woods back there, he might have been right," said Murphy. "There's still so much I don't understand. Why didn't Grandma tell us we had an uncle? Shit, why didn't Mom ever mention him? And why the fuck did they bury him in the woods like that?"

"I don't know," I said. *But he's wonderful*, I almost told her. *I listen to his sermons after you fall asleep at night.*

But I didn't say a word. Something felt wrong about it, like this secret wasn't hers, like she wasn't ready yet.

Ready? Ready for what?

"Anyway, I'm going to bed," said Murphy. "It's like four A.M., and I got to get some sleep tonight. Grandma will probably make me cut down a whole goddamn tree by myself tomorrow. I swear the old bitch is just trying to wear me out."

I hated when Murphy talked shit about Grandma. But I didn't feel like getting in a fight this late at night, so I held my peace.

"Good night, Murphy," I said.

"Whatever," she said.

And eventually I fell asleep.

THROUGH THE BLANK STAR-STREWN WORLD I
ran, the campfire in the distance, the monster after me. Always,
the monster after me. But he was slow. The campfire had long
disappeared into the black, and the stars above me had grown
brighter, stranger. I knew daylight should be coming, but daylight would never come. There was only the chase, only the
monster and me. I could hear him suck breath through his
nose, the strangled sound his throat made, the clomp of his
feet on the ground. He was misshapen, he staggered when he
moved, he ran with a kind of loping lurch. It was horrifying, I
was disgusted by him, I was disgusted by the eyeless gray face
every time I looked over my shoulder.

I knew he would never stop running, he would never quit.

But I also knew that I could run faster.

THE NEXT DAY GRANDMA LED ME THROUGH
the fields again. The Hummingbird Grove was alive with movement, bright blossoms blooming midair only to flitter away
from one feeder to the next. The sun cast a haze through the
trees, a sort of glow that made everything dreamy and unreal.
Wildflowers unleashed themselves in gashes of yellow across
the green. The place seemed suffused with life, a garden where
only miracles could grow. Grandma and I sat down in supplication, but before we could begin, I asked her a question.

"Grandma, did you have a son?" I said.

The smile fell right off her face.

"Why ask a question when you already know the answer?"
she snapped. I started to apologize, but she hushed me. "It's
okay. I know y'all followed me. Well, I didn't know it at the
time, but I figured it out later. Quite a thing, spying on an old
woman in her grief like that. It's a personal moment, standing

over the grave of your child. You don't know that kind of pain. You couldn't possibly."

"I'm . . . I'm sorry," I said. "We didn't mean to break your trust. With all you've done for us, taking us in like this, protecting us from Horace. It wasn't right, and I'm sorry."

Grandma sucked in a deep breath and let it out slow. She looked back at me with eyes gray and sad and wore-out.

"No, Lee. It's my fault for not telling you the truth, mine and your mother's. She never told you about Jeremiah? Not even a hint?"

I shook my head. "Not a word."

"Well, that just about breaks my heart," she said. "Figures, though. It's not an easy thing to talk about, losing a brother like that. Especially one as close as they were. I should know. I lost my sister when I was just a girl. Never quite got over it, even now."

"Just seems weird that she wouldn't have mentioned him."

"It's not like I talk about him either. Not with other folks, anyhow. That's something about our family, Lee, something rotten. We don't talk about grief or pain. We just bottle it up until it becomes unbearable, until it explodes on us, until it's so big and overblown it can't help but ruin things."

"Yeah," I said. "I noticed."

"It's a terrible habit," she said. "One we ought to break, if any one of us ever had the guts to." She sighed again, waved a hand in front of her face like she was brushing the whole thing aside.

"Anyway, Jeremiah. My one and only son. What would you like to know about him?"

"Just, you know, what he was like. All that."

"Where to start? He was a sweet boy." She paused, her finger on her cheek. "No, that's not the right word for him. He was luminous, my Jeremiah, a magnet for attention. If he walked into a room, no one bothered to look anywhere else. Even in a field—even in the Hummingbird Grove—it was hard not to let your gaze fall on him. And it wasn't just that he was a beautiful child, which he was, of course—about the most handsome and lovely boy you ever laid eyes on. It was something else about him. Charisma? No, that's not strong enough. He was more like a whirlpool, I reckon. He could suck you right in if he wanted, whenever he wanted, and you'd be glad for the attention. That's just the way he was.

"But oh, so smart, and so kind. He was a seer like you, except greater, more magnificent. The things he witnessed, the visions he imparted to us—it was like they weren't fit for mortal beings. They were so full of light they could make you weep for joy. He had this way of speaking, mind you. It wasn't so much his words but his voice, his cadence and melody. Every syllable out of that boy's mouth was music, and when he spoke it was like he was casting a spell. Because the spoken revelation has power, more so than any words written down, that's just the truth of it. Yes, Jeremiah was just about all I could see, that I assure you.

"Maybe it's my fault, the way I doted on him. I know it made your mother jealous. Who wouldn't be jealous of a parent's obvious favorite? With their father gone and a farm for me to run all by myself, I didn't have the time or energy to focus on the both of them. And Jeremiah was so much. He filled every room he was in with his smile, his voice. Every day your mother was left by the wayside."

I knew exactly how that felt. I mean, Murphy was no transcendent talker, but she and Mom understood each other in a way they never bothered to try with me. I knew what it was like to be the left-behind one, the ignored one. It made my heart break a little for my mom. I wished I could tell her that I loved her, that I forgave her for ignoring me. I wished I could tell her anything at all. The grief hit me then, harder than it ever had before.

"Oh, now I've got you crying, haven't I?" said Grandma. "I'm sorry, Lee. I didn't mean to harp on about such sad things."

"Please, tell me more," I said. "It feels good to talk about this stuff, even if it does hurt. I guess I just don't understand why Mom never mentioned Jeremiah to us."

"I won't lie to you, Lee," said Grandma. "Jeremiah's death just about sucked all the fire out of me. I couldn't hardly pick my head up off the pillow, much less keep the Farm running. A lot of that labor fell on your mother, and that wasn't fair at all. Probably why she ran off like she did. Me flat on my face, dark depressed, doing nothing. I despaired of my life. I wanted to die. And it's a miracle I didn't. I think your mother took my grief hard, the overwhelming sadness I felt. When your momma ran, she ran for her life, that I do believe."

"What saved you?" I said.

Grandma looked up at me, eyes gone bright again.

"Well, I had a vision," she said.

"What kind of vision?"

"I'll never forget it. Your mother had been gone about six months. I'd stopped eating, for the most part. Our hired folks had all left, took off for greener pastures, not wanting to be at the beck and call of a woman so miserable she couldn't drag herself out of bed. I want you to know, Lee, that I nearly did kill myself. I had a knife. It was Jeremiah's knife, one he would carry around, same as any boy carried around a knife. I had it sharpened and ready. I said my prayers to the Spirit, for it to receive me, to float off into the ether and join my boy. And as I pressed that cold metal to my skin, the room seemed to fade away, the walls and ceiling and floor, until it was just me hovering there in the black, floating like a hummingbird. A light appeared like a window, and through it I saw the Farm, all fixed up and painted and green, a gravel road spread out in front of it. And on that road was a big loud black car, a boy and a girl inside of it, coming slow up my driveway. I remember it same as I remember my mother's name. It burned itself on my heart like that. I knew just what it was too: My grandchildren sidling up the road, come to join me. Come to bring the good times back.

"What I'm saying is: Lee, honey, you saved me. You and Murphy. I've been waiting twenty years, and it finally came true." She put her arm on my shoulder. "Let me tell you, son, it was well worth the wait."

Grandma started crying, and I cried too, and we held each other, and I don't know, I'd never felt loved like that. Not before or since.

That's when I saw him.

It was the boy from my visions, and I finally knew who he was.

Standing before me was Jeremiah Sanford, right there in the Hummingbird Grove. His hair was blond as milk, his skin soft, his eyes a deep and wondrous blue. He stared out at me, dressed in a black suit, a preacher's suit. He was hazy, and he seemed to ripple in the wind like he was made of something thinner than air—not a ghost, but something like that. Jeremiah had this pained look on his face, a kind of silent agony, full of regret. I guessed it hurt, watching me with his mother like that. I knew that he wished he could hold her, that he could reach out and be held. But he was dead now, a ghost or a vision, some leftover memory burned into this place forever.

"What is it?" said Grandma. "What do you see?"

Jeremiah held one finger up to his lips in a *hush* gesture.

"Nothing," I said. "I don't see anything at all."

And he smiled at me.

Grandma stood up to leave.

"Is it okay if I stay here a little longer?" I said. "I think I just need a minute after that one."

"Take all the time you need," said Grandma, and she made her way back to the house.

Jeremiah approached me, and the light followed him, as if he brought the brighter world with him, as if everywhere he stood that world bled into this one.

"You have questions for me, Lee?" he said.

"That's you on the tape, isn't it?" I said.

He nodded.

"But you sound so much older in them," I said, "like you're my age."

"This is the form my body takes in this world, in the daylight," he said. "I am powerless to change it."

"I knew it had to be you on that tape. I knew it had to be your voice. Jeremiah, I need to know what's happening here. I mean, with the town, with those people in the grocery store."

"You enjoyed it, didn't you?" he said. "All the attention."

"I mean, sure I did. Who wouldn't?"

"Those are your people," he said. "They are the ones who believe in you."

"Why would they believe in me?" I said. "You're the leader. You're incredible on the tape, the way you told them your visions, the way you made everyone in the room feel exactly the way you did. When I try to talk about my visions, everyone just gets annoyed. Even when somebody will listen, like Grandma, they don't see what I see or hear what I hear. I can't make it make sense to them."

"But you're a poet, aren't you?" he said.

"I mean, I try to be," I said. "How did you know that?"

"Lee," he said, "I have much to show you."

"Why can't you just sit me down and explain everything to me?"

"Because it isn't sufficient to simply hear it. To understand, you need to see it and feel it as well."

"I don't understand."

Jeremiah laughed.

"You, Lee, are so much in love with words, and words are the most deceptive of all. No, you must see and feel and taste the Spirit, all that power. You must know the future as I know it, experience it as I have. Only then can you believe."

"Believe what?"

"That you are a prophet, the same as I am. That your visions have a value and a purpose. That you were chosen by the Spirit before you were born, raised up for exactly this purpose. You must believe, and then all the others will come to believe through you."

Could this possibly be true? But how? I was the misfit kid, the loser with no friends. My mom had barely even liked me. Why would the Spirit pick me? How could I be some kind of great leader?

"You think I'm mistaken, that I lie to you?" said Jeremiah. "Well, you'll see. Go ahead—address the Hummingbird Grove, and it will respond."

"But what do I say?"

"The Spirit will give you the words in the proper time. Focus on the Spirit and the Spirit alone. Can't you feel the light inside of you? Can't you taste it like honey on your tongue? Have faith, Lee, and speak, and the words will come."

I stood up and stared deep into the Hummingbird Grove, into the constant motion of the birds whirring like the cosmos, into the stillness of the forest around us. Jeremiah walked up behind me and began to murmur some sort of chanting prayer in my ear, like the kind I heard Grandma do over the grave in the woods.

I decided it was time. I decided I would have faith in myself for once.

I opened my mouth, and I spoke.

But it wasn't my voice that came out—it was Jeremiah's, same as it was on the tape, the one full of such joy and power that it sounded like it came bearing priceless gifts. It was the sweetest, saddest voice you ever heard in your life, and it was mine now.

The words were nonsense—they were just syllables, just sounds, like the Pentecostal people I'd seen overcome on TV. It was melodic, meaningless so far as I knew but pure and right as music.

The hummingbirds ceased their darting and whirling, and they stood still in front of me, an army of red-throated baby angels waiting at attention.

"Shut your eyes," Jeremiah whispered in my ear. "Give yourself over to the Spirit. Never mind the words. Let the words be what they may. Let the Spirit flow through you like wind through the mouth of a cave. Let go until you vanish and there is nothing left but the Spirit."

I cleared my mind and focused as hard as I could, and I spoke whatever words came to me. I talked and I talked until I felt something rise up inside of me, and I began to sing, a melody I'd heard before—the song Cass sang under the Split Tree—but with my own words, with whatever words the Spirit gave me. I sang and I sang, and my voice became like sunlight, and it fell down on the trees and the grass and the flowers, casting everything in a golden haze.

"Open your eyes," said Jeremiah.

I did as he said.

The Hummingbird Grove was filled with animals. Birds hunched in the trees, sparrows and cardinals and blue jays and mourning doves, watching me wide-eyed. Rabbits had gathered, standing on their hind legs as if awaiting a command. A family of deer stood nearby, a doe and a buck and three fawns, and the buck bowed his tangle-crowned head before me.

"They're listening," I said. "They're hearing every word."

"Not just them," said Jeremiah.

I looked out past the Hummingbird Grove, past the garden, to the trees surrounding us. People were there, dozens of them, maybe hundreds, standing stock-still, watching me. They were all naked, pure as God had made them, like they'd just tumbled out of Eden, and they gazed upon me, eyes wide with wonder and faith, like I was everything they'd been waiting for.

"They will come from all over for you," he said. "They will hold your words dear to their hearts, dearer than all else. They will forsake husbands and wives for you, and children will abandon their parents. They will all come to follow you."

"But why?"

"Because the Spirit chose you before the foundation of the world. You were raised up for exactly this purpose."

"Can it be true, Jeremiah?" I said. "Can that be the reason for my visions? Could I really be destined for all of this?"

"The Spirit never lies," he said.

"But it's been wrong before," I said. "I've seen visions that didn't come true."

"Each vision is a world," he said, "a possibility. You will not be the victim of fate, who must suffer the winds of change like all the peasants of this world, if you only choose not to be. You are no peasant, Lee. You are a prince of this earth. The reality you seek is that which you will. That is your power, Lee. That is your truth."

I left the Hummingbird Grove with my heart reeling, the happiest I'd ever felt in my life. I finally knew the purpose of all my visions. I was to be a leader, a guide for this community, a force for good in the world. I was so happy I just sort of wandered around the woods, all the way to the Split Tree. I didn't know why, but I had a feeling something new would be there if I looked. I stuck my arm deep into the hole and pulled out another tape, this one dated 12-1-88.

I also found a note scribbled on a piece of paper, folded and dropped into the tree. It said, "COME TO THE TENANT HOUSE TONIGHT. AFTER MIDNIGHT."

Holy shit. It was an invitation to go hang with Cass and them. Of course I would be going. There wasn't any way on earth I'd miss something like that.

It made me wonder a little bit if it was Cass leaving me these tapes. But how would she have copies of my uncle's sermons? That didn't make any sense. I had told her I'd be coming back to the tree to check for things, and she'd left me a note, that was all. I slid the tape and the note into my front overalls pocket and was about to head back to the house when George Urquhart stepped out of the woods. I tried to pretend like he hadn't scared me.

"This is your favorite spot to spy on me, huh?" I said.

"Shit," he said. "I seen you come out here, looking like you were on a mission. You pulled a tape out of that tree. Never seen somebody do something like that before."

I clutched the pocket where the tape was hidden, pressed it close to my heart. He wasn't getting this thing from me without a fight.

"Whoa there, boss," said George. "I ain't after your tapes now. I come to fetch you. Granny wants to see you. Don't worry now, she won't kill you or nothing. She just wants to talk."

I wasn't sure what to do. What did Jeremiah want me to do?

I felt a stirring in my heart then, just a little whisper. *Go ahead. After all, you are a prophet of the Spirit. What can they do to you?*

"Promise," he said. "You'll be safe. She's only an old woman with some questions."

"Okay," I said. "I'll come."

And I followed George down the path that led off of my grandma's land to where the Urquharts lived.

It took a while, the trail overgrown and winding, the trees thick and gnarled in this part of the woods. I realized for the first time just how massive the Farm really was, how deep the old western woods went. Eventually the trees broke and we came to a clearing with a gravel drive leading past it. Busted toys were tossed about the yard, and a rusty Ford pickup sat out front, flies buzzing around its open window. A row of ratty lawn chairs stuck up from a yard full of kudzu and weeds. A grill lay tumped over on its side, spent charcoal scattered on the grass. And in the midst of all that chaos, the Urquhart house rose like a tumor on the lot.

It stood a leaning, crumpled two stories, gutters hanging off the roof, the chimney caved in. The windows were all busted out with garbage bags and cardboard taped over them, and the front door barely hung on its hinges. I followed George inside, the boards bending under my every step. In the living room the TV played talk shows while the Urquhart girl slept on the couch, snoring. Somewhere up a creaky flight of stairs with a busted railing I heard the sound of a baby crying. I wondered where its mother and father were, who else was up there in the darkened rooms.

"Stop gawking and come on," said George. He led me to the kitchen, where the Urquhart grandmother was waiting on me. The place was filthy—dishes piled up in the sink, a refrigerator grumbling in a corner, the thick scent of something odd bubbling on the stove. The grandmother sat at a little round table, squat and hunched over as a mole. She wore a dirty blue dress and had a big warty nose that made her look like one of those cheap fortune-tellers you see in New Orleans. She had an old yellow-paged legal pad and a Bic pen in front of her. The room was dark, a single purple candle burning on the table between us.

"Welcome," she said, "to this shithole I call home. Have you a seat."

"Thanks," I said. "I guess."

I sat down across from her. George stood over by the refrigerator and lit a cigarette. He leaned against the wall, this weird smirk on his face, just watching me.

"It wasn't always like this, you know," said Mrs. Urquhart. "Not ten years ago, this was a good place to live."

"What happened?"

"Used to be I cared," she said. "Used to be I had some pride in myself, in my family. But we're cursed, I understand that. There's no fighting time, what it does to you. So I gave up on trying to be respectable. Now all I want is my boy back."

"Your boy?" I said. "You mean Carl?"

"Mmm-hmm. My boy."

"Well, I don't know where Carl is," I said, "so I don't see how I can help you."

Mrs. Urquhart shut her eyes a minute and hummed to herself like she was saying some kind of weird prayer. I looked over at George, but he just frowned and sucked on his cigarette. All the while Mrs. Urquhart kept on humming.

On the wall behind her were old pictures, snapshots in frames, same as at Grandma's. I took a look at them, waiting on Mrs. Urquhart to finish whatever it was she was doing. They were of a happier sort—families together, everyone smiling. Some of the photos looked like they went back a hundred years. A tall, lanky man with short black hair was in several. I guessed that was Carl. He had dark brown eyes and a kind smile, and he seemed like the sort of person you'd miss when he was gone. I hoped they found him, and soon. In another picture, an old framed black-and-white one, stood three men in suits. They had black hair and great billowing mustaches, and they looked rich and healthy, like they'd live forever, like they were the happiest folks in the entire world.

"My daddy and his brothers," she said. "Recognize them?"

Mrs. Urquhart still had her eyes shut. How had she known I was looking at that picture?

"I've never seen that photo before," I said, "so how would I recognize them?"

Mrs. Urquhart smiled a little, just a flicker in the left corner of her mouth. She grabbed the yellow legal pad and pen and started scribbling, her eyes still shut. She was drawing frantically, long black slashes across the page, and a picture came into form. It was a snake and some stars, a sickle moon, and three figures hunched on the ground. She wrote something small in the margin, something tiny and scribbled that I couldn't read. Mrs. Urquhart yanked the paper free and held it over the candle flame. It caught, the edges blackening, smoke pouring up from it. But it didn't smell like normal burning paper. No, there was something else to it, like sage, some kind of spice or herb, and I began to cough from the smoke. The flames spread, touching her fingers, but Mrs. Urquhart didn't drop the paper. She clamped it tight in her little crone hand, the ashes crumbling onto her palm.

Mrs. Urquhart opened her eyes. They stared deep into mine as if they were some kind of open window she could crawl through.

She took a deep breath and blew the ashes right into my face.

I gagged on them, the smell was so strong, the ashes all in my mouth and nose and eyes. I jumped up, knocking my chair over, but she grabbed my arm in a claw grip so tight it hurt.

"You see them now?" she snarled. "You see them?"

The light in the Urquhart's kitchen dimmed and went black.

I found myself standing in the campfire world, the night wild and alive with stars, the wind smearing the light across the sky.

The Gentlemen were there, but they wore suits this time, and I realized they were the Urquhart brothers, all three of them. They sat in the dirt to the left of the campfire. Across from them sat a tall blond man with glasses. He wore ratty old clothes like a tramp, but he looked arrogant, and his grin had something of a sneer to it. Between them was a large metal tray with three bone-colored dice lying on it. They didn't look like normal dice—no dots on them, just symbols. An eyeball and a snake and a dagger showed faceup.

The middle Urquhart brother spoke.

"The game is on, Mr. Sanford?"

Holy shit. The blond guy was my great-grandfather. I could see it now, kind of. I could see his resemblance to Jeremiah.

"The game is always on, old friend," said my great-grandfather, grinning wickedly in the firelight. "The oldest struggle there is. I want what's yours, and I want it all."

"And if we win?" said the middle Urquhart.

My great-grandfather laughed. "If you win, I'll pack my shit up and leave this place. I'll stop bothering you altogether. I'll give up my claim to this land, to this world. You'll never hear another word from me again, that I promise you."

"That isn't enough," said the middle Urquhart.

"Fine, fine," said my great-grandfather. "If you win, I will be yours. Every last member of my family from my daughter on down will serve you from now till the end of the line. You'll be our kings."

The Urquharts huddled together, whispering back and forth.

"We accept," said the middle Urquhart. "Cast the bones."

The bones? Were the dice carved from bones? It made sense—the color, the rough shape of them. This was old magic, I knew deep in my heart, something that was a part of me, that maybe always had been.

"You first," said my great-grandfather.

"Very well," said the middle Urquhart.

He picked up the dice and rolled. They clanked and pinged across the plate, landing on a falling star, a sickle moon, and an hourglass.

My great-grandfather began to laugh then, to cackle horribly in the windy night. I saw him slip a single die from his coat sleeve into his left palm. He passed it to his right hand smooth as a magic trick, and I knew for a fact that not a single one of the Urquharts had seen it. Only I could, from where I was standing. My great-grandfather scooped the other dice and rolled, cupping the extra one with his pinky. Again, he was smooth about it. If I hadn't been standing so close to him, looking over his shoulder, I wouldn't have even noticed.

The wind blew, and the fire flickered, and a shadow fell over the moon. In the sudden darkness I couldn't see what he had rolled. I couldn't see what the dice read before my great-grandfather swooped his hand across the plate and scooped them back up. But I could tell one thing from the looks on the Urquhart brothers' faces.

My great-grandfather won.

The light in the world began to change. The stars shivered and vibrated, and the moon sped away as if it were yanked on a string, as if the whole world moved in fast-forward. The desert ground sprouted trees, flowers in swirls of color, numerous as the stars. The moonlit desert had become a sun-sparkled garden. And in the middle of it stood my great-grandfather, laughing, dancing, and spinning. With yellow butterflies circling his head like a halo, he began to sing. He had this thunderous deep voice, and the whole forest resounded with it.

The Urquharts had vanished along with the moon and stars. They had no place in this daylight world, not any longer.

There was only my great-grandfather and the world he would go on to create.

Slowly the light dimmed and faded, and I came to in the Urquharts' house.

My eyes burned, and my mouth still tasted like ash. George stood smirking in the corner. I wondered if he knew what I'd seen. I wondered if he'd ever been to the campfire world at all.

"So you see?" she said. "You understand that none of this belongs to you. Your great-grandfather cheated."

Something snuck into me, a hardness in my heart. I heard a whisper in my ear, Jeremiah speaking through me.

"I saw nothing of the sort," I said.

Mrs. Urquhart frowned at me.

"Is that so?"

"Indeed," I said, the word not even mine, like I had nothing to do with it at all. "What I saw was my great-grandfather play a game and win. I don't know what kind of game it was, but I saw your father and his brothers lose it. Lose their lives, lose their claim to this land, lose whatever it was that they bet. So I'll leave you be now. Thanks for showing me my great-grandfather. He seemed like a hell of a guy."

I stood up to go.

"I thought you'd be different," said Mrs. Urquhart. "A kind boy with a good heart. That's how George described you, anyhow, and it gave me hope. But he was wrong. You're just as bad as all the rest of them."

"Coming from you," I said, "I'll take that as a compliment."

George Urquhart took a step toward me then, his fists balled up like he was ready to fight. And I got scared a minute. There was no way in hell I would win a fight against George Urquhart.

"Sit down, George," said Mrs. Urquhart. "The boy made his decision, just the same as his uncle did."

"My uncle?" I said. "What do you know about Jeremiah?"

Mrs. Urquhart smiled.

"A hell of a lot more than you do," she said. "Now get the fuck out of my house."

"With pleasure," I said.

And I left.

I WAS PRETTY SPACEY AT DINNER THAT NIGHT. I kept wondering about the Urquharts, about what had happened in their house. I wanted to ask Grandma about it, but I didn't want to do it around Murphy.

So I kept my mouth shut about everything. It was weird how far apart my sister and I seemed to be drifting. Murphy was so tired after all her work that day—Grandma made her chop firewood all day even though it was summer and we had plenty already, and I was absolutely forbidden to help—that she barely spoke a word to me all through dinner.

"Go on to bed, Murphy," I told her after she declined Grandma's dessert. "I'll finish up the dishes myself."

Murphy shot me a look like she knew I was up to something, but I guess she was so tired she didn't care.

"Whatever you want," she said. "I don't even give a shit anymore."

And she slumped upstairs to bed.

Grandma had made peach cobbler for dessert, and the two of us sat there together in silence and ate.

"I saw the Gentlemen again," I said after a while. "They were playing a card game with your father."

Grandma raised an eyebrow at me.

"What else did you see?"

"I saw your father win, and the darkness of the world changed to light, and the desert became a garden."

Grandma clapped her hands. "That's my daddy for you. I wish you'd known him. It was like the sun rising in your heart every time he walked into a room."

"But what was that game they were playing?" I said. "What kind of dice were those?"

"Folks had strange ways of deciding things back in those days," said Grandma. "I wouldn't worry much about it if I were you. That kind of game is gone from these parts, and dice like those are long forgotten. We have to focus on the future, Lee. We're trying to build something here from what your great-grandfather started. Try not to worry about the past so much. After all, we can't change it any, can we?"

"No," I said. "But it seemed weird to me, how my great-grandfather won. It seemed like he cheated."

Grandma leaned in close to me, staring me straight in the eyes.

"This doesn't have anything to do with the Urquharts, does it?" she said.

"It might," I said.

"You can't be trusting those people, Lee," she said. "They are trash, I already told you. Treacherous. You mustn't believe anything they show you."

"I won't," I said. "I promise."

"Good boy," said Grandma. "Now get these dishes done before too late. We got us a big day tomorrow."

After Grandma went to bed, I finished cleaning up and headed to my room, Murphy already sleeping in her bunk. I pulled out the tape recorder and laid my ear against the speaker and pressed play. The tape garbled and moaned for a moment, and I was afraid the player would eat it, spew out a bunch of tangled black ribbons. But after a second it caught itself, and soon I heard Jeremiah's voice belting out into my ear. I wanted to hear everything, to memorize it, to take it into my heart like Gospel. This was my truth now too, wasn't it? The first part of the sermon was lost to time and distortion, so this one started somewhere in the middle.

"The greatest threat to the human soul is loneliness. Yes, I'll say it again—loneliness is the scourge of the world. For people were not meant to live apart. Separate, cut off from the light of community. Have you not felt this longing in your own soul? Light calling out to light, even as the darkness of the world seeks to swallow you whole?

"Friends, that is not our destiny.

"No, we have found each other, and the light inside us has answered the Spirit's call. We are being gathered together, swept from all across the world by the winds of the Spirit, our burning lights stitched into the sky. We together have become a new constellation, a sign for the world to see. A world that is not worthy of us, that never understood us in the first place, and we will change that world, transform it in our own image. Because we are one here, all of us—one body, one soul, one mind, one family.

"And together we will do magnificent things."

The tape ended with shouts and applause from the congregation, or whatever they were. I mean, people were going nuts. And how could they not after hearing something like that? Because it was true, everything Jeremiah said about loneliness. I knew that pain, I knew it in my heart and bones. And if what he said about loneliness was true, wouldn't he also be right about community, about the power of all of us together?

I wished I could have seen him speak. I wished I could have been there.

I waited until I thought it was around midnight, when it would be time for me to go to the tenant house. I hid the tape player and slid out of the bunk as quiet as I could. I pulled on my clothes and snuck out of the bedroom.

IT WAS BRIGHT AND CLEAR OUT, THE MOON A
sign in the sky welcoming me into the night. I walked through
the field, past the big, strange, empty barn, dark with its
secrets, Murphy sleeping fast in the house behind me. I'd
never been out in the Farm at night without my sister, and
I felt a little bit like a jerk for leaving her behind. But how
many times back home had she climbed out of our window
to go meet with her friends, and had she ever asked me to
come along? Hell no. So maybe it was okay if I did something
without her. Maybe it was okay if I struck out on my own
for once.

I followed the birch trail to the tenant house. Along the way
I could hear them, the laughter and music—joyful this time,
not eerie and strange like before—and soon I came upon a few
kids around my age, sitting in plastic chairs around a small fire
in a gravel pit in front of the house.

They all looked at me as I walked up, the music loud and blaring from a stereo inside the house, the window left wide open so it would blast into the yard. Nobody said a word, and for a second I nearly turned back and walked myself right into the darkness and my own bedroom.

But then Cass came laughing outside, a beer bottle in her hand. She wore a blue dress with flowers all over it, and when she walked it swished around her ankles. Cass could have been from 1967, or she could have been from the future. She could have come from anywhere.

"It's Lee!" she said and ran up to give me a hug.

I didn't know what to do with my hands, so I just stood there and let her pull me close.

"Dude," she said, "you give the worst hugs."

"Sorry," I said. "I'm not much of a hugger."

"It takes practice," she said, and it was like she was seeing right through to me, to how awkward and friendless I was, like my own loneliness was scrawled in big letters on my forehead.

A redheaded kid stood up and walked toward me. He was short and wore a sweaty gray T-shirt.

"This is the famous Lee, huh?" he said, shaking my hand. "Heard a hell of a lot about you."

"Oh," I said, taken aback. "I hope not."

"Ha!" said the redhead. "Didn't tell me he was funny too, did you, Cass? I'm Stephens. Welcome to our lovely little outhouse."

"It's not that bad," said Cass. "Remember, his grandmother's our landlord."

"No insult intended," said Stephens. "All in good fun. Lord knows she rents it to us cheap enough."

"It suits our purposes," said a tall kid in a Cubs hat who was smoking a corncob pipe. "I'm Luther. Pleasure to meet you."

We shook hands. Mom always said to shake hands hard as you could so people wouldn't think you were a wuss. Horace liked to break your palm, he squeezed your hand so tight. I tried to do something in the middle, just your average grip and double pump. I know, I was analyzing the shit out of my handshakes, but that's how awkward I was. I put every action I took under the same withering microscope.

"We have our own private driveway," said Luther, pointing to the far side of the house, "where we park the van. Leads us straight to the main road just past the border of the property. All in all, not a bad setup."

"You guys are in a band, right?" I said. "I think Grandma mentioned that."

"Indeed," said Luther. "It's our trade, how we make money."

"Oh come on," said Stephens. "We don't make any money."

"This is true," said Luther.

"But making money isn't the point, is it?" said Cass. "The point is just to make our own noise, you know, and to make it with as much heart as we possibly can. There's beauty in that too, right?"

I had the feeling that this was an old argument, one they'd all had a million times before. I didn't mind listening in on it. It made me feel like I was one of their friends.

"It would be cool not to be broke, though," said Stephens.

A kid with a shaved head sat on the roof, a beer in one hand and a cigarette in another, squatting like a medieval gargoyle. I wasn't sure how long he'd been up there.

"Who's that guy?" I said.

"Oh, that's Jack, our lead singer," said Stephens. "Dude's weird."

"Thinks he's psychic," said Luther. "He's always trying to channel the Spirit. Crazy stuff, you know?"

The Spirit. How did they know?

Of course I didn't think it was crazy. It was hard to call anybody insane when you'd spent your whole life seeing things that weren't there. But I was trying to make friends and not be weird, so I kept my mouth shut.

"Jack does his own thing," said Cass, shrugging.

"Cool with me," I said.

She laughed. "Is it? Is it cool with you?"

I could feel myself blushing hugely, so I stared at my feet.

"Jesus, I'm sorry," I said. "I guess it doesn't matter what I think."

"I'm just fucking with you, Lee," said Cass. "Relax already." She smiled her crooked-tooth smile at me, and I got shivers all over. "Anybody need a beer?"

"Of course," said Stephens.

"Come on," said Cass, grabbing my hand. "I'll give you the tour."

The tenant house was bright and dusty, lit by lamps and candles scattered across the floor. It was remarkably tidy for how many folks were living in it. There was a shelf full of books, old ratty hardbacks and mystery novels. Someone had dragged a couch into the room, probably from the dump, but it looked as if it had been washed, hand-scrubbed and cleaned up. Recording equipment was set up everywhere, microphones and speakers and a small mixing board, even a laptop. In fact, the place seemed kind of nice. Homey, even. Musical instruments lay all over the place—electric guitars and amps, a big Rhodes piano, and a red Tama drum kit. Other instruments too, old stuff—a banjo, a washtub bass, an acoustic guitar, a violin.

"This place is fucking awesome," I said. "It's like a real studio, you know? Like The Band at Big Pink or something. You're really doing it."

Cass grinned at me. "That's the plan, anyway." She led me to a small kitchen area, reached into a mini fridge, and handed me a beer. "Would be cool to have my own room though. Only two bedrooms for the four of us."

"I hear you," I said. "Since we moved here I've been splitting a bunk bed with my sister."

"Murphy, right? Why didn't she come tonight?"

"To be honest," I said, "I didn't tell her."

"Good boy," said Cass.

Stephens stuck his head in the window. "Hurry up with the beers already."

Cass switched the record—they had an actual record player with stacks of vinyl piled around the stereo—and we hurried outside.

"Guys," I said, "this place rules."

"Amen to that," said Luther. He lifted his beer, and we all drank.

I'd never really had much beer before. Seeing my mom drunk all the time didn't help, and I always figured I'd leave the boozing to her and Murphy. But again, I was trying to make friends, and it seemed fun.

"Cheers," I said, and took a gulp.

"Yep, we live in a real fucking paradise," said Stephens. "I ain't being ironic about that either. I mean it. I've waited my whole life to find a spot like this."

"It's true," said Luther. "I mean, we're in nature, first off. And not just any nature. Powerful nature. There's a spirit to this place, an energy here. You can't tell me you don't feel it."

"No," I said. "I know exactly what you're talking about. It's like the whole Farm has an electricity to it, like you live closer to the bone here."

"You a writer or something?" said Stephens.

"Kind of," I said. Cass raised an eyebrow at me. "I mean, I try to write poems."

"I'd love to read some of your poetry sometime," said Cass.

Yeah, that was never going to happen. I never showed anybody anything I wrote, not that anybody'd ever asked to see it before. I figured I'd better change the subject quick.

"So what brought y'all to Benign?" I said.

"Nice deflection," said Luther.

"I did deflect, didn't I?" I said.

"Absolutely you did," said Cass. "But no worries. I'm sure I'll read your poetry soon enough. But as for your question, Stephens and Jack grew up here. I came from Kentucky, and Luther's from Mississippi."

"I just don't get why you guys would come here of all places," I said. "I mean, I'm glad you did, but how did you hear about the Farm?"

"You kidding me?" said Stephens. "Your grandmother's a fucking legend. The Farm was a pretty amazing thing back in the day. An actual utopia."

"What do you mean?" I said.

"You know, how it was like the perfect society and all that," said Luther. "Share and share alike, everyone's equal, no one left behind."

"I have no idea what you're talking about," I said.

"Dude," said Stephens. "That is crazy. How do we know more about your family than you do?"

"The Farm was a kind of commune," said Cass. "It got national coverage in the news and everything. It would have gone on forever had your uncle not died. How do you not know any of this?"

I didn't know if it was the beer already going to my head (yeah, I'm that much of a lightweight) or what, but that kind of got to me a little bit. I mean, I knew from the tapes of Jeremiah's sermons that people came to the Farm to hear him preach, and Grandma had said other folks used to live there. But I had no idea it was famous. I hated that I'd missed everything, that nobody had ever even bothered to tell me. It made me pretty mad at my mom, to be honest with you. This was my legacy too, you know? It was where I came from.

"Well, my mom didn't talk about her past much," I said.

"That's a fucking shame," said Stephens. "My dad used to live on the Farm, and he never shuts up about it. Said it was the happiest time of his life. That's part of why I hooked up with this crew and moved out here. I wanted to see if it lived up to the hype."

"And does it?" I said.

They all looked back and forth at each other like they had some kind of secret.

"It remains to be seen," said Luther.

A foot stomp and a wolf howl sounded from the roof.

"Oh shit," said Stephens. "Jack's onto something."

Jack was waving his arms for everybody to hush.

"Quiet down now!" hollered Jack from the roof. "I got an announcement to make!"

Stephens ran inside and cut the stereo off. The rest of us stood below, watching Jack, the moon bright and wild behind him, the heavens full of all their stars.

"The Spirit," he said, "requests a song. An Irish ballad in the key of D." He cleared his throat. "Shall we?"

Jack began to sing then in a thick Irish brogue, some old song about a wedding day. You could tell it was one of those hundred-year-old ballads, the melody too sweet and sad and beautiful to be anything new.

And it *was* beautiful, one of the best things I'd ever heard in my life. By the second refrain, we kind of knew the tune, and everybody raised their drinks and joined in each time it came around. It felt so good to lift my voice up with all those guys, hollering loud as I could some heartbroke ballad about some- one who probably never existed. It was better than church, my voice just one among a whole chorus of them, feeling it tangle and mesh with the others until we were a crowd, one loud voice bellowing out into the night sky.

It felt good to belong, is what I'm saying. I was about the happiest I'd ever been in my life.

And then I had a vision.

It was the staggering kind, the sort that threw me to my knees, that made my whole body shake and quiver, a full taste- and-sound-and-sight vision, one where it felt like reality had been torn open and the guts of the world were revealed.

I saw things the likes of which I'd never seen before.

All the singing stopped.

"What is it?" said Cass. And then, like she already knew: "What are you seeing?"

I don't know why, but I started speaking then. I told them everything.

How I saw the sky become fleshy, pink, and it sprouted eyeballs, big bright blue blinking eyes, and lightning fell down in great musical notes, striking the earth in the sweetest tones. How fire spread across the Farm, lapping up the birch trail and through the woods and into the house itself, the music of the fire a shivering, melancholy sound. How I saw all of us burning but none of us hurting, none of us in pain, all of us lit alive by fire and the sound it made, the words of our hearts turned straight into music. How the ground opened up before me, the great gaping mouth of the world, and from that mouth came a roar like a lion's, a noise that shook the earth.

When I finished talking I was on my knees, crying, my throat gone scratchy and parched. All of them were staring at me, even Jack, dangling himself half off the roof to better hear.

"Holy shit," said Luther.

I knew I needed to apologize, that now they would all think I was weird or crazy, that I was some kind of psycho loser kid with a screw loose, that they would reject me same as everybody else, maybe even kick my ass for what I'd just done, for telling them about my visions.

Cass grabbed me and pulled me to my feet.

"I'm sorry," I said. "I don't know why I said all that."

But Cass wasn't angry. Cass kissed me.

It was my first kiss, wild and electric, and I felt it down to my toes.

When she pulled away I felt weak and blubbery, like my knees might give out and I'd fall crumpling to the dirt.

"That was art," hollered Jack. He jumped down from the roof and grabbed me by both of my shoulders. "It was the Spirit moving, man, flowing straight through you. It was like poetry, you know? Something beautiful. That's how I want my music to be."

I couldn't believe it. There was no higher compliment.

"Poetry?" I said. "Really?"

"Hell yes," he said. "It was like I was there, you know? I could feel it, I could see it just the same as you could."

That's when I finally understood it.

I didn't have to turn my visions into art, into poetry. My visions already *were* art. Maybe the Spirit could speak my visions through me, same as it did for Jeremiah. Maybe if I couldn't write my visions down, I could talk them, write them in the air with my voice, cast them like lightning through the sky. Maybe, if I spoke them just right, I could scald them into the brains of everyone who heard me. I could change them forever. Isn't that what poetry was, really, what all art was for? To make people see what you see and feel the hot burning life you feel?

Yes, that was it exactly. That was exactly what I was born to do.

"I feel like I finally know my purpose in life," I said.

"Goddamn," said Stephens. "Somebody get this man another drink."

So I took another Budweiser. And then another one.

I think I drank a lot of Budweisers. And also some clear liquid straight from a bottle. And then some other things.

That's when the night started to get a little blurry for me.

I remember dancing by myself while Stephens played the banjo.

I remember trying to sing my mom's favorite Kate Bush song a cappella and failing miserably.

I remember being inside the tenant house and Cass pulling me onto her sleeping bag when everyone else went outside to smoke. I remember kissing her frantically, my mouth all over the place, trying to make sure I got her on the lips.

I remember her laughing, holding me close, telling me I was wonderful, telling me that I was everything she had been waiting for.

I don't remember anything after that.

I JERKED AWAKE. MY HEAD POUNDED, AND I thought I might vomit. At first I didn't know where I was, and then I remembered. I was in the tenant house, still fully dressed, on a pallet on the floor, wrapped up tight with Cass.

Oh shit. Cass.

She rolled over and blinked her eyes at me, all sleepy and confused.

"What's the matter?" she said.

"I have to go," I said, scrambling to my feet. "I'm sorry."

I ran out of the tenant house and into the woods, still half drunk, the stars scattered and burning above me. I snuck in the house and down the hall, my head aching, my stomach starting to swirl. I was going to puke, I knew that. The house was so dark, so quiet, and I staggered up the stairs as silent as I could. The second-floor hallway was pitch black and lightless, every footfall of mine making the floorboards holler.

The bathroom wasn't far, just a couple of doors down from our bedroom. I stepped inside, the room so dark it might have been a closet, and fumbled a moment with the light switch.

Finally I flicked it, and fluorescent light flooded the room.

A man in a gray suit stood in front of me. He was tall and old, strands of white hair swooped across his bald head. In his hand he held a knife.

I was so scared I couldn't move, my scream caught in my throat. He stared at me, red-eyed and pleading, a tear spilling down his cheek.

"Are you certain?" he said. "Are you sure there's no other way?"

I stood there dumbly, trying to find my words, trying to do anything other than gasp for air.

"Very well," he said.

I thought he was going to kill me. I thought he was going to murder me in my grandmother's bathroom. I held my hands up and staggered back against the door, trying to protect myself.

The man lifted the knife to his neck and slid it across his throat. Blood erupted from his neck like music, like all the words he had been too afraid to speak out loud, all the dreams and wishes and thoughts he'd stored up his whole life now finally set free.

I flung the door open and tripped into the hallway. When I looked back, the man was gone.

He was never there at all. It was a vision.

I crawled back into the bathroom and shut the door behind me and vomited, trying to be quiet about it, trying not to wake a soul. After a few minutes I guzzled water from the tap and stumbled to the bedroom. I shut the door and locked it.

"You okay?" mumbled Murphy.

"Just a stomachache," I said.

"Holy shit," she said. "Are you drunk?"

I just stared at her, my eyes all red and bloodshot. I must have looked like I was about to puke again, because Murphy slumped back on her bunk.

"Sleep it off," she said. "But tomorrow you've got some explaining to do."

I climbed up into my bunk, and soon I was asleep.

MORNING CAME, AND I FELT LIKE ABSOLUTE shit. My head was a screaming throbbing nightmare, my guts ached, and my throat was ripped raw from all the puking. Light hurt, sound hurt, the bird chirps outside my window were like jackhammers.

Murphy peeked over the edge of my bunk.

"Aww, Lee's first hangover," she said. "Horrible, isn't it?"

"Miserable."

"I wish I had a camera. Wish I could document this moment forever." She grinned a little bit. "This wouldn't have anything to do with a certain girl in the tenant house, would it?"

"Leave me alone," I said and stuffed my pillow over my head.

"Serves you right, all the shit you used to give me on hangover mornings."

"I didn't know it was this bad."

"Well, you do now," she said. "Need a glass of water or anything?"

I pulled the pillow off my head and looked into Murphy's eyes. They were sad a little, concerned for me. She wasn't just fucking with me.

"Yeah," I said. "That would be great."

Murphy left for the bathroom. I tried to raise my head, and my stomach got all swirly, and I thought I might puke again. There was no way I could do any chores, not today. I didn't even dare go outside. I hoped Grandma wouldn't be pissed at me. I hoped I hadn't just wrecked everything forever.

Murphy came back with my water. "Here you go," she said. "I looked everywhere for some Advil or something, but it doesn't look like Grandma keeps pills around. Big surprise there."

"Man, she's going to be so mad," I said.

"Oh, come on," said Murphy. "I'll tell her you have a stomachache, that you caught a bug or something. It'll be no big deal."

"Thanks, Murphy," I said.

"No problem. But later, when you're feeling better, we got some talking to do, okay?"

"Yeah," I said. "Okay."

Great. How the hell was I supposed to explain everything to Murphy? My head hurt too bad to think about it. I rolled myself over, scooting as far away from the daylight streaming through the window as I could, and I fell asleep.

Grandma woke me up around noon with a plate of crackers and a bowl of soup and a weird beige-colored smoothie-looking drink.

"Here," she said. "This will make you feel better."

"I don't think I can stomach anything right now," I said, "but thanks, Grandma."

"Come now and drink," she said. "It'll do you good."

I really didn't want that drink. I really didn't want anything to touch my stomach, lest it come screaming right back out again.

"Lee," said Grandma. "I really must insist. I've lived a long life, and I know how to deal with a hangover."

Shit. How did she always know?

"Fine," I said, and I took the glass from her and drank. It tasted like grainy sludge with some weird herbs or something floating around in there.

"What is this stuff?"

"My home brew," she said. "It never fails. Now drink up."

"I don't think I can handle any more."

Grandma reached over the bed and grabbed the bottom of the glass and tilted it toward my mouth. I gulped and gulped and gulped until the liquid was all gone. Grandma pulled the glass away, and I lay back down, gasping.

"You'll feel better in no time," she said, smiling at me. And then she left, shutting the door behind her.

I wasn't sure, but I thought I heard the lock click like she had turned the key from the outside.

Why would Grandma lock me in here? I thought.

I fell back asleep.

IT WAS THE AFTERNOON, I KNEW THAT FROM the way the sun slanted across my room. Something had woken me up—something was wrong. I wasn't alone in the room. There was someone else there with me.

My closet door creaked open.

There stood the Hobo, tall in his boots, his eyes wild. He stepped toward me, the floorboards creaking under his feet.

It was like I was paralyzed, like I couldn't move at all. This wasn't real, I told myself, it was a vision, it wasn't happening.

I wanted to scream, I wanted to cry for help, I wanted to do anything but lie there, still and dumb.

He was standing right next to my bed.

The Hobo reached a scarred hand over my body and laid his palm on my forehead. It felt hot and sweaty, the blood pumping strong beneath his skin.

He began to chant, to mutter and groan, like he was praying, like he was a priest anointing me.

The light in my room flickered and dimmed, like the sun was just another cheap electric bulb, and the whole world plunged into darkness.

I stood in the night world again, the black endless place where the stars whirled wild and strange above me.

I knew I'd been running for hours and hours, days and nights and weeks on end. I was so tired. My sides ached, my head throbbed, my feet were blistered.

And all the while the monster was gaining on me.

I saw the Gentlemen's campfire burning far off in the night like some last beacon of hope, and I ran toward it, I ran with all my heart. The stars fell around me in long silver arcs, the sky slashed with color and light. Something was happening, something was changing in this world, and I was afraid.

With the last bit of my strength I made it to the fire, and I fell facedown into the dirt. I couldn't run anymore, I could hardly move. The three Gentlemen watched me, their faces passive, like they weren't surprised to see me here, like they'd been waiting on this moment for a very long time.

The first Gentleman, the one with the eyes so perfect and blue, spoke.

"It has already happened," he said, "and it will happen again."

The second Gentleman, the one with the smile, spoke.

"He was kept separate for years and years," he said, "but you are the door."

The third Gentleman, the comforter, stretched his hand toward me, granting me peace, granting me serenity.

"In the woods the secret is spoken," he said, "and it is made flesh."

He gazed past me, a sadness in his eyes.

I turned my head to look over my shoulder.

Behind me stood the monster.

I knew that now I would die. I knew that now I would be ripped to shreds by the monster, my limbs would be separated, my bones broken, my organs scattered. I could hear it clomp up to me, the sucking gasping sound of its throat.

The monster had come for me. It was time.

But it stepped past me, limping around the fire to where the Gentlemen sat.

The monster grabbed the first Gentleman, the one with the perfect blue eyes, and lifted him to his feet. It jabbed its fingers into the first Gentleman's eye sockets and gouged his eyes out. It held them, bloody and quivering, the nerves dangling from each eyeball like a comet's tail. The first Gentleman's body slumped over into the dirt, blood flowing from his empty sockets.

The monster crammed the first Gentleman's eyes into his own sockets, and they burned beautiful and blue as stars.

The monster stepped over to the second Gentleman, who sat smiling peacefully into the flames, though his eyes seemed sad. The monster grabbed his jaw in both hands, bracing his foot on the Gentleman's shoulder, and yanked. The jaw ripped off the second Gentleman, a horrible tearing sound like the snapping of tree limbs in a storm. It hung bloody and gangling in the monster's fist, and I watched in terror as it fixed the jaw to its face, strange and snarling as a Halloween mask.

The monster stood in front of the third Gentleman, who rocked back and forth in the dirt, singing this quiet little song, a chant almost, in a language I couldn't decipher. It was like he was praying, like he was singing last rites for himself, like he was preparing himself to die.

I couldn't move. I couldn't speak. I could only lie there and watch.

The monster took his long fingernail and slit the third Gentleman's chest open, a long gash like from a surgeon's knife, and blood flowed from his wound, blackening his clothes. The monster bent over his body and shoved both palms into the wound, cracking the sternum, prying the ribs apart. The monster plunged its fist into the wound and pulled out the third Gentleman's heart. It lifted the heart, still beating, up to the moon as some kind of offering, as a tribute to the sky and stars, the Milky Way and Mars and the cosmos, the whole universe watching.

And I watched as the monster ate the third Gentleman's heart, swallowing it, sucking the heart down its throat.

IT WAS LATE WHEN I FINALLY WOKE UP, THE
sound of rain and thunder booming. The sky was dark, and I
realized I'd slept through the whole day.

I thought I'd still be hungover from the booze and the
visions, but I felt weirdly great. I guess Grandma's health juice
or whatever really did the trick.

Pretty soon I heard Murphy bounding up the stairs,
and she banged on the door like she was trying to knock it
off its hinges. I got out of bed and unlocked the door and let
her in.

"He is risen," she said and laughed a little. "Feel up
for dinner?"

"Yeah," I said. "Surprisingly."

"Good," she said, "because Grandma made a fucking feast."

"I believe it," I said. "Let me get dressed, and I'll be
right there."

Murphy wasn't kidding about it being a feast. I mean, Grandma had cooked us the biggest dinner I'd ever had—pork tenderloin, mashed potatoes, corn on the cob, this weird lemon asparagus bacon wrap thing, and parmesan risotto, with banana pudding for dessert. For whatever reason, I was starved. I ate until I thought my eyes would roll back in my head. Murphy polished off three servings herself. I'd never eaten so much in my life.

"Now get some rest, children," said Grandma. "We have a big day tomorrow."

"More chores?" said Murphy. "Or do we have to go back to the creepy-ass village?"

Outside thunder rumbled, and the windows flickered with blue lightning.

"Whatever we're doing," I said, "it'll be a whole lot nicer in the sunshine. Hope this storm passes."

"Me too, Lee, dear," said Grandma. "Good night, children."

Grandma kissed us both on the cheek and left, humming to herself.

We got started on the dishes, me washing and Murphy drying, both of us working in silence. After a minute Murphy finally asked the question I'd been waiting on all night.

"Where were you last night?" she said.

"I was at the tenant house," I said. "At a party."

"Why didn't you take me with you?" she said.

"I don't know, why didn't you ever take me with you back home?" I said. "To anywhere you ever went?"

It came out meaner than I'd meant it, and I could tell I had caught Murphy off guard. But it also felt really damn good to say, to finally let that out.

"Because I didn't think you'd want to go."

"Is that right? You thought I just loved staying home by myself all the time?"

"No," she said. "I guess not."

"You didn't bring me because you were embarrassed of me," I said. "Your weird brother with the visions, all fucked up in the brain. I bet you never even told anybody you had a brother. You just pretended I didn't exist."

"That's not fair," she said.

"Seems pretty fucking fair to me," I said.

"Oh yeah, totally," she said. "I mean, you get to frolic in the meadows all day, having your little visions, while I do all this manual labor, working my ass off, and it's exhausting. You get treated like royalty by Grandma and by this whole fucking weird-ass town, and all I do is get shit on."

"Grandma loves us," I said. "We'd be lost if it weren't for her."

Murphy slammed a cup down on the countertop so hard she cracked it.

"What is with you? It's like Grandma has you wrapped so tight around her little finger you'll do whatever she wants."

"Look," I said, "maybe you can't understand how I feel because life has always been good for you and everybody likes you. But my life was shit back home. People hated me, Murphy. I didn't have any friends at all. I couldn't sleep at night. I had these dreams, these visions, and I never understood why, not until I came here. Grandma is the first person in my life not to treat me like a freak. Mom didn't even like me."

It was true. I was speaking honestly to Murphy for the first time in my life. It felt horrible, but it felt good in a way too, like a release, like I'd had this scream buried deep in my chest my whole life and I was finally letting it out.

"Mom loved you," said Murphy. "You know that."

"Yeah," I said, "but she didn't like me. It was always just you and Mom learning to box. You and Mom talking sports. You and Mom out at the range shooting guns. And me? Nobody cared what books I ever read or what movies I wanted to watch, the old black-and-white ones where everybody's beautiful all the time. Nobody read any of my poems, nobody gave a shit that I even wrote them. And don't get me started on the visions. Both of you just looked at me like I was some kind of freak, and you always have. But not Grandma. Grandma loves me. She even likes me. So do Cass and the kids at the tenant house. So does everybody in this whole town. And you can't stand it. That's why you're being such an asshole about all this."

"You better watch your fucking mouth, big brother," said Murphy, her finger in my face, just like Mom used to do. Just like Horace.

"Or what? You're going to kick my ass? You're no better than Horace."

Murphy swung once. Hit me square in the eye, knocked me flat.

I looked up at her from the floor, my face already throbbing.

"Shit," she said. "Jesus, I'm sorry."

"Fuck off, Murphy," I said, and I scrambled upstairs before she could see me cry.

I LAY IN MY BUNK, ALONE AND FURIOUS.

Murphy and I had never really fought before, not like this. I mean, as much as she didn't always like me, at least Murphy had my back. I probably should have told her all my secrets already, but I didn't want to, not yet. Something told my heart to wait, that the time wasn't right. And I trusted that feeling. I was starting to trust my feelings more and more, to believe that where they were leading me was right. It was working out pretty great so far. And if Murphy didn't understand, if she couldn't be happy for the changes I was going through and all the beautiful things happening in my life, then maybe I didn't need her after all. If my sister couldn't support me now, when I was finally finding my place, then what good was she to me?

I rewound the second tape and played it again and again, Jeremiah's words flashing like hummingbirds through my mind. I shut my eyes and listened while thunder grumbled outside, while the rain pattered on my window.

"So how do we escape the whirling gyres of our fate? How do we step outside of history, of the cycle we were doomed into? How do we not only reflect the light like our mother moon but become the light itself? How do we cast off the darkness of flesh, jealousy and strife and envy, the need to be superior to others? I ask you, who needs to be better than a hummingbird, all movement and color and light, sipping the sweetness of the world? Who needs to be anything more than a flower birthed only for beauty, to spread its food and seed so more beauty can abound?

"How do you find freedom from the tyranny of self, from your own selfish desire? You can satiate it, and yet be hungry only for more. You can gather for yourself all the money in the world and gorge on food and possessions and sex until that desire consumes you. Is that freedom? You can mortify the flesh, deny it, flagellate it out of yourself, bleed that desire dry until your very humanity is gone. Is that freedom?

"Or is freedom to be found together, in community, everyone working for the good of all? Is freedom not the sound of a thousand voices rising together in one roar, a thousand tiny lights shimmering together in a great bonfire so huge the world can't help but take notice? A tower to heaven isn't built by one single hand, no. It takes a multitude with one heart and one purpose and one vision. And this tower will not be baffled by many tongues, it will not be thwarted by any jealous deity. No, this tower is no physical thing, no work of the flesh. It is the power and glory of the Spirit working together in all of us, in every hand and heart and mind, to accomplish something beautiful.

"It is all of us gathered, a family, bonded by the Spirit, working together in power and in light."

I listened to Jeremiah's words, and I knew he was right. It was everything I could have ever dreamed of. The end of loneliness forever.

The family I'd always wanted.

I WOKE UP TO OUR BEDROOM DOOR SHUTTING. I didn't even remember falling asleep. The tape had ended, so it must have been well after midnight. Thunder boomed outside, and rain rattled the windows. Murphy stood there in her overalls, holding a flashlight.

I lay still, pretending to be asleep.

"I know you're awake," she said. "Look, I'm sorry."

I didn't say a word.

"I'm sorry. I'm sorry, I'm sorry, I'm sorry," she said. "Those are all the sorrys you're going to get from me."

I kept my mouth shut. It was going to take more than apologies to get me to talk to Murphy again.

"Anyway, I think you should know about upstairs. I just went to the third floor. It's not an attic. It's a dorm or something."

I rolled over and faced her.

"What do you mean?" I said.

Murphy smiled a little, like she was glad I'd cracked and spoken to her.

"I mean there are like ten bunk beds up there," she said. "With sheets and stuff. It's all set up for people to come and live."

The Farm. The congregation. They were coming back. I was so happy I could hardly stand it.

"Don't you think that's weird?" she said.

"Yeah," I said. "Crazy. I wonder what it's all about."

"I don't have a clue, but I'm going to find out."

"How?"

"Well, while you were laid up in bed all day being hungover, I was up on the roof cleaning the gutters, and I got a pretty good view of the place. I mean, the whole Farm—the pond and the trees and the fields and everything. And I saw something in the woods. Something big and metal glimmering out there in the sun."

"What was it?"

"I don't know," she said. "But Grandma's hiding something, and I'm going to find out what it is. Are you sure you don't have any idea?"

"Nope," I said. "I don't know a thing."

Murphy climbed up to my bunk so we were at the same eye level.

"Why don't I believe you?" she said.

"That's your choice, Murphy," I said. "I can't do a thing about it."

Murphy scowled.

"Whatever. I'm going to check it out."

"In the rain?"

"Yes, in the rain. It's like eighty degrees out, I'm not going to catch the goddamn cholera or something."

"Well, good luck."

"You're not coming?"

"No, I'm not coming."

"Seriously? You're going to send me into the woods to investigate something in a rainstorm alone? What kind of brother are you?"

"A smart one," I said.

She glared at me. "If only Mom could see us now."

Why did I suddenly feel like she actually could? Why did I feel like Mom was in the room with us and speaking to us, begging us to listen, but neither of us had the eyes to see her or the ears to hear her voice? Maybe I did need to go with Murphy. After all, the third Gentleman had said there was a still a secret in the woods, hadn't he? I'd thought he meant Jeremiah's grave, but maybe there was something else out there. Maybe Murphy would lead me to it tonight.

"Okay," I said. "I'll go with you."

"I knew you'd come around." She aimed the flashlight at her face. "It's time to go exploring. Into the woods. Into the darkness."

And she clicked the light off.

I guess Murphy was trying to be funny, but I don't know. It scared me a little.

OUTSIDE THE RAIN FELL FAT AND WET AND warm. Mud gurgled and splattered with our every step. The trees bent in the wind, waving their branches wild like people at a Pentecostal church. Lightning lit the sky in blue and pink and purple, the clouds torn and scattered. This was no normal storm. It was a sign, a vision that all could see, a promise that something big was coming, something that would change everything.

"You sure you want to do this?" I said.

Murphy nodded. "I want answers, Lee. And I can't figure any other way to get them."

Whatever answers you find, I thought, *you might not like.*

I followed my sister through the rain-ripped night. Lightning roared into the forest, sparks shooting up from a far-off tree. The noise was deafening, a thunder cannon. I wondered if that tree had split down the middle like the holy spot where I'd found the tape recorder. I wondered if Grandma had hidden the tapes there or if somehow Jeremiah had done it from beyond the grave. It wasn't impossible. No one was ever really gone, not in memory or substance. We breathed them in the air, they were permanent wrinkles lodged in our brains. Their cells somehow made up our bodies, and we ate the plants that grew from them. All of life was connected, I could see that now, and I was a part of it all too.

"Come on," hollered Murphy.

She was nearing the edge of the trees, almost to the small path that led to Jeremiah's grave. I realized I hadn't been there since the night we saw Grandma crying. It hadn't made sense for me to visit his grave because Jeremiah wasn't dead to me. He was a part of me, in my blood and mind, in my genes. I'd seen my great-grandfather in the campfire world, playing the mystic game with the dice. There was magic there, power in our bloodline. I knew now that I came from a long line of seers and prophets, even beyond Grandma herself. I wondered if that history was written down somewhere, if there were stories of our ancestors speaking before great crowds, maybe as tribal chieftains in Europe, maybe as weird soothsayers in Rome. I didn't even know where our family came from. Mom said it wasn't important, all that mattered was where we were now. I didn't believe that anymore.

I stopped at Jeremiah's tombstone. Small fires, little flames, red and strange and weightless as hummingbirds, hovered over the grave.

"Oh my god," I said.

The rain didn't even seem to touch them, like the fires burned and whirled so hot that water avoided them altogether.

"What?" said Murphy. "What's there?"

"The flames," I said. "Don't you see them?"

Murphy grabbed my arm.

"Lee, there's nothing there. Now come on. Shouldn't be much farther."

But I could see them plainly, tongues of fire flickering in the wind and rain. I wanted to touch them. I reached out over the grave.

"Come on," said Murphy, yanking me onward, past the grave and onto a side trail. "This will take us to the northern edge of the property. That's where I saw it. I'm positive."

We tromped on, thunder booming, the rain shuddering me down to my bones. My shirt hung tight and wet against me like a second skin. It was like we had wandered into a hurricane, and Murphy only wanted to take us farther, into some dark discovery.

"Jeremiah," I whispered, "what am I doing here?"

We walked farther, branches whipping our faces, snagging our clothes, the rain pelting us so hard it stung. My shoe got stuck in the mud. When I yanked it out my whole foot was covered up to my ankle. I wondered where all the creatures of the forest were—all snuggled up in their dens, in their nests, in the warm little nooks of trees. I didn't know how anything survived a night like this in the wild.

The woods were denser here, the trees all tangled together with no clear trail through. It was hard going, especially in the rain. Part of me wanted to turn back, to go back to the house, to get warm and dry again. My shoes sank deeper into the mud, and I was scared of losing one. I didn't want to have to walk back barefoot. This was stupid, and we were going to get in trouble, and whatever Murphy was going to find out here, I knew it was something she couldn't possibly understand. I was the one with the visions, I was the one who spoke to Jeremiah. Murphy had her own role, sure, whatever that was, but she was dealing in things beyond her, things not meant for her.

But I couldn't quit now. The Gentlemen had promised me a secret out here, and I was going to find it.

Lightning flashed, a bright gashing bolt that pierced the tree veil above us and revealed the forest in light. I saw something in the woods, a hooded figure not twenty feet from me, a walking shadow among the trees.

I grabbed Murphy by the arm.

"Murphy," I said. "There's someone out here."

"No, there isn't. Enough with your hallucinations already."

"I'm not kidding, Murphy. I saw somebody. They were dressed in black, and they had a hood on, like some kind of monk or something."

"On a night like tonight? We're in the middle of the woods, Lee. There are no monks here. It's just one of your visions or whatever. The only people stupid enough to be out on a night like this are us. Now come on. It can't be much farther."

But in my heart I knew we weren't alone out there. I felt eyes all over me, hidden creatures waiting in the dark, watching.

"We're almost there, I know it," hollered Murphy over the wind and rain.

We stumbled out of the woods into something like a clearing, where the trees were sparser, more spread out, but still thick enough for secrets, a hiding place. About fifty feet away I saw a dirt path that led out of the woods. We were standing in a bend not far from the main road, in a little enclave.

Something was hidden there, something big. In the rain and lightning I made out a car, mud-slathered, with brush and tree limbs covering most of it. This was deliberate, I knew. Someone had brought the car here to hide it. Murphy yanked off some of the camouflage.

Lightning struck, a web of fire strung across the heavens. I could see the thunderclouds up there flashing, beating like a heart, a living being with eyes and a brain and a consciousness, not God but something like God, glowering down at us.

"Holy shit," said Murphy.

It was a police cruiser under the leaves. It was Horace's sheriff car.

"I told you I saw somebody in the woods," I said.

"He's here," she said. "Oh my god, he's here in the woods with us."

"We have to go," I said. "We have to go now."

We turned back toward the house as lightning crashed above us. Did you know lightning strikes downward and upward as well? It's the way the earth and the clouds speak to each other, the touch between them, heaven reaching down to earth and earth reaching back. It's a communication, lightning is, the flash and boom of vision, of light and energy transferred.

That's what it's like, I thought. *That's what happens to me when I see.*

Wind ripped limbs from trees and dashed them to the ground, crashing around us. This was no ordinary storm. Hail began to fall, chunks of ice flung from the sky, pelting us, smashing through the trees. When I passed Jeremiah's grave, red fire was strewn all about, moving like plasma, a burning aura around the whole thing that was so bright I had to shield my eyes.

"Come on!" said Murphy, yanking me past it.

We made it to the yard, and it was like a battlefield, the grass dotted with white hailstones that seemed to glow in the dark, the barn roof pinging with every stone that fell. I saw funnel clouds whip and whirl in the sky, swirling like exits out of this world, gateways to the next. I didn't know if they were real tornadoes or if I was having a vision. I realized I never really knew what was there and what wasn't, actually, and maybe it didn't matter at all. Maybe the old man at the gas station was right and time was just a dot, and everything happened all at once, in one great thunderclap. Maybe my visions were glimpses into other worlds where other possibilities happened, and any moment Murphy and I could slip through from one to the next and never even know it.

Reality was flimsy like that, I realized, just a series of open doors and long hallways, all of us passing from world to world and existence to existence and never once being the wiser. Somewhere out there was a universe where Mom had never died and Jeremiah had never died and Murphy and I had never been born, and it seemed like a good world, possibly a better one, all the congregants of the Farm still here, laboring together happy and beautiful with no need for Murphy and me at all. It was strange to imagine a better world without yourself in it.

Lightning struck the barn, sparks flying like a flicked cigarette from a car window, the embers scattering across the black pavement of the sky. I covered my head and sprinted through the mud, two steps behind Murphy, toward Grandma's house. It loomed blackly at the far end of the field, a many-eyed monster in the dark.

We made it to the back door and scrambled inside, muddy and wet and hail-pelted and terrified.

"I'll grab the keys to the Trans Am," she said, "and we'll get the hell out of here."

"What about Grandma?" I said.

"Oh for fuck's sake," she said. "Grandma will be fine. We'll write her a letter. Let's just grab the keys and go."

"No," I said. "I'm not leaving without Grandma. You get the keys, and I'll wake her up. You don't even have to talk to her, okay?"

"Whatever," she said. "Let's just hurry."

I sprinted to Grandma's room, and Murphy ran past me to ours. Grandma lay sleeping in her bed, her face calm and still and peaceful, like it was the best sleep she'd ever had in her life, like it was nothing but good dreams playing on repeat in her brain. I almost hated to wake her. "Grandma, get up. Horace's here."

She rolled over and blinked her eyes at me.

"Jeremiah?"

For a moment my heart stopped, and I caught my breath, wondering if she could see him with me, if he was so visibly here now. But no, she'd just woken up from sleep confused. I was about Jeremiah's age, that was all, and she had confused the two of us.

"No," I said. "It's me, Lee. Our stepdad is here. The killer. His car is here. We found it in the woods."

"You kids have been sneaking out again?"

"Come on, Grandma," I said. "That's not the point. Horace found us, and we're in danger. We have to go."

Grandma snapped awake. "Horace?" she said. "He's here?" Grandma threw back the covers and jumped out of bed. She grabbed a pair of jeans from her dresser and pulled them on. I peeked out her window, rain and hail pelting the glass like an army of souls begging to be let in. I'd never seen a storm like this one. Not even in my visions.

Murphy burst into the room. "You got a gun, Grandma? We might need it."

"A gun?" she said. "Why yes, I suppose I do. There's a shotgun in the kitchen. I keep it for coyotes and the like. It's not loaded, mind you."

"Where are the shells?" said Murphy. "And can you hurry it up?"

"I'm moving," said Grandma. "Trying to find my house keys. You don't have to bark at me, Murphy."

"Bark at you? Are you fucking kidding me?" said Murphy. "I'm trying to save our lives. Horace is here. He's been here awhile, since at least this afternoon. He's a killer, and he could be fucking anywhere. We have to go, *now*."

A bang sounded from upstairs, from the third floor, like something had tipped and fallen over. Footsteps creaked across the hardwood above us.

Someone was up there.

"Oh shit," said Murphy. "He's in the house. Horace is in the house. Grandma, hurry!"

I grabbed Grandma's raincoat and flung it at her. Lightning flashed pale light over the room, and I was aware of every shadow, every lingering darkness. Horace was in the attic, and he was coming for us.

We ran out of the room and downstairs—Murphy, Grandma, and me.

"Grandma, get the shotgun," said Murphy. "Where are the shells?"

"Kitchen cabinet."

I went for them, and they were just where she'd said they were. I grabbed as many as I could and handed them over to Grandma. I only hoped Horace was still upstairs on the third floor. I hoped we could make it out of the house before he got to us.

"Head for the Trans Am," said Murphy. "I'm driving."

We ran out the front door and into the mud and rain. Hail slapped against the gravel drive, pocking the car. Horace would have a fit if he could see this, I thought. And then I realized he could see it, that he was fully goddamn aware of it, and that terrified me. I felt it all the way through my body, the terror of my stepdad the murderer, the one who had chased us all the way here, the one who would probably kill us dead for what we knew about him.

We were nearly to the car when lightning crashed above us and a brief flash illuminated the driveway. A black-cloaked figure stood next to the Trans Am, unmoving, rain lashing down around him. Something metal glinted in his hand—a gun or a knife, I couldn't tell. His face was hidden in shadow, but it had to be Horace. Who else could it be? He must have beaten us down here. We froze, barely twenty feet of gravel drive between us and Horace.

"What do we do?" said Murphy.

"The barn," said Grandma.

"Are you serious?" said Murphy.

Horace took a step toward us.

"There's no time for this shit," I said. "Run!"

We took off around the side of the house, toward the back lot. Grandma kept up with Murphy and me just fine. Maybe it was the rain and mud, or maybe she was just in that good of shape. Grandma was like that—stronger than she looked, swifter and smarter and faster. Grandma always had a plan.

"There's a radio in the barn," hollered Grandma as we crossed the field. "I never told y'all about it because the outside world is a distraction. Besides, the barn's sturdy. We can barricade ourselves in and call for help."

"I'm not locking myself in," said Murphy. I could barely hear her over the thunder and rain. "We need to leave, not hole up somewhere without an exit."

On the far edge of the field I saw another figure in a black cloak standing at the tree line. I looked behind me, and there was Horace, all hooded and coming after us as well. I didn't understand.

"You see that?" I said and pointed toward the woods.

There were more of them now, stepping past the tree line. Lightning shot a camera flash around us, and I could see six or seven of them, hooded and walking toward us.

"The fuck is going on?" hollered Murphy.

We made it to the barn. The hooded figures were closing in. Every time lightning struck they were steps closer, moving like a film with missing footage, scenes cut in half, motions jagged. It seemed impossible—the way they moved, the night, the storm, all of it. It was more like something from my visions than anything from real life. Grandma held the shotgun under her arm and yanked a huge key ring out of her jeans pocket, and she set to work on the lock. It was hard going in the rain and hail, and the key kept slipping. Thunder crashed around us, so deep and loud I felt it in my chest, and my heart thudded with it.

All around us the figures came closer.

"Hurry, Grandma!" I said.

"Almost got it," she said. The lock fell into the mud. Grandma grabbed the big barn door and pushed it open. We ran inside, and I slid the door closed, bolting it from the inside.

The barn was utterly dark. Only the slightest sliver of lightning flash blinked under the door. I heard a kind of groan from the back of the barn, an animal noise. But it could have been the wind, or the rain and hail, or just my imagination. It could have been anything or nothing at all.

"Where are the lights, Grandma?" I said.

"No lights," she said, nothing but a voice in the darkness. "Just the lantern. Hold on."

I heard a flick, saw the small spark of a lighter trying to catch, until a flame shone and a small pale glow illuminated the barn.

The lantern light wasn't much, but it was enough to show me that the barn didn't look like any barn I'd ever seen before. There wasn't any equipment in this barn, no hay or straw, no farm tools scattered about. Instead, rows of wooden benches sat on either side of a long walkway leading up to an elevated platform, a kind of stage. The walls were covered in what had to be more of Mom's murals. But these were grander, more triumphant somehow: A young boy with the sun as his halo. A fiery pale moon dangling in a star-slathered sky. A cup full of golden coins overflowing. An orchard full of hummingbirds, the fruit dangling from the trees alive enough to eat. They felt like stained-glass windows, like they were pictures meant to tell a story, symbols crammed full of meaning. It was Mom's masterpiece, there was no question about that.

This wasn't a barn, and it never had been.

"Welcome, Lee," said Grandma, the lantern glowing her face gold. "Welcome to your church."

"My church?" I said.

"What is this, Lee?" said Murphy. "What the fuck is going on here?"

"All will be explained, Murphy, dear," said Grandma, "in due time. But I must insist that you watch your mouth. This is a church. It is holy ground. Your mother helped build the place, after all. You should be able to respect that, shouldn't you?"

Something thrashed between the pews, something big, a kind of creature. It flopped back and forth on the ground, a massive worm of a thing, chains clanking on the barn floor. I knew it was the monster from my visions. He had finally caught me. I was afraid, I staggered backward, I wanted to run. A fat rusted-metal chain snaked out from behind the pews, fastened to the barn's center beam.

"Oh, don't fear, children," said Grandma. "He's harmless, see? I got him all chained up for you."

Grandma set the lantern down. She grabbed the chain and pulled it backward into the aisle between the pews. Again I marveled at how strong Grandma was. It scared me a little. She dragged the creature into the light.

"Oh my god," said Murphy.

Wrapped in chains, swaddled in garbage bags, a gag over his mouth, lay Horace. Blood was caked on his forehead, and his face was covered in bruises. He looked like he'd been beaten and starved for days, like she'd just dragged him out of a ditch on the side of the road.

"He got here before y'all did," said Grandma. "He prattled on and on about you kids and how worried he was about y'all. Cried about your mother too, the hypocrite. I poisoned him, naturally. Drugged his coffee, and he slopped right over. Kept him locked up in here this whole time. Neither of you children figured it out. Didn't think Lee would, sweet as he is. Jeremiah would have found out immediately, though he was a bit more devious than you, Lee, dear, so don't take it as an insult. Kind of disappointed Murphy didn't. Would have liked to see the look on her face when she figured it out, when she learned her own role in this plan. When she learned her place in this world."

"My place?" said Murphy. "The fuck are you even talking about?"

"*Language*," growled Grandma, the veins in her neck bulging, her teeth bared like a wolf's. She took a deep breath and let it out slow. "You are the guardian." She spoke softly now, daintily. "The protector of the prophet. That is your one and only purpose in this life, Murphy, dear, same as it was your mother's: To protect your brother. To protect him from people like this filth here."

She kicked Horace in the chest as he grunted and whined.

"Grandma," I said. "Who are those people out there?"

"Go ahead and find out," she said. "Open the barn door, Lee. Don't worry, they won't hurt you. Quite the opposite."

"No wonder Mom left," said Murphy. "You're stark raving insane."

Grandma ignored her. "Open the door, Lee."

I looked at Grandma, and I looked at Horace all tied up on the floor. He didn't seem so fierce anymore. He seemed like a wounded bleating creature, barely a man. For the first time since the day Mom brought him home, I looked at Horace— bloodied, gagged, writhing on the barn floor—and I wasn't afraid. Not one bit. I felt nothing but hatred for him.

And I loved it.

Grandma had caught Horace for us, protected us from him, saved us when no one else would bother. Grandma had taken care of us, just like I thought she would. I looked down on Horace, his eyes wide, his gag thick and crusty with blood, the man who had murdered my mother, weak and helpless on the floor.

I stared Horace in his terrified, blood-rimmed eyes, and I spat in his face.

Let me tell you, it felt good. It felt powerful. *I* felt powerful. I felt like the world was mine for the taking, like I could do anything I wanted on this earth, and for the first time ever, no one could stand in my way.

I grabbed the lock on the barn door.

"No, Lee!" said Murphy. "Don't do it. We don't know what those people want with us."

"Actually, Murphy," I said, "I think I know exactly what they want."

And I threw back the bolt and slid the door open.

THEY STOOD HOODED AND DARK IN THE entranceway to the church, ten or twelve in all. But with the lantern light splashing over them, they didn't look so fearsome. For one, those weren't cloaks they were wearing, no mystic order druid robes. Just raincoats, the big kind fit for tromping around in the stormy woods at night. I moved aside, and they stepped into the church one by one, clomping the mud off their boots at the door so as not to track anything on the floor. They stood in a slumping line in front of me and dropped their hoods.

Sheriff Bearden with his cockeyed grin, a toothpick between his teeth.

The old man from Piggly Wiggly, Wilmer Jenkins, the one who had kissed my hand.

The lady from the gas station, her graying ponytail all frizzled from the heat and rain.

Stephens's father, Mr. Brownderville, grinning and proud, looking like he wanted to slap me on the back.

And Cass. There stood Cass, her hair rain-soaked, her eyes deep and beautiful and alive in the night.

The rest of them were there too, Stephens and Luther and even Jack. They smiled at me, finally revealed for who they were, for why they'd come to the Farm in the first place.

Several other people I recognized from my ride through town, many of them older folks. I could see glimmers of their younger selves, devout, eyes big with love of Jeremiah, as I stared at them in the lantern glow. It felt like all of time was present in that room, the past as well as the future, all of it happening now, in this very moment. I knew that Jeremiah was there, and the Spirit he served, and Mom as well, together in that church. I never felt more loved, less alone, than I did in that moment.

I had finally found my place in this world.

"We came because we needed to see," said Wilmer. "We needed to see it with our own eyes, that our Jeremiah is back, that he's come back in you."

"I was told I would see him again before I died," said the ponytail lady. "He promised me that in a dream." She reached out and touched my face, her fingers wet and cold. "I wanted to believe. I wanted to know."

I watched them, their raincoats dripping on the church floor, their faces bright and expectant as lightning crashed behind them.

"You all came for me?" I said. I looked at Cass, her crooked-tooth grin, the way the lightning lit her bright and wild. "Even you?"

"Jeremiah spoke to me in a dream too," she said. "He was beautiful, standing in this perfect garden, his voice like a song. He told me all about you, how I had to move down here to your grandmother's land. How we were destined to meet each other. I left home and moved here, all for you."

"And for the Farm," said Stephens. "So it could come back, and things could be good in the town again."

"So they could be better than they ever were before," said his father.

"Every song I write is for you," said Jack. "The Spirit gives me a song, and I sing it, and the songs are yours."

"I told them tonight was the night," said Grandma. "Tonight you would come here, and you would take up your calling. I saw it in a vision." She smiled. "Mine are nowhere near what yours are, Lee, dear, but they are powerful in their own right."

"We came to witness and to intervene, if need be," said Sheriff Bearden. "The Spirit has a plan, it always does."

Murphy grabbed my arm. I'd completely forgotten she was there.

"Lee, what the fuck is going on?" she said.

"I don't know if I can explain it," I said. "I'm not sure if I totally understand it myself."

"Your brother is a prophet, Murphy," said Grandma. "Same as his uncle was. And you are his guardian, his keeper, just as your mother was meant to protect your uncle. She failed at this, and the boy died, and with him died our family, our Farm. We had to excommunicate your mother, send her off into the world, to somehow bring about Jeremiah's return. We knew he wouldn't leave us for long, that his spirit was here, wandering the woods. I myself saw him in his suit by the pond, and I swear to you he walked clean across the surface of the water, causing not a ripple. But mostly I saw him in the Hummingbird Grove, same as you did, Lee. That's why I took you there day after day. I knew that was where he was most powerful."

Murphy whispered, "We need to get the fuck out of here. These people are all nuts."

"No, Murphy," I said, "they aren't. It's true. I've seen Jeremiah. I've heard his voice whisper mysteries, and I've seen his visions, his secrets. Jeremiah is very much alive, and he talks to me. He talks through me."

"You're kidding me."

"I'm not," I said. "I see him all the time, and I have ever since we got here. I think he's been sending me visions ever since I was a baby."

Murphy stared up at me, eyes gone wide open with terror, like she was just seeing me for the first time, like she'd never really looked at me at all.

I felt a stirring in my heart then, a kind of tremor deep in my soul that shook me down to my bones. I could feel something happening, a brightness to the air, a glimmer on everything around me. I was going to have a vision, I knew it—a big one, more vast and important than anything I'd seen so far. This vision would change me. It would crack my soul wide open.

"What's happening to you?" said Murphy.

I tried to answer, but I couldn't. My heart was beating near out of my chest, and I could feel my pulse in my fingers and toes, in my eyelids. My whole body thrummed with power, and the hairs on my arms and legs stood up. I felt like a human lightning rod, like a fork about to be shoved in a light socket.

Grandma gripped Murphy's shoulder, her hand like a claw.

"Don't you know?" she said. "Your brother is having a vision."

I staggered, my eyesight gone swirly, my head all foggy and strange. It was coming now, it was happening, it would strike me like lightning, it would sear me to my marrow, it would burn me clean, it would change me forever. I felt the ground quake beneath me, the whole earth a sick feverish shaking thing. A moan erupted from Horace's gagged mouth, a kind of long sad whine like a kicked dog makes. Thunder boomed above us, lightning striking the church roof, shaking the whole building.

I fell to my knees.

It was like the church roof had been torn off, the storm roaring above us, and I saw past the rain and the clouds and the stars to what lay beyond. I could see the whole universe alive and breathing, lit on fire from within. I could hear the deep burning heart of the world, feel the lava in its core, the rivers of its bones. I saw a pair of pale eyes gazing down at me from the darkness, a god's eyes.

The Spirit had come.

I heard a sound like a whirlwind, I heard the voices of a thousand stars screaming, and everything went black.

I was in the starlit world, the campfire burning, the corpses of the three Gentlemen gore-slathered and strewn about. The second Gentleman was stripped naked, and I saw that the monster now wore his suit.

The monster turned to face me, and I saw him truly for the first time.

It wasn't Horace, this monster chasing me. No, it wasn't a monster at all.

Before me stood Jeremiah Sanford, his face illuminated by starshine. He was the one from my visions, the one the Gentlemen kept apart. He appeared as a child in the daylight world of the Hummingbird Grove, but part of him was trapped in the campfire world, his spirit imprisoned as a monster. I understood now: I was the door through which Jeremiah would enter the world again, the way he would become whole.

I tried to speak, but no sound would come from my throat. I raised my hand in a kind of wave, and Jeremiah raised his back at me. I took a step forward, and he took one as well. I moved left, and Jeremiah moved perfectly with me, as if in a mirror. We walked closer to each other, and soon I couldn't tell if he was mimicking me or if I was mimicking him or if we were the same person all along.

We stood face-to-face, Jeremiah my height, his eyes the most perfect blue I'd ever seen, the eyes of the first Gentleman.

He smiled at me, the smile of the second Gentleman, and I knew I was smiling too.

A wind blew through the empty place, and the stars seemed to shiver above me, and I felt the third Gentleman's heart beat inside of me.

Something changed.

When I looked in front of me, I didn't see Jeremiah Sanford. I saw myself. And when I looked down at my body, I was wearing a black suit, my hands ghostly pale. I stared into my own eyes and saw Jeremiah's bright blue ones staring back at me.

I felt dissolved, the boundaries of myself disappearing, the whole universe swooping into my soul. I became a part of everything.

I saw myself standing in a suit, a congregation of people around me, old people, folks young and beautiful, all races and ages alike, hollering and singing and dancing while I spoke to them, my voice rising high and lovely above the crowd like honeysuckle on the wind. I told them my visions, and they lapped up every single word. They loved my visions. They loved *me*. It was glorious. It was my calling.

I felt Jeremiah whispering into my ear, breathing his breath into me, his words and spirit and life.

And then I was back in the barn with Murphy and Grandma and the rest, Horace's body writhing on the floor. But I still heard Jeremiah's voice, sweet and rich as honey, bellowing out over the rain and storm and wind.

"… and before me I saw a rift in the earth, an open growing maw, and from it streamed smoke of black and yellow and green and purple, a living haze, a cloud of fire. And in the haze I saw the moon and stars and all the night sky, a new world becoming, and I perceived a presence so great and strong and powerful I fell to my knees, the gash in the earth spewing up smoke and vapor, incense, perfume, power. I heard a voice bellow from inside the maw, as if the earth itself were speaking. 'You are my true disciple, and in you my Spirit is present. Lead my people.'"

I realized it was me speaking those words. It was my voice, but the same cadence, the same pitch as Jeremiah's. Jeremiah had been training me all this time, teaching me how to see like him, how to hear like him. Most importantly, he'd been teaching me how to speak like him. When I opened my mouth, out came his beautiful, melodious song of a voice, his words, his heart, his thoughts. They were lovely, and they had power. And now they were mine. Now I had power. Now I would gather the Farm together, a newer, better church. I would have a new family, people who loved me, people who needed me. It would be the start of something beautiful, all of us together, working toward a perfect world.

I believed in him. I believed in the Farm. I believed in myself.

"Alone we are weak, we are nothing," I spoke. "But together—yes, together we can be a power unlike any the earth has ever seen."

"I've missed that voice," said Wilmer. "By god, I heard it every night in my dreams."

"He has come back," said the woman with the ponytail, tears filling her eyes. "He truly is the second coming of Jeremiah."

Cass just smiled at me, the light of the whole world in her eyes.

"We will be a family again," said Grandma. "It'll be just like things used to be."

Murphy stared up at me, wonderstruck, dumbfounded, while the rest of them gathered around me.

These were my people, my family.

I would lead them, and it would be glorious.

IT WAS ONLY SIX DAYS UNTIL OUR FIRST GATH-
ering—which was what they called Farm meetings, where I
would talk about my visions and address the whole congregation about our future—and I was pretty nervous about it. I still
had so much more to learn and only a week to do it. Frankly I
didn't know how that would even be possible.

People were already showing up too. The night after we
discovered the church, fifteen people had come to live at the
Farm. It wasn't just old folks, either, the leftovers of the original congregation. It was their children and grandchildren, even
a few people Murphy's and my ages. All those people bustling
around the house that first day, setting to work in the fields,
was almost like having a big family full of cousins and aunts
and uncles like people always had in movies. Grandma set up a
big table in the living room, and she had food cooking all day,
the fridge stocked full. Everybody was given a task. It would

take a long time to get the Farm self-sustaining again—years, maybe—but it would be worth it. And all of it depended on me, on my ability to lead, to let the Spirit move in me. Like I said, I was pretty fucking nervous about it.

So I decided to run off that first afternoon and hide at the tenant house. At least I already knew those guys liked me.

I walked up as Cass and Luther were arguing about politics. Stephens sat in a lawn chair watching them, looking bored. I took a seat next to them, all of us gathered around the dormant fire pit. I had no idea what Cass and Luther were talking about, but I heard words like "egalitarian," "proletariat," and "pseudo-Marxist bullshit," so I knew pretty immediately that I was in over my head. I didn't care, though. I loved the language of it, the big ridiculous words that concepts carry. Cass was so beautiful and so much smarter than me. I could have listened to her talk for hours. She was clearly winning the argument. You could tell by how hard Luther was puffing on his pipe, great big dragon plumes of smoke pouring out of it. I was a little concerned their conversation was going to break out into a fistfight.

"Don't worry," said Stephens. "They're always like this."

Jack walked by playing a banjo, singing "Come Fly with Me" in a redneck croon.

"And is Jack always like that too?" I said.

"You know it."

Stephens offered me a warmish High Life, and I took it even though it was only three in the afternoon.

"Don't tell Grandma, okay?" I said.

Stephens shrugged. "You're the boss."

"The boss?" I said.

"No," said Cass, her argument briefly paused. "The leader. You're our leader, Lee. Not our boss."

Our leader. That was still a hard thing for me to wrap my head around. It was something I never would have aspired to, not even a month ago. I only wished Mom could be here to see it, to see how I had taken Jeremiah's place and brought the Farm back. Maybe it would have changed the way she thought about my visions. I wondered if she hated them because they reminded her of Jeremiah, who had all these magnificent visions and then died before they could come to pass. Maybe that was why she had refused to believe in my visions.

I finished the beer and said goodbye to those guys and walked over to the Hummingbird Grove. Grandma had spread the word that the Grove was forbidden, like it was a sacred spot just for me. It was a powerful place. I knew and understood that now. It had been my mom's favorite place, and it was Jeremiah's. He was waiting for me, standing there same as if he were real, a physical being. We talked for a while, him giving me advice, preparing me for my duties to come. After half an hour or so I just up and asked him something that had been on my mind lately.

"What are you?" I said. "I mean, are you a ghost or something?"

"I'm myself," he said, "or at least the most lasting part of me. I survive through the power of this place."

"The Spirit?" I said.

He nodded. "It's an old entity, from a time long before people walked the land. Very few are left in the world, and most are dormant. But the Spirit is active here, and it has allowed me to linger."

"I'm glad it did," I said. "Thank you for choosing me."

"It was fated," he said. "I saw it long before you were born, when I was split between the two realms, between the dark and the daylight, in fragments. The Spirit showed it to your grandmother as well. This is how it must be, how it always had to be. You're here now, and you can carry on my work. Because the light must grow brighter for the darkness to diminish. And never forget: We are the light-bringers."

"The light-bringers," I said. "I like that."

"It's what we do here, our work. We're building a place on this earth for everything the world disdains. For kindness, for gentleness, for work and togetherness. There is no competition here, no fighting, no backstabbing. Everyone has work, and everyone eats plenty. The Farm is the first of what will be many. It's my own grandfather's vision, truly, handed down to my mother. He's the one who wrestled control of this place away from the Urquharts and their darkness to create a kingdom of the light."

Hummingbirds swirled around me, a bright-flecked crowd of tiny flames, a burning holy cloud.

"And now it's mine," I said.

"Yes," he said. "All yours."

That night Grandma gave me my own room. It was the store-room we'd found, Murphy and I. She moved all of the boxes out, cleaned the place up, gave me fresh sheets, all that. I felt grown, separated off from Murphy and my whole childhood, full of purpose. Everything was changing.

Murphy came to see me before bed. To be honest, I was surprised. I felt like she'd been avoiding me all day. She didn't acknowledge me at dinner, didn't look up from her work when I came to say hey. I could understand that. It was a lot to take in, what I was to become, what her place in the whole grand plan was. But in a sense Murphy had always been my protector, right? Didn't she beat up the kids who picked on me when we were younger? Didn't she have my back always? Murphy would come around—she just had to. My sister loved me, and that was just a fact.

Murphy sat on the edge of my bed and whistled.

"Nice digs," she said.

"Yeah, no more bunk beds."

"Got to be honest," she said, "I kind of enjoyed sharing a bedroom with you."

"It could have been worse."

I thought about our rooms back home at Mom's old place. It seemed like a lifetime away.

"I just wanted to ask you something," she said. "Do you really believe this stuff? That you're the prophet meant to lead this community and all that?"

"Yes," I said. "I really do."

Murphy bit her lip and nodded at me.

"Well, did you ever figure out why Mom and Grandma stopped talking? Why Grandma never came to visit even though you were the chosen one or whatever?"

"Grandma told us in the church. She said Mom was supposed to protect Uncle Jeremiah, and she failed. That's why Mom had to leave."

"Don't you think it's just a little bit fucked up that Grandma never cared enough to try and get to know us?"

"No, I don't, Murphy. I think Grandma knew we would come to her when the time was right."

"Was that in one of her visions? Or did our ghost uncle tell her that?"

I glared hard at Murphy. I felt Jeremiah standing behind me, could picture the bright burning of his eyes, could feel his anger toward Murphy.

"You don't have to believe in me," I said. "But you can't stand in my way either."

We sat in silence a moment. It was strange, all the people in the house, the noise of their feet overhead, people coming and going, everything. I loved being in the middle of all that life, knowing I had a place in it, knowing that it circled around me. Why didn't Murphy love it too?

"I guess that's that, then," she said. Murphy stood up from my bed. "Good night, Lee. Hope your dreams aren't too apocalyptic."

THE NEXT DAY—FIVE DAYS LEFT TILL THE FIRST
Gathering—I woke up to a problem, something I wasn't quite
sure how to deal with.

That problem was Horace.

Sheriff Bearden had moved Horace to an old toolshed out
back. It was less secure and secret than the church, but since it
would be hard to have the Gathering with my chained-up stepfather flopping around on the floor, it seemed like the toolshed
was a pretty good bet.

Let me make this clear: I hated Horace. I hated what he had
done to Mom. I hated what he'd done to our family.

Still, it was hard to be in that shed with him bloodied and
bound and duct-taped to a chair. It was hard to smell the filth on
him after days of being starved and unwashed, hard to look at
his blood-spattered, busted-lipped face, hard to look him in his
blackened, red-rimmed eyes. It was hard to act all brave in the
face of a man who had so often scared the ever-loving shit out

of me. So I walked into that toolshed with its one bare hanging light bulb more than a little afraid, even though Grandma was with me and Sheriff Bearden was waiting outside with his gun.

I stood there in front of Horace, and I didn't know what to say. I didn't really even know what I was doing there.

"You're to face him," was all Grandma had told me. "The Spirit will show you what to do then."

The Spirit—right. More and more I heard the voice of the Spirit talking to me, telling me things, usually in the voice of Uncle Jeremiah. I wasn't sure if the Spirit *was* Jeremiah or if Jeremiah had been so close with the Spirit that it just took his form now as a matter of convenience. To be honest, I didn't understand much about the afterlife. My visions had never really taken a turn into that realm, for better or for worse. I figured with more practice I could get a glimpse here and there, maybe like that guy St. Paul knew who got swept up into "Third Heaven," whatever Third Heaven meant. Did heaven have levels like a skyscraper, and the better you were, the higher the floor you wound up on when you died? Maybe I could write a poem about it.

Grandma gave me a *well, go on* kind of look, so I cleared my throat and gave it a shot.

"Hi, Horace," I said.

He grunted into his gag, eyes wide, staring up at me.

With fear. I realized Horace was afraid of me, of what I could do to him.

What could I do to him, really?

And that's when I understood: I could do anything I wanted to Horace. I had the law on my side, right? At the very least, I had the law outside this door with a shotgun. I had the Spirit in me, I had my visions, I had Grandma and the Farm. Every single bit of that was power. And what did Horace have, bloody and bruised and stinking of piss and sweat, useless, duct-taped to a chair?

Horace had nothing at all.

I felt Jeremiah near me, praying over me.

Do not be afraid, whispered Jeremiah, *for you are not alone. Speak, and the Spirit will come to your aid.*

I took a deep breath and tried again. I looked down at Horace, and it was like I could see his fear, a great gray-black mass of it swarming his brain like an infection. It was almost palpable, his terror of me, of what I could do to him. I could do this. I only had to let the Spirit speak through me.

"Hi, Horace," I said again, but I was smiling this time. "Grandma, loosen that gag on his mouth."

"You sure about that?" she said.

"Horace isn't going to try anything, not now. He's too hungry, and he's too scared. Besides, I have some questions for him."

Grandma pulled the gag out of his mouth and dropped it on the dirty floor. He gasped a little at the stale air, and when he spoke his voice was soft and brittle, whittled thin by days spent bound on the church floor.

"I didn't kill your momma," he said. "No matter what they tell you, I didn't do it. I loved her."

Was he telling the truth? He seemed sincere about it. But I knew what I'd seen in my visions and what we'd found in the trunk of his car. No, Horace was bullshitting me, same as always.

"Stop lying to me, Horace," I said. "I'm sick of it. I'm sick of the way you treated Murphy and me, the way you swooped in and wrecked all of our lives. I hate you for that. I hate you for what you did to my mom."

It fell on me then—not a full vision, but a glimpse of something. I saw Horace at home, just a boy, with his shirt off, hunched on his knees in front of his bed. I saw a man standing over him, bald and potbellied, a cigarette burning in his mouth. I saw a belt wrapped around his fist, the buckle end dangling down like a whip. This was Horace's father, I knew immediately. I saw him raise the belt above his head while Horace cowered beneath him.

It was just a flash, an instant, and then I was back in the tool-shed, Horace looking up at me, his eyes cracked, his voice just a husk.

"Please," he said. "I didn't do it, Lee. I didn't kill your mother."

I looked down at him, and all I could see was that boy about to be whipped, staring right back at me. Staring at me the same way he had stared at his father.

I couldn't help it. I turned and ran out of the toolshed. I vomited in the grass next to Sheriff Bearden's boots.

Grandma came outside, frowning at me like she was disappointed.

"It seems we still have quite a lot of work to do," she said and walked off toward the house.

I was pretty down after that. All day I couldn't shake these nagging thoughts, like maybe I wasn't cut out for this, like I would never be good enough, I would never be what Jeremiah was. I was so afraid of failing him, of failing Grandma, of failing our entire community. That's what I found myself telling Cass later that night.

"You're still new to this," she said. "You're still learning about yourself and about the Spirit. You'll be a great leader, and people will open their hearts to you, to the Spirit and to our message."

I was at the tenant house, sitting by the fire pit outside, no one but Cass around. We'd been talking long into the night, and eventually, one by one, each of the other kids had gone inside, leaving just the two of us. It was a windy night, the clouds racing in gray blurs across the moon, all the stars fighting up there just to be seen. I was a little drunk, sipping red wine from a plastic cup. I still wasn't very good at holding my liquor. Cass kept laughing at me.

"I feel scared," I said. "Like maybe this is all too much for me."

"It's not, though," said Cass, putting her hand on mine. "You have a kind, pure heart, Lee. You were given this gift for a reason: to help the world. You would never twist things to your own end." She smiled her crooked-tooth smile at me, and my heart did a backflip in my chest. "You keep what's best for the Farm, what's best for the community, in mind. You'll do what's best for us—I know you will. I have faith in you."

I have faith in you. Had anybody ever said something like that to me before? Not that I knew of. Not Mom, not Murphy, nobody. But how could I be worthy of another person's faith?

Cass grabbed both of my hands and held them, her brown eyes flashing witchy at me in the firelight like she was casting a spell on me, like she was looking deep into my soul. I could feel my pulse throbbing, my heart beating out of my chest. Up above us the clouds whipped by, ghost ships in the sky.

"I believe in you," she said, "because you are destined for this. We are destined for this together. It was written a long time ago. Time happens in a blink, all of it at once. A collision of things, the instant of everything. There are two worlds, the daylight and the darkness, and we are of the daylight."

I watched the fireglow flicker across her face.

"Come inside," she said. "I have the back room all to myself tonight."

And I followed her into the darkened doorway of the tenant house.

THE NEXT MORNING, GRANDMA AND I TALKED over the plans for the coming months. I asked her what I was supposed to do at the Gathering to come, how I was supposed to grow a community, much less lead one.

"That's part of why what we're doing with Horace is so important," she said. "It's training for what you will do with entire crowds, with multitudes. Knowing what the crowd wants, precisely what words will break through to their hearts. Just by being in your presence they will be won over, they will come to believe in you, to believe in us. That is how our community will grow."

"But isn't that, like, cheating in a way? That they'll only believe in me because I'm telling them what they want to hear?"

"Honey, what's the difference, so long as they believe? Because we are the light-bringers, remember? We banish darkness from the earth. Anyone who opposes us is the darkness.

Is it not better for them to come to the light by any means necessary?"

"I guess," I said. "I just thought they would come because of me. I mean, because of us, the Farm, how good it is."

"Lee, that's why they'll *stay*. Because we are good, and we do help the world. That's the truth. Sometimes people just need a little push to take that first step. And that's what you'll be giving them."

"But I'm not giving Horace a push. I feel like we're torturing him."

"Horace is a threat," she said, "and threats need to be eliminated. Did he not cause your mother's death? And knowing what he does, couldn't he destroy the Farm and everything we've worked so hard for? Everything my son died for? Isn't it better this way, to bring him into the light? Would you prefer for us to kill him?"

"No," I said. "Absolutely not."

"Then it's settled. The lessons will continue, though not necessarily with Horace quite yet."

"What does that mean?" I said.

Grandma just smiled all secret.

"Watch and see."

With four days left before the first Gathering, the whole Farm was busy preparing. Nearly everyone would be there by then, even the stragglers. I knew more would come soon. They would journey from far and wide to join our family, to hear my visions, to hear the secret wisdom Jeremiah and the Spirit had in store for them. Already my eyes were becoming sharpened, my visions brighter and clearer. Sometimes it was hard to keep straight what was real—what was objectively there right in front of me—and what existed purely in the other plane. The worlds were becoming intertwined, like the way colors bleed through one page and onto another.

The Spirit was drawing other people to me too, working in me to bring them into the fold. Like this one woman, maybe about sixty-five or seventy, who came walking up to me in the fields. I'd never seen her before. She had hair down to her butt and a kind of embarrassed smile on her face. She held a wicker basket in her hands with a blanket over it, like she was going to a picnic.

"I made a thing for you," she said and offered me the basket.

"Thank you," I said. "Um, I don't think we've met."

"Oh shoot, gosh," she said. "You're right. I'm Willamette Darling."

"It's a pleasure," I said. "I'm Lee Sanford."

"I know who you are," she said and blushed a little bit. "That's why I made this for you. Go on now, open it."

I pulled the blanket back from the wicker basket. I didn't know what I was expecting—maybe cookies or some kind of jam or a cake or something. But instead there was this strange tiny thing at the bottom of the basket, maybe the size of my fist. It was a corn husk doll with a little knitted suit on it, a dopey grin like a clown's hand-painted onto its face. It was kind of cute, maybe, if you squinted right.

"It's a wardle," she said. "You like it?"

The woman looked up at me with eyes so kind and innocent they might as well have been a toddler's.

I thought about what Cass had said to me, that I should try and use whatever gifts the Spirit had given me for good, to help people. I wondered what it was that Willamette needed, what had brought her to the Farm in the first place.

"Um, what's a wardle?" I said.

"A little critter I invented," she said. "I'm always making them out of stuff I find at home. Pine cones and corn cobs and straw, little bits of string, you know. Got a whole house full of them, only don't nobody want them."

She's lonely, a voice whispered to me, maybe Jeremiah's, maybe the Spirit's. *Don't you feel it?*

"I don't recall Grandma mentioning you to me before," I said. "Were you one of the original folks at the Farm?"

"Gosh, no," said Willamette. "Always wanted to be, but I was too scared to ask. Besides, my brother told me I was being foolish, that nobody would want me here."

"Where's your brother now?" I said.

"He died. Just last year."

"I'm so sorry, Willamette."

"It's okay. He wasn't too nice to me. He'd drink too much and smash my wardles. He'd say, 'Look at your little friends, Willamette. The only friends you'll ever have.' And he'd toss them right out the window."

What does this woman need from you? What does she want?

Something happened then, and I caught another glimpse, like what had happened with Horace. I saw Willamette Darling at home by herself, making her little creatures, piecing them together from debris and trash, from things she had collected from the forest. I saw her building them with care, speaking to them, laughing, her wardles gathered all around her. I saw her pick one up—a round-looking bucktoothed thing made from a gourd—and kiss it on the check, swaddling it like a baby.

And then it was gone. I was back in the field, talking to Willamette.

It was a short flash into Willamette's life, but it told me enough. What Willamette wanted was the same thing all of us want: to be loved, and to be accepted for who we are. She was testing me to see if I was going to reject her just like her brother had.

"Well," I said, "your wardles are welcome here, as are you."

"You mean that?" said Willamette.

I got a feeling then, a little burning around my throat, like some golden light was bubbling up in there. I knew whatever I said next would be right, would be exactly what she needed to hear, what her heart longed for.

"Your creativity is a gift," I said, the words flowing easy as breathing from my mouth as if by instinct, as if I didn't have to try at all. "It is one of the truest gifts of the Spirit. It was given to you to express what is deepest in your heart, to tell the truth about yourself and about this world. Don't ever let anyone convince you that your gift doesn't matter, that it doesn't have a place here. Because I assure you that it does, and it always will."

Her eyes got all big, and they filled up with tears like she was about to bust out crying at any moment, like that was the nicest thing anyone ever said to her in her life.

Willamette Darling hopped up on her tiptoes and kissed me on the cheek. Then she waddled off, crying, before I could say another word about it. I was stuck there, blushing, holding my wardle.

I had done that. I had made her that happy all on my own. All because I had seen what was happening in her mind. And my words were true, weren't they? It wasn't like I had lied to her or anything. Not exactly. Besides, I knew in the moment before she kissed me that she was a part of the Farm forever now, that she would follow this community to the ends of the earth if I asked her to.

The Spirit was moving, was working in me to draw them near.

You're awfully pleased with yourself, aren't you? whispered Jeremiah. *But that was easy. There will be harder battles ahead. You must practice. You must prepare.*

And I would. There was no other choice.

That night in my new bedroom, I sat worrying over what Jeremiah had told me. How could I grow? How could I be ready in time?

Grandma came to see me before bed, and I asked her that same question.

"The Spirit will work in you to grow and form you as it pleases," she said. "You can't go on worrying all the time. Do your part, and the Spirit will provide."

"But how do you know that?" I said. "What if I'm just a failure?"

"You are many things, Lee," she said, "but a failure isn't one of them. The Spirit is your birthright—it's in your blood, same as Jeremiah's. It even flowed through your mother, though she rebelled against it."

"Really?" I said. "The Spirit spoke to Mom too?"

"Yes," she said, "though not in exactly the same way. Can I show you something?"

I nodded at her. Grandma left the room and came back with a big leather suitcase-looking thing with a lock on it. She dropped it on the bed and unlocked it with a tiny gold key from her pocket.

"Go on," said Grandma. "Take a look."

I flipped the thing open.

It was full of parchment paper, big sheets of it, on each one a painting.

"Your mother did these," said Grandma. "I kept them hidden because they don't bring back the best memories. But I thought you would like them."

I took them out one by one. They were beautiful but strange, almost surrealistic: Shrouded figures gathered around a glowing campfire. An old woman with pink teeth and a third eyeball bulging out of her forehead. A garden of unbelievable brightness, swirling gyres of reds and blues and purples shining against utter darkness surrounding them.

"They're visions, aren't they?" I said.

"Yes," she said. "They're Jeremiah's visions. He spoke them to her, and she painted them as he told them. It was like they had twin minds sometimes, like the Spirit could flow between them in a curious way. The paintings were the only way Jeremiah allowed his visions to be remembered other than the recordings we made. He refused to ever let them be written down lest they become merely words and lose their power."

I thought about my own attempts at writing poetry from my visions, how shitty they all turned out. "Why does writing them down make them lose their power?"

"Well, Lee, all of our beliefs spring from direct experiences of revelation," she said. "We have no written canon, no fixed doctrine. What we believe is fluid, alive. You speak the words of the Spirit, and the Spirit moves. When you write something down, when you nail it finally to the page forever, you murder it, you suck the life straight out of it. Just the way that seeing the musical notation on a page cannot compare to actually hearing the song, to feeling the wind and air of it hit you right in the face, to breathing the music into your lungs and letting it filter into your blood. That's why the tapes are acceptable, because Jeremiah's voice has a power all its own. Your mother's paintings show versions of Jeremiah's visions, but they don't fix their meanings down. And I have to hand it to her, they evoke the Spirit quite well."

I gazed at the paintings, each one a sacred thing, a vision of power and color and light. I could have looked at those paintings for hours and hours. Some of them were like visions I had seen myself, and the feeling Mom had drawn from them was something close to magic. They seemed perfect, miraculous even, thrumming with power. In that moment I felt closer to Mom than I ever had in all my life.

"Don't stay up too late," said Grandma. "And Lee? Do me a favor. Keep those away from Murphy, won't you?"

"Why?" I said. "I think she'd want to see them."

"Just trust me, please," said Grandma, and she closed the door behind her.

After a while I put the paintings back in the suitcase and slid them under my bed for the night.

WITH THREE DAYS LEFT BEFORE THE GATHER-
ing, Grandma took me into town to buy a new suit.

"A leader needs a suit," she said, "and a nice one, not like that old thing you wore to the funeral. Clothes inspire confidence. Never forget that."

I asked if Murphy wanted to go too, but she declined. It was hard for me to believe Murphy would turn down an opportunity to leave the Farm, even if it was only for a few hours, but she wasn't having it.

"I think I'll just stick around here awhile," she said.

Murphy was getting weirder and weirder, and every day I felt like I understood her less. I would see her lurking around the Farm, watching all the newcomers with this kind of strange look on her face, like she was sizing them all up for a fight. I didn't like it, not one bit. Something felt wrong to me in my gut, like maybe the Spirit was telling me to be cautious around her.

Or maybe I was just overreacting. If Murphy didn't want to come to town, she didn't have to. To be honest, it was kind of a relief. I liked spending time alone with Grandma. I felt like I could be myself around her more easily, that I could talk about Jeremiah and all our plans for the Farm, how great everything was going to be. I would have felt pretty self-conscious doing all that with Murphy around.

Benign was full of smiling people that day, folks hollering and waving at us, person after person walking up to shake my hand. It was hot out, and everyone had that sort of flushed scurrying look that Southerners get when they're working their way from air-conditioned room to air-conditioned room. I was starting to learn everyone's names, even the folks who weren't part of the Farm, folks who were just locals and curious about me. I was shaking hands, telling jokes, all that, like I was some kind of politician or something.

The weird thing was, I was kind of good at it. Me, who couldn't hardly hold a conversation with a stranger not a month before. Maybe it was having Jeremiah with me, ghostly all the time, or maybe it was just my newfound confidence and purpose, but I *liked* all the small talk and glad-handing, I liked meeting people's kids and grandparents, aunts and uncles and cousins. I liked everybody knowing my name, everybody wanting to know me. And so what if it was mostly older folks? When you've been ignored and disliked as long as I had, you'll take any kind of attention you can get, and from anybody. And those people liked me. Hell, they *loved* me. Just for being me. You should have seen Grandma, the way she smiled at me, how proud she was. I never felt so loved and accepted in my whole life.

I even saw Mr. Cartwright, sweating and shaky, come walking up to Grandma and me, wanting to say hi to us. I'd never seen a man so fearful as he was of my grandma, but he was still brave enough to try, and I respected that. When I realized she was about to ignore him, same as usual, I figured, what the hell?

I stepped in front of her and stuck my hand out.

"How are you today, Mr. Cartwright?" I said.

I swear to you, the man looked up at me with tears in his eyes. He didn't take my hand—he wouldn't dare.

"Thank you," was all he said, "thank you so much," and he stumbled away.

"Taking charge of things now, aren't we?" said Grandma.

"I'm just trying to give the man a fair chance," I said.

"Well, he did get you safely through an evening at the Clock, I'll give him that. And don't look so surprised. Not much happens in this town without me knowing about it one way or the other. Now come along, we've got work to do."

After a couple of hours of that kind of thing, I started to feel pretty good about myself.

That's why, when Grandma was chatting up the seamstress about an alteration for me and I saw this sweet-looking old lady beckoning at me through the window, I figured I would step outside and say hi to her.

She was a short woman, bone-skinny, probably in her seventies or so, standing under a shade tree just across the street. She wore one of those pink dresses you see old ladies wear in church sometimes, even though it wasn't Sunday. A huge purse dangled from her left hand, stuffed full of something and heavy, from the way she was straining to hold it.

I walked on over to her.

"Hi, ma'am," I said.

She smiled real big at me. "You're Lee, aren't you? I knew that was you the moment I saw you. I used to know your mother, did you know that? She was a rowdy little thing, but sweet. And your dear uncle. Aren't you just the spitting image of him."

"Why, thank you," I said, though it wasn't true. I didn't look a thing like Jeremiah.

"It's the Spirit in you," she said. "So much the way it was with him."

I started to thank her again, to tell her how grateful I was for her kind words, when she swung her purse up hard and walloped me in the face with it. There had to be bricks in it, a concrete block or something, because I went down, and hard. My vision was splotchy, and I could taste blood, like she'd busted my nose.

The woman hunched over me, her eyes gone fierce.

"Yes, I can smell the evil reeking off of you," she said. "Do you even know what you're doing? What you're capable of?"

The woman drew a big gleaming knife from her purse.

"I have gone down that road before, yes I have. I lived in that world for a time. And it was not right. I lost my daughter. I lost everything."

She crouched on top of me, her knees on my chest, pinning me down. My head still swam, and I could barely focus my eyes. I could do nothing to stop her.

"I won't let it happen again," she said. "Not here. Not like that."

The woman raised the knife above her head and brought it down in one swift plunge.

Something tackled her off me. It happened so fast and my head hurt so bad, I couldn't tell who it was. I saw the woman roll someone off of her, and I saw her knife lodged deep in the person's chest. She got up to run and fell back over, hollering, her shinbone bent at a weird angle.

That's when I saw him clearly, the person who had saved me. He was tall and gangly with a big beard and wild hair, and his clothes stank, barely rags. He lay on his back, gasping these tiny little breaths like a fish does when you lay it on the river-bank to die.

It was the Hobo.

I crawled over to him, staring like it was a dream.

"But you aren't real," I said. "You're just a vision in my head."

The Hobo reached his hand out to me and touched my face softly, and I flinched backward. He died staring at me, his eyes full of pain, sadness.

He had saved my life.

I WASN'T HURT THAT BAD, BUT GRANDMA
rushed me home and shut me up in my bedroom anyway.
No one was allowed to come and see me, not even Murphy.
I figured she would be pretty pissed off about that, but there
wasn't much I could do about it. Eventually this guy named
Dr. Thompson showed up to check on me. At least Grandma
said he was a doctor, or he used to be, anyhow. Dr. Thompson poked and prodded at me and shined a flashlight in
my eyes.

"He'll be fine," said Dr. Thompson. "Just a headache. Keep
him in bed the rest of the day, but try not to let him fall asleep
for a while, if you can."

When he left the room, I asked Grandma why that lady had
tried to kill me.

"Not everyone is a friend of the Farm," she said. "Not everybody is on our side of things."

"You mean like all the people at the Clock Without Hands?"

Grandma nodded. "I mean those people precisely."

"But I didn't see that lady there the night we snuck in."

"That's because she used to be one of us, and she still keeps some of our ways. Her daughter was very sick, and she brought her to Jeremiah. But there was nothing anybody could do for the poor girl, not at that point. Her daughter died, and she blamed your uncle for it. Poor misguided woman."

Grandma left it at that. My head throbbed, and it was hard for me to keep things straight. It was like my whole life was just a tumble down a huge hill, things just happening and happening without me having any control over them at all.

"I just still can't believe that the Hobo was real," I said.

"Yes, honey," she said. "It would appear that he was real indeed."

To be honest, the thought of it made me want to vomit, and I nearly did, right there in bed. The idea of him looking in on me at night, sneaking around the house, hiding in my closet. This man, so obsessed with me, haunting my whole childhood. Following me. God, it was awful. Being watched like that, spied on. What all had he seen? What did he know about me? I felt, I don't know, *defiled* in some way. Like I needed to shower and scrub his eyes off of me.

But the Hobo was dead now, and he'd saved my life.

I still don't know how I feel about that.

There was a commotion outside, dogs barking, people hollering. I went to the window to look out.

The Urquharts stood in the driveway. They were dirtier, more ragged than before, and they looked angry. The mom's face was all red, and it was obvious she'd been crying.

The grandmother held a snake by its jaws. I recognized it. It was a cottonmouth, alive and squirming in her fist.

In her other hand she held a knife.

She lifted the knife to the snake's throat and slit it, grasping the creature's head while its tail whipped around in a frenzy, the blood running down its body and onto the dirt. When it stopped wriggling she tossed it on the ground.

One by one, the Urquharts turned and left, the dead snake a bloody S on the driveway.

Grandma sat back on the bed, chewing her lip.

"What in the hell was that?" I said.

When Grandma spoke, her voice shook, like it was painful for her to say the words.

"That man you call 'the Hobo,' the one who saved your life—that was Carl Urquhart."

There was no way. It wasn't possible.

"How?" I said. "I thought he was missing."

"He was, for years and years," said Grandma. "Not anymore."

"It just doesn't make sense. I mean, I spent my whole life terrified of him. He would watch me through my bedroom window while I slept. I would wake up and see him there, staring at me. I saw him on the night Mom died. I thought he was a vision, like an omen of doom or something. I thought he meant that I was going to die."

"Well, I guess if he was an omen, he meant the opposite of death for you," said Grandma. "He meant life."

"But George said he hated us, that all the Urquharts hated us. Why would he risk his life for me?"

"Since when have you spoken to George Urquhart?" said Grandma.

I stammered a little about how George had come to see me a couple of times.

"You are not to be seen with any Urquharts, do you understand me?" she said. "Now listen to me. The Urquharts have opposed the Farm, and all us Sanfords, ever since I was just a girl. The Urquharts hated us, always have, because my daddy won this land off them long before I was born. The Urquharts always swore they'd been cheated. Trash does that, Lee—blames other people for their problems, won't take responsibility. Truth was, the Spirit wanted us to have this land, chose us to bring its message to the world. See, there are forces aligned against us. You do know that, don't you, Lee? There are two sides to this power here, and they are always at war with one another."

"That's what the Gentlemen said. 'There are two worlds, and they are the same.'"

Grandma smirked. "They would say that, wouldn't they? No, they are not the same, not exactly. But they are always in conflict, and the conflict is what makes this world. We are light-bringers, and we come to heal this world. Those who oppose us are of the darkness, and there is no light in them. From what you tell me, the Gentlemen were a sort of prison for Jeremiah, his aspect divided. You had to free him from that realm, Lee, and you did it. For that I will be forever grateful."

"Why did Carl save me if his family hates us so much?" I said.

"Well, the truth is, Carl and that wretched mother of his tried to kill your uncle when he was about thirteen or so. Gave him a poisoned piece of candy. That's why I cook all of your food myself, yours and Murphy's, and I don't allow any outside snacks. It just isn't safe."

"But why was he spying on me? Why did he follow me my whole life?"

Grandma seemed to grow smaller, like she was curling in on herself, drawing her bones closer, fresh pain brimming in her eyes. I was amazed how after so many years, the hurt of losing Jeremiah hadn't dimmed at all. In that moment she seemed so small and fragile, like a doll of herself, like someone could snip a single thread and she would unravel, collapse into a tumble of old bones and dust.

The moment passed, and Grandma sat up straight again. She took a deep breath and let it out slow, and a fierceness replaced the pain in her eyes.

"Because after your uncle survived," she said, "Jeremiah won Carl Urquhart over. And he grew to love your uncle, more than his own family, more than himself, even. He swore to protect Jeremiah, to give his life for him. Of course, Carl was such a nuisance about it that Jeremiah put a curse on him, took away his voice. He forbade Carl from interfering unless Jeremiah's life was in danger. After he failed to protect Jeremiah, I guess he just moved on to you."

That didn't make any sense to me at all. How could someone go from such deep hatred, from wanting to murder a person, to loving him, to risking their life for him?

"It isn't so strange," said Grandma. "Didn't Saul want to murder Christians before he converted and became Paul? It was the same with Carl and your uncle. Carl persecuted Jeremiah, and then Carl came to see the light."

"But how?"

Grandma raised her eyebrows at me.

"Lee, honey, what do you think we're doing with Horace? You are learning to win people to our side, little by little. Why not start with your worst enemy, the person who hurt you the most? If you can win someone like that, then you can win anyone at all. You can win the whole world."

I heard Murphy stomping around in the hallway, same as she'd been doing for hours now, the door locked to her. I couldn't figure out why Grandma was so intent on keeping Murphy away from me.

"Why don't you like Murphy?" I asked Grandma.

"It's not that I don't like her, exactly," said Grandma. "It's just that I don't find your sister to be a particularly affirming presence at the moment. I do believe she hurts our cause more than she helps."

"But she's my sister," I said.

"That may well be," she said. "She is your sister by blood, sure. But is she your sister in the Spirit? Is she one of us?"

I wasn't sure what the answer to that question was, and at the moment I didn't quite care.

"Just let me see her for a minute," I said. "Otherwise she's liable to kick the door down."

Grandma relented and unlocked the door. Murphy came bursting in, all kinetic energy and worry.

"Jesus Christ, are you okay?" she said. "They told me you were almost killed, and then she locked me out of your fucking room all day."

"I was only trying to let your brother rest," said Grandma.

"Yeah, well, I've been pacing the halls like a goddamn maniac," she said. "You could have just let me say hello or something."

"You have fifteen minutes," said Grandma.

She got up and left us, giving Murphy a little scowl on the way out, and shut the door. Murphy and I were alone together in my bedroom.

"I'm fine, I'm fine," I said. "To be honest, I don't really want to talk about it."

"Is it true?" she said. "About the Hobo. That he was real?"

"Yeah, Murphy. He was Carl Urquhart, apparently. And he saved my life."

"You know that's the single creepiest thing I ever heard, right? That dude peeking into your bedroom at night, following you around ever since we were kids, like the goddamn boogeyman."

"Really he was more like my guardian angel, when you think about it."

"Yeah, I guess so," she said. "He saved your life when I couldn't. I should have been there. I should have protected you, like Grandma said."

"No," I said. "Murphy, that's not your responsibility."

"Maybe it should be," she said, and she gave my shoulder a squeeze. "I'm glad you're okay, Lee. I'm glad that crazy lady didn't kill you."

"Me too, Murphy."

"I guess I'll be seeing you around then," she said, and she went back to her room.

I sat there in the quiet of the room, wondering. Was I Murphy's responsibility? I kind of always had been. That's what

Grandma said in the church, that she was my protector. Maybe Murphy was coming around to everything. Maybe she'd be a part of this family yet.

I knew the Spirit could win her over. It just had to.

I wouldn't bet on it, came a whisper in my ears.

Was Jeremiah telling me that? Or was it my own mind? It was becoming so hard to tell the difference.

THE NEXT MORNING AT BREAKFAST, MY FIRST
Gathering only two days away, Murphy ran up to the table all
frantic and angry.

"I need to talk to you," she said to me. "Right now."

"I'm sure it can wait until after breakfast," said Grandma.

"It certainly fucking cannot," said Murphy.

"It's okay, Grandma," I said. "I'll be right back."

I followed Murphy into the hallway. She held out a piece of
white sketchbook paper.

"Look at this shit," said Murphy.

The drawing showed the earth ripping open, like in an
earthquake, and a cloud of night pouring out, the moon and
stars erupting like a volcano, the night seeping out of the earth
in a black plume.

"That's . . . that's my vision," I said. "The one I had in
the church."

"I fucking well know it is, you jerk," she said. "How did this get in my head?"

"Murphy, this is wonderful," I said. "It's a miracle. I mean, when did you learn to draw like that?"

"I didn't learn," she said. "I just did it, almost in my sleep. It was like I was in a trance. What the fuck is going on here?"

The Spirit is working, I thought, but I didn't say it.

"I'm serious, Lee. This is freaking me out."

I had to be careful here. I had to say it just right.

"You know, Mom used to paint Jeremiah's visions," I said. "You saw them on the church walls. Maybe that's part of your role here as well—to paint my visions, just like Mom did."

"But I don't want to paint your visions," she said. "I don't want to paint anything at all."

"Don't you see, Murphy?" I said. "You're a part of the Spirit's plan whether you like it or not. You belong here. You're a part of all the beautiful things that are to come."

"Fuck off," she said and ran off to her room.

I got to be honest, that hurt. But I was encouraged a little bit too. The Spirit was working. The Spirit was moving, even in Murphy.

Later that day I was walking in the fields when I met this kid with stooped shoulders and unbearable acne. He might have been nineteen. He came loping up to me all furious with this ungainly stick-man stride, like his limbs were too stiff and long, like he was a marionette controlled by a drunk guy. He got right in my face and sneered.

"Look, what's all this about?" he said. "You hippies or something? I live in this county, and I have a right to know."

I was a little taken aback. I mean, he really looked pissed, like he wanted to kick my ass. But I held my composure and fake smiled, waiting for the Spirit to give me words. I was getting better and better at doing that.

"We aren't hippies, no, sir," I said.

"*Sir*," he said. "What a laugh. Nobody calls me sir. I'm just Byron, thank you very much."

That was something. Maybe I could work with that.

"Well, I'm Lee," I said. "And what do you do for work, Byron?"

"Nothing."

"You don't have a job?"

"Oh, I got a job all right," he said. "I work the counter at the Shell station over in Merton. Press some buttons and sit on my ass. It's as close to nothing as anyone could ever do and still get paid for it. I'm like a big human ear, you know? I hear things—gossip, talk of the town, all that. That's how I come to find out about you people."

"And why did you decide to pay our community a visit today?"

He shrugged. "It's my day off. What the hell else was I going to do?"

Listen, whispered the Spirit. *Pay attention.*

"You didn't want to stay home on your day off, did you?" I said. He shook his head. I saw a glimpse of a woman in a grey terry cloth bathrobe scowling over a pot of boiled hot dogs. "Because your mother is home, right?"

"She's always home," he said. "Never leaves, not for anything."

I could see images now, more and more of Byron's life flashing before my eyes like a projector cast over the real world straight from Byron's mind.

"And she's angry at you, isn't she?" I said.

"What would you know about my momma?" he said. He was getting angrier and angrier, his face flushing red.

"She makes you help in the kitchen and beats you with a whisk whenever you mess up," I said. "It doesn't hurt, but it makes you feel stupid. Everyone makes you feel stupid, isn't that right? And what does your father do?"

Byron's jaw hung open, and his fists were balled at his sides. He looked like he was about to snap, about to bust my jaw open.

"Leave my daddy out of it," he growled.

But I couldn't stop. I couldn't help it.

"He wears sweatpants and drinks beer all day," I said. "He watches your mom whip you, and he laughs, doesn't he? Doesn't he, Byron?"

I thought the guy was going to strangle me. I thought he was going to pin me to the ground and bust my teeth out. He drew his fist back, and I waited for the blow to land, for him to knock me senseless.

But Byron flung his arms around me and collapsed onto my shoulder, weeping.

"No one wants me," he said. "No one wants anything to do with me, not at all."

"I do," I said, and I meant it, I really did. "I want you here. You belong here with us. With all of us. You're part of our family now."

"Thank you," he said.

And he wept and wept.

Well done, Lee, whispered Jeremiah. *Well done indeed.*

I wanted to tell Murphy what had happened with Byron, but she wouldn't hardly speak to me. I guess she was still freaked out about the whole painting thing. I wondered if I showed her Mom's art, whether she would be more excited about what the Spirit was doing in her, how it was changing her.

I knocked on her door.

"Murphy?" I said. "I got something to show you."

She opened the door and glared at me.

"If it involves this spooky goddamn religion of yours," she said, "I want nothing to do with it."

I stepped inside and shushed her a little bit.

"You got to stop insulting this Farm," I said. "It's bad for people to hear you do it. It hurts our cause."

"If I had my way," she said, "I would stomp your cause into the fucking ground."

"You don't mean that," I said. "You can't."

"Oh, I mean it," said Murphy. "I hate this place. I hate what it's doing to you."

"It's making me great," I said. "It's making me into a leader."

"Is that what you think you are?" she said, a mean little smirk on her face. "Lee, the great leader of the people? Or are you just Grandma's little puppet?"

I was so angry I could have spat. I wanted to scream at Murphy, to slap that grin right off her face. But then I felt something different, a stirring inside me.

"It's okay to be jealous of me, Murphy," I told her, my voice placid, calm, not quite my own. "Though I can say it's not a very becoming look for you. Jealousy makes you small, Murphy. It makes you pathetic."

"How about you get the hell out of my room right now?" she snarled.

"Okay," I said. "If you wish."

I stepped backward, and she slammed the door in my face.

I told you not to trust her, whispered Jeremiah. *She is not one of us, and she never was. Send her away now.*

Maybe he was right. Maybe Murphy would never give in to the Spirit. But I couldn't just throw her out, could I?

She was my sister.

I lay on my bed that night, listening to Jeremiah's tapes. Grandma had them all in her bedroom in a safe, shut tight. I guess she was the one hiding them in the Split Tree all along. She gave me a certain tape, marked special for me.

"You'll enjoy this one," was all she said.

I closed the window and shut off the lights and pressed play.

"Every human being is a collision." Jeremiah spoke in a whisper, private and personal, as if this were a sermon for only me to hear. "Two worlds smashing into one, forming something new. No doubt, children, that this is an act of violence. There is no creation without violence, no sacrifice without the shedding of blood. Is violence desirable? No, but sometimes it is necessary in this fallen world. The things that form us are no less violent than the cataclysm that created this world. Did you know the earth itself was formed from a collision, two planets slamming into each other, fused into one? Our beautiful world and all the abundant life it contains—our very selves, all we know and love—are the result of the most awful violence. Because in the right hands, and for the right purpose, violence and creation are the very same thing."

The darkness of the room began to churn and swirl like smoke rising up from a fire. I wasn't sure if I was listening to a tape anymore or if Jeremiah was there in the room with me, walking in the shadows, so real I could reach out and touch him.

"If we are to escape our isolation, our loneliness," he said, "then we must be created anew. Our only hope in this light-starved world is to burn so brightly that all of humanity will turn to notice. We must transcend, collide like an errant planet with the Spirit of the world, to burn and fuse into something new, into pure light. We must cast aside that to which we formerly clung, sacrifice what is most dear, pitch it into the fire so that we may all rise together like smoke, an offering to the Spirit, a sacrifice pleasing to it. We must undergo the violence that leads to creation, the shedding of blood that can make us beautiful, as we were meant to be. Only then may we transcend. Only then can the world ever become what it was intended to be, a splendor of light.

"Yes, Lee. To burn and to glow. That is freedom. To become pure light. The violence of collision. The violence that leads to beauty. There is no other pathway to freedom. Not in this world nor the next."

I lay there in the darkness, holding my breath.

THE DAY BEFORE OUR FIRST GATHERING, I spent all morning sitting in supplication in the Hummingbird Grove, talking to Jeremiah.

"I have something to show you," he said, and he placed a cold hand on my forehead.

Suddenly I was by the pond, but I wasn't in my body. I was some floating hazy spirit that didn't exist, that could watch everything from far away, and I knew I was in the past somehow, I knew I was seeing something very old and forgotten.

There were two teenagers at the pond, a girl and a boy. The girl had long brown hair, and she swam confident and alone while the boy lay on the bank, napping, sunning himself.

I knew the boy immediately. That pale hair, the long thin body. It was Jeremiah. He lay back, his eyes shut, arms behind his head for a pillow, a great smile on his face. I wondered what he was dreaming of, if he was having visions, if he was seeing his whole beautiful future stretched before him, the Farm and all it could be, his people, his congregation. The sun shone down on him like a spotlight, like the whole world existed just to draw attention to him.

I saw Carl Urquhart standing a little ways off from the bank, peeking through the trees. He was much younger, and his beard and clothes weren't so ragged yet.

The girl—my mother—hollered at Carl.

"Get away, you creep," she said in a voice that sounded exactly like Murphy's. "Give us some privacy for once."

"Oh, let him be," said Jeremiah, from the bank.

"No," said Mom. "I'm sick of him following you around all the time like your creepy goddamn shadow." She motioned to Carl. "I said to get!"

Carl Urquhart took a few steps back into the woods.

"Not far enough!" hollered Mom. "Keep on going! Don't stop until you get to the house!"

And Carl Urquhart slunk off, looking over his shoulder every few steps. Mom watched until he was gone.

"I hate that guy," she said and dove underwater.

I watched her swim around while Jeremiah dozed on the bank. I wondered how tough it had been for my mom to grow up with someone like Jeremiah as a brother. It was hard enough growing up with Murphy, who was friends with everyone, who Mom loved the most. I couldn't imagine what it would have been like having to compete with Jeremiah for your mother's affection, not to mention all the other folks hanging around all the time. I felt bad for Mom then, like maybe I'd never understood her, like maybe I hadn't tried hard enough while she was still alive.

But then Mom's head snapped up out of the pond and she grew still. A water moccasin glided past her, its neck arched with some strange dignity, kingly, like it was above all the other creatures, like everything else at the pond existed only to fear and worship it. I watched it slither across the water as if it were on solid ground, slickly sliding toward land.

Toward Jeremiah.

Mom followed the snake out of the water as she searched the bank for some kind of weapon. She grabbed a stick, a broken-off tree branch thick as my arm. If it wasn't rotten, it would do as a club. The snake was on the grass now, so close to where Jeremiah slept. If Mom woke him now and he jerked too quickly, the snake would bite him for sure. I watched her creep up quiet toward the snake and raise the stick, ready to bash the moccasin's head in.

But then Mom froze. I watched the look on her face, a kind of confusion, or maybe anger, or maybe it was just that she couldn't figure out how to attack the snake without putting her brother's life in further danger.

The snake slithered right up to Jeremiah, skipping his bare leg, past his chest, sliding right up to his neck like it knew what it was doing, like some divine wretched force was guiding it. I wanted to scream, to holler at him to wake up, to snap Mom out of her reverie. But it was a vision, only a vision. I couldn't make a sound. I watched as the snake drew close to him, right up to Jeremiah's face, gently, as if it were going to whisper a secret in his ear.

And then Mom lowered her club.

The snake bit.

Hard. It clamped down on Jeremiah's neck. I watched as he kicked and thrashed, but the snake wouldn't let go. It didn't seem possible, a snake holding on like that, pumping so much venom into one boy. It seemed like some kind of evil mistake, the opposite of a miracle.

And Mom didn't do anything. She just stood there and watched.

The snake detached itself and seemed to vanish into the grass as if it had never existed, as if it was never there at all.

"You have to help me," said Jeremiah, his neck already swelling, his face breaking out in a sweat. "You have to hurry."

But she didn't. Mom just stood there and watched him.

Jeremiah staggered to his feet and began to walk. He tried to holler for help, but his voice was all ragged, and it came out barely a whisper. He walked past the pond and into the woods like he was trying to make it to the Farm but he'd lost his sense of direction. He was wandering, hopeless, aimless. Mom followed a few steps behind him, silent, her bare feet padding softly through the grass. Eventually they came to the Split Tree.

Jeremiah stumbled there and fell against the tree trunk. He leaned back and stared at the sky, panting, groaning in pain.

As his throat closed up and his eyes rolled back in his head, Mom knelt beside Jeremiah and held his hand.

Until Jeremiah grew still.

I jolted out of my vision, gasping for air like it was me who had been snakebit, like my throat was the one closing up.

Was that vision true? Did it mean that Mom killed Jeremiah? Or not killed him, but let him die? Was that why she hid the Farm and Grandma and everything else from us? Was it all just her guilt?

Jeremiah stood there before me in the real world, a sort of white glow about him. His eyes shone blue and pure, as if lit by an inner light.

"Jealousy is a powerful force," he said. "It can corrupt anyone, even those closest to you. Even your own sister."

I thought about Murphy back at the house, off sulking in her room.

"Murphy doesn't believe in me or the Farm," I said. "But she'd never turn on me like that. She'd never kill me."

"Perhaps not," said Jeremiah, his voice gone sad and wise, like he knew so much more about the world than I did and he had learned every last bit of it through pain. "But it's dangerous to trust one single person too much, to rely on them alone. That's what the community is for—to balance each other, to protect each other. There's a power when all of us are together, a love stronger than anyone can understand. An abiding love, not easily broken. A love that can hold on far beyond the grave, long after death. That's what you deserve, Lee. A family who believes in you. Who will stand by you and your visions. Who will love you forever, unconditionally. Not like your mother, and not like Murphy either."

"But she's begun drawing my visions now. The Spirit is moving in her."

"Yes," said Jeremiah, "but the Spirit was present in your mother as well. Some people wield that power for noble purposes. And some use it to hurt."

I began to cry, thinking about Mom, how she had betrayed Jeremiah, how she had probably never even loved me at all. Murphy too, how strange she'd been toward me ever since the night in the church, the way she resented me for how beloved I'd become, for how important I was now.

Jeremiah laid his hand on my shoulder.

"You don't need your mother anymore," he said, "and you don't need your sister either. You have me, you have your grandmother, and you have the Farm. We are your family now, your community. We love you so much, and we'll never leave you."

"Promise?" I said.

"I swear it," he said, "with all of my heart."

We stayed like that, Jeremiah's hand on my shoulder, the light of him granting me peace.

COME AFTERNOON, I MADE HORACE CRY. I MEAN, big tears.

I spoke to him about our mother.

It was Grandma's idea. I didn't want to, not in light of what I'd learned about her from Jeremiah, but Grandma insisted that was the way to Horace's heart. He still wouldn't admit to killing Mom, but he was so full of pain, so full of sadness and regret. He told me how sorry he was for the way he had treated us back home, for how angry he always was.

It was a strange thing to hear. I mean, if he loved her so much, why did he kill her?

Then I remembered: Horace was an asshole, a horrible, horrible person. Sure, his father had been abusive, but that didn't excuse the way he treated Murphy and me. It didn't excuse any of what he'd done.

But I was winning him over slowly. I figured in a week or two I would break him. Maybe he wouldn't love me the way

Carl Urquhart had loved my uncle, but he would stay here, and he would serve us. Maybe I could make him live in the woods, only bring him around to shovel shit and dig ditches. Work like that would suit Horace, strong as he was. At the very least, I'd never have to look at his face again.

And yeah, it was all pretty fucked up, what we were doing. But something needed to be done about him, or else Grandma and Sheriff Bearden and the whole Farm would be in serious trouble. Wouldn't it be better my way? I could probably make him happier too, make him love his shitty life out in the woods.

I could make Horace happy if I wanted to. I could be merciful like that.

Tomorrow was the first Gathering, my big coronation, the start of a new era in my life, in the life of the Farm, maybe even in the life of this whole world. The church had been cleaned out, the floors scrubbed and sparkling, the lawn tended, the preparations made. I could feel the Spirit thrumming in my heart, feel it rush through my veins, the tingle of it in my bones. Jeremiah followed me like a shadow, my guide and comforter. And my people seemed to love me. They really did think I was someone special, chosen. Sometimes they were even afraid to talk to me, scared to shake my hand.

I knew I could be a good leader. I was on the true path, my heart was right and pure, and I would guide the Farm into the future.

Maybe I could be greater even than Jeremiah.

THAT NIGHT I HAD A VISION.

Oh man, did I ever have a vision.

I saw myself, clad in a black suit like Jeremiah's, standing on the stage in the church. I was older, maybe in my twenties, and the church was huge, a brand-new building even bigger than the one that was there now. It was fancy, with red carpets and oak pews and flowers all over the place, everything bright and shiny and new. Light streamed through the stained glass windows showing pictures of my visions, mystical symbols the Spirit had shown me, and the whole place took on a glimmer like we were already in heaven, and light suffused everything around us.

I looked taller and handsomer than I ever imagined I could be, and when I spoke, it was my voice, but it was Jeremiah's too—it was the perfect synthesis of the two of us, like we were speaking together in perfect harmony. Usually when you hear your own voice in a recording or something, you hate the sound of it, but my voice was wonderful. I loved hearing it belt out wild and loud over a crowd of believers, every single last one of them loving me. They loved the words pouring out of my mouth like a flood of dreams, of benedictions and curses and blessings, of the right ways to live and the wrong ways to die, of all the good and true things that lay in the hidden heart of the world. I could listen to myself make pronouncements and illuminate dreams all day and night for the rest of my life, it sounded so good.

I was magnificent, is what I'm saying. In my vision I was everything I ever dreamed I could be, a leader of people who adored me. It was confirmation that my visions were in fact a gift, that what once had gotten me punished and shunned was a blessing to the world, the most precious anointing. It meant I wasn't a freak, wasn't one of the afflicted, but a set-apart one, a chosen one, holy in my own right. It was proof that Mom hadn't died in vain, that her death had led me to the Farm, where I could find my destiny, where my gift would reach its fulfillment. Every moment in my life had been part of a grander plan, the good and the bad, and all of it existed to bring me here.

I would lead the Farm, all my true believers following my every word. And oh, according to this vision, there would be many of them spanning the globe, and my visions would be broadcast loud for the world to hear. All people would know my name.

I saw Cass onstage beside me, leading the congregation in song. I saw Grandma and Sheriff Bearden, my right- and left-hand guards. I saw Mr. Cartwright in the front row, sober for the first time, grinning and clapping, singing hymns with his eyes closed. I saw Wilmer Jenkins and Willamette Darling and Byron and even Kent Knoll in the crowd, with eyes shut, hands outstretched, receiving every word and song from my mouth as if it were a gift, as if it were the dictation of the Spirit itself. Which of course it was.

Everyone was there, all of them, everyone I had ever known. There was only one person missing: Murphy wasn't there. My sister, who should have stood at my side, my sworn guardian, my keeper since we were kids. I looked everywhere in the room, but I couldn't find Murphy.

But then I saw her, or someone who seemed to be her, lurking in the darkest corner of the room. Murphy had changed. She looked monstrous, her eyes narrowed into slits, her teeth grown into fangs. Yes, there was Murphy, always creeping around the fringes of things, the spoiler, the ruiner, the one who would try and steal it all from me. Had she not rejected the Spirit as it had brought forth talents in her? Had she not rejected me as a leader, the Spirit's own chosen prophet?

This was a warning. I couldn't trust Murphy anymore. I would beware of her from then on. She didn't belong here, and she would never truly be one of us. Murphy was someone I was supposed to leave behind. She was a traitor, and her faith was weak. I didn't need her anyhow. I had Grandma, and I had Cass, and I had anyone I wanted to protect me. I had Jeremiah, I had the Farm, I had my new family, and they were enough. I felt the Spirit spread out and cover the world, swallowing every trace of darkness, bathing the earth in light.

I had everything I ever wanted and more.

It was a glorious vision.

The best I'd ever have.

GRANDMA SHOOK ME AWAKE.

She wore a white dress that came down to her feet, like a wedding dress. She had a leather satchel slung over her shoulder, and in her left hand she carried the shotgun.

"Get dressed," she said, "and be quiet about it."

"What's wrong?" I said.

"Nothing at all," she said. "There's just one thing we have to do before the Gathering. Come along now. It's time."

"Time for what?" I asked, but Grandma only told me to hurry.

I got dressed, and we crept quiet out of my room, walking soft down the hall as if this journey into the night were secret, as if the rest of the Farm could never know about it.

Outside, Grandma lit a lantern. The night was balmy and loud with bugs, with tree frogs and insects, the hot swirling forest call of the night. I liked to pretend the cricket sounds were the stars hollering their light down and the breeze from the wind was just the song of the moon. I followed Grandma's lantern through the black like it was a rogue star loosed from the sky. Grandma guided me toward the toolshed next to the barn, the one Horace was chained up in.

Grandma creaked the toolshed door open, but she left the electric bulb off, as if anything but lantern light would somehow spoil things. Horace slumped in his chair, duct-taped and bound, his eyes fluttering awake. He moaned a little, the gag muffling the sound, and he stank. Somehow he was worse even than he had been the last time I'd seen him. I shivered, revulsed by him, and in that moment I hated him more than I had ever hated another person in my life.

"Good," said Grandma, as if she could sense my thoughts. "You'll need that."

Grandma propped the shotgun against the shed wall and laid her satchel on the concrete floor. She pulled out a small pouch and took to sprinkling the contents in a circle around Horace, chanting quiet to herself all the while.

"Grandma," I said, "what are you doing?"

But still she wouldn't answer me.

When the circle was finished, Grandma grabbed me by the hand, and together we knelt in front of Horace while she prayed.

"Spirit, the hour has come," whispered Grandma. "The night is yours, and the stars and moon are yours, and the woods are yours. We kneel in supplication, asking for your indwelling presence, for your anointing on Lee, the prophet you have chosen for yourself. Bind yourself to him, your spirit to his spirit, your essence to his bones. May he speak with your words, and may he see with your eyes. May the nations kneel before you."

Horace, gagged, watched us, his eyes wide and confused.

"I don't understand, Grandma," I said. "What's happening?"

"Every true prophet must bind himself to the Spirit," said Grandma. "Your great-grandfather taught me that. And there can be no binding without a sacrifice."

"A sacrifice?" I said. "What are you talking about? I'm winning Horace over, just like you asked me to. Soon he'll believe in me. He'll be one of us."

"That's never been his purpose, Lee, not really," she said. "That's not why I saved him, kept him bound in the church for you, though for a time he proved a useful toy for you to practice on. No, I always had other grander plans for Horace."

From her satchel Grandma removed a knife. It was long and slender and ridged, a steak knife, the very same one I'd seen her use in our kitchen.

Horace began thrashing in his chair, jerking against the duct tape.

"I can't do this," I said. "There's no way."

"But you have to," said Grandma. "It's for us, for your family, your people. This is how it's always been done since your great-grandfather first took the land from the Urquharts. There is no other way."

Horace screamed, his voice muffled by the gag, and yanked harder against his bonds. The chair shook and rocked, and for a moment I thought he'd knock it over.

"Be still!" screamed Grandma, pointing the knife at him, and Horace obeyed.

It made me feel good, a little bit, to see Horace so scared, to see him cower away from Grandma. And then I remembered the glimpse I'd seen of him as a child about to be whipped by his father.

I took a step backward, away from the circle.

"Don't fight it, Lee," said Grandma. "Your great-grandfather killed his own daughter to gain the power of the Spirit, my twin sister. He cut her throat, and the blood bound the Spirit to him for all his life. We drew lots, she and I. And my sister went willingly. She understood the price that had to be paid. I dreamed of this for myself, I always had. But my daddy wouldn't let the Spirit pass on to me. He said it had to be a male child, his heir—that's what the Spirit commanded. It hurt me. I wanted what you have, Lee, what Jeremiah had. But the Spirit chooses who it chooses, and it has chosen you, the same as it chose your uncle. We all have to make our own sacrifices."

"That lady who tried to kill me," I said. "Is that what happened to her daughter?"

"The girl was willing," said Grandma. "It was her choice, her gift to our community. She was nearly dead anyway, the cancer all in her bones. All Jeremiah had to do was make a tiny slit up each wrist"—Grandma made a slicing motion with the knife—"and he held her in his arms while she bled away. It was quick and quiet and nearly painless. And the girl was taken up into glory."

Grandma held the knife out to me, but I was afraid to take it. I backed myself against the wall of the shed.

"I would gladly have died for this community," said Grandma. "But I was the one the Spirit chose to live. Just as the Spirit has chosen you."

"I can't do it," I said. "I can't just kill somebody."

"But this is the scum who killed your mother!" said Grandma. "The wretch who spent his days on this earth terrifying you, ruining the life your mother built for you and your sister. Spoiling every last thing he laid his hands on. Don't you remember? Don't you hate him, Lee? Don't you loathe his very bones?"

I did, I realized, and I felt the hate rising up in me. I heard whispers now, the Spirit speaking to me, the voice of Jeremiah chanting around me in a language I couldn't understand. I felt the air alive and electric, the space between worlds grown thin, flimsy as paper.

"Take the knife, Lee," said Grandma. "Take it and do what must be done. For your people, for your family."

Her eyes peered into mine, the same strange brown as Mom's, yellow-speckled like the last autumn leaf.

"You're a good boy, Lee. You know what's best for your people. You're not even sacrificing an innocent, not like Jeremiah did, not like my own daddy did. You're killing someone who hurt you, someone who deserves it. You're serving justice right here on the Farm."

Grandma grabbed the front tuft of Horace's hair and yanked his head back, exposing Horace's wide white throat.

"It'll be so quick," said Grandma, holding the knife out to me. "Just slide it right across his throat, one flick of your wrist. It will barely take a second."

"But what's the shotgun for?" I said.

"Sometimes it takes a body a long while to die," she said. "You just have to slit his throat, that's all, spill his blood, make the sacrifice count. Afterward I'll shoot him if you want so he doesn't have to suffer too long. I'll put him down like a sick dog, and it won't bother me any to do it."

My ears full of the Spirit, my heart beating wild, the very blood in my veins throbbing, I realized I wanted to take that knife. I wanted to feel that power in my hands, the power to shed blood, the power to invoke the Spirit, the power of life and death in my palm.

The door to the toolshed burst open, flinging moonlight across the floor. There stood Murphy.

"Go back to your room, Murphy," said Grandma. "Your brother and I have business here."

"If it concerns my brother," said Murphy, "then it's my business too."

Grandma let go of Horace's hair and pointed the knife at my sister.

"You don't know what's good for you and what isn't," said Grandma. "You don't care about our community."

"You're right about that," said Murphy. "I think you're all fucking crazy. Come on, Lee, we're leaving, right now."

"Shut your mouth, you little bitch!" snarled Grandma. "You're just a meddler, same as your mother. I should have killed her a long time ago and raised you kids myself."

Horace ripped his hands loose then. I don't know how he did it after days of being starved, but the brittle arm of the old wooden chair he was taped to finally snapped, and he tore himself free and fell to the floor. He scrambled to the corner of the toolshed and grabbed for the shotgun. Grandma leapt on top of him, stabbing the knife into his back over and over until he lay still. Murphy scrambled for the shotgun, and Grandma tackled her to the floor, straddling her body, pinning Murphy down, her left hand clasped over Murphy's mouth.

"Your stepfather here ruined our sacrifice," snarled Grandma. "Made me kill him myself." She held the knife tight against Murphy's throat, and a trickle of blood slipped down her neck. "Can't be spilling any more of that—it's too precious. It's got to be you who does it, Lee. We need a sacrifice tonight. You have to kill your sister."

"But I . . . I can't . . ."

"You must," said Grandma. "If Horace isn't dead, he will be soon, by my hand. He's no good as a sacrifice now. But your sister is a traitor. She doesn't care about this community, she said so herself. She's jealous of you, Lee. She's selfish and spoiled. I thought all this work on the Farm would humble her, would teach her how to give instead of just taking all the time. But your sister will not learn, Lee. She will have no life in our world to come. So go on, grab the shotgun. You don't have another choice."

I remembered my glorious dream, my vision of the future, with Murphy the snake lurking around. Was this what I was supposed to do—kill my sister? Was that the only way for the Farm to prosper, for the beautiful life that I foresaw to come true? Was Murphy the only thing standing between me and the world I wanted?

I walked over to the corner of the shed and picked up the shotgun.

I knew that if I killed Murphy, it would be for the greater good, for our community and maybe for the whole world. I remembered how in my vision they had watched me, all those adoring people, millions worldwide listening to my every word, my own gospel of love and peace and harmony. It was everything I wanted, more than I had ever dreamed of. I started to cry, I was terrified and ashamed, but I knew what I had to do.

"You must kill her, Lee," said Grandma. "Murphy will ruin us. She'll take it all away again. She'll spoil everything."

"But she's my sister," I said. "We can let her go. Murphy will leave. She won't bother us again. We can find somebody else."

"That's a lie, and you know it," said Grandma. "I'm doing this to protect us, Lee. I'm doing this for our community—for your true family."

I was crying so hard I could barely see, and the gun trembled all heavy in my hands.

"The Spirit is on my side, Lee," she said. "The Spirit knows that it is right and true that Murphy should die. Ask Jeremiah. He'll tell you."

And there he was, standing before me, a pale figure in a black suit, handsome and brave and brilliant, my whole future, everything I'd ever wanted to be.

"Oh, Lee, my beloved disciple," he said. "We have come so far together, you and I, and our journey is only beginning. This is the sacrifice of which I spoke, the violence that leads to creation. All you must do is spill your sister's blood, and everything you've ever wished for will come true."

I knew no one else could see him, no one could hear him but me. Grandma watched me, the moonlight glimmering in her eyes, Murphy struggling beneath her, that knife held tight to her throat. I stepped closer to them and pointed the shotgun at Murphy's head. I couldn't look at her face. I couldn't look her in the eyes.

"I'm going to move my hand," said Grandma, "and then you shoot. Do you understand?"

I shook my head. "I don't think I can do it."

"You have to," said Jeremiah. "Don't you know how beautiful this world can be? How loving and how pure? We can have a family more perfect than anything you could ever imagine. And your sister is trying to ruin it, same as my sister ruined it before. Don't let her, Lee. Be strong. Be a leader even greater than I was. Become who you are destined to be."

I saw my vision again, my glorious future, the adoring enchanted crowds singing the words I taught them, the hymns of my visions.

All of those people loving me.

I knew what I had to do.

"Do you see him?" said Grandma, her voice pained, pleading. "Can you see my son?"

Grandma moved the knife from Murphy's throat, giving me a clear shot at my sister's face.

"Lee," said Murphy. "Please."

I pulled the trigger. The kick from the gun half knocked me to the ground.

The shot hit Grandma square in the chest. Her body flopped lifeless to the floor, the gore of her flung all over the wall of the shed. Jeremiah vanished, gone.

Murphy screamed. Her arm was bleeding. I thought I might have shot her too.

"You okay?" I said.

"I . . . I think so," she said.

I helped her up, trying not to look at Grandma's body, trying not to see the damage the shotgun had done. I couldn't stop shaking and crying.

It was over. I had ruined everything.

"Thanks, Lee," said Murphy. "You saved my life."

Horace moaned from the floor. I guessed he wasn't dead yet.

Murphy ran to Horace and helped him to his feet. Blood ran down his back and legs and onto the floor.

"You dying?" said Murphy.

Horace, all haggard and starved and blood-soaked, his shirt ripped in gashes from Grandma's knife, shrugged at her.

"Doubt it," he said. "Don't think she stuck me anywhere too important. Want to hand me that shotgun there, Lee?"

I looked at Murphy, and she looked back at me.

"You can trust him," she said. "I promise."

I gave Horace the gun.

"Just follow behind me," he said, "and we'll get us the fuck out of here. How's that sound?"

We walked out into the hot summer night, mosquitoes swarming us, as the members of the Farm began to stream out of the house and into the yard, curious.

Sheriff Bearden ran up to us in his underpants.

"What the hell happened here?" he hollered.

Horace pointed the shotgun at him.

"Back up now," said Horace. "You already gave me about a week's worth of reasons to pull the trigger."

Sheriff Bearden backed away from us. The members of the Farm were all gathered in the yard now, watching us. They were like a flock of penitents, all in their white pajamas, staring wide-eyed and strange at me.

"Tell them to back the fuck up," said Horace, "and give us a clear path to the car."

"Out of the way!" hollered Sheriff Bearden, and the Farm folks scattered.

I couldn't look them in the eye. I couldn't bear to see what they thought of me now.

"Move it, kids," said Horace, and we obeyed, walking around the side of the house and into the driveway. The night air felt heavy, and the clouds were sparse and gray, the moon just a scrape of bone in the sky. We walked to the Trans Am, Horace behind us, the shotgun trained on Sheriff Bearden.

Only when we reached the car did I turn to look.

There stood Grandma's house, dark and strange-eyed, my home. And in the front yard was the community, all my people, everyone who believed in me. They stood hangdog and watching, their bare feet stuck with mud, as their prophet abandoned them. As I abandoned them. I was supposed to lead them. I was supposed to save them. In that moment I loved them all so much I thought my heart would burst.

I saw the pain and disappointment on their faces. I saw how I was failing them, each and every one, how I was destroying their faith, what they'd dedicated their lives to, like I was the prophecy that hadn't come true.

And then there was Cass.

"I don't understand," she said. She was crying, her face a mess of hurt and anger and bewilderment. "This was my purpose. It was what I was supposed to do with my life. How could you do this to us? How could you do this to me?"

"I'm sorry," I said.

"Get in the car," said Horace. "We ain't got time for this shit."

I saw the blood dribbling from his back, how it spread over his arms, how his hands shook when he held the gun. I realized he was going to collapse soon, that it was taking everything in him not to keel over and pass out.

Sheriff Bearden must have seen it too. He lunged at Horace, grabbing for the shotgun. Horace blasted him right in the chest. The man slumped over backward in the dust.

The blast seemed to cancel everything. Nobody spoke, nobody moved. Only the wind shuddering through the trees, the night birds calling, the strange croaking jungle sounds of the Southern night. All of the community out in the open, the moon and stars shining down on them in their pajamas. They looked like dirty angels. They looked like a choir come down from heaven, Cass in the lead, the most holy communion of people ever assembled, and I was letting them all down.

It was the worst feeling I'd ever had in my life. It was worse than Mom's death.

"I'm sorry," I said again.

We got in the Trans Am and left.

MURPHY EXPLAINED THE WHOLE THING TO ME on the drive back. That is, she explained as much as she could before Horace started losing consciousness. The rest she told me while we waited in the emergency room.

I was numb, empty, and all cried out, and Murphy talked fast, but I caught most of it.

She said, "After I realized Grandma had gone completely nuts and you started talking in that weird-ass old-timey preacher voice, I knew I had to move quick to save us. No offense, big brother, but you were pretty much a lost cause at that point, so I knew I had to do it myself. I just had to bide my time until the moment was right.

"The day you went to Benign to get your stupid fucking suit, I snuck out to that toolshed while the guard was off taking a shit. I ripped the gag off Horace's face and took one of Grandma's kitchen knives and pointed it right at his head. I said, 'Tell me right now why I shouldn't let them kill you.' And Horace got to talking. He had a whole hell of a lot of things to say. About how the Farm was a cult, how Mom was raised in it, how after her brother died she ran away and barely escaped with her life. How a lot of folks weren't nearly so lucky. How Mom had started seeing some of the old cult members—Sheriff Bearden, for one—sneaking around our neighborhood, spying on you. How she knew that they would come for us soon, you and me, to fulfill whatever vision Grandma first had about Jeremiah and Mom and the Farm. We were their second chance, I guess. That's why Mom had Horace adopt us, even though we never would have consented to it. Mom knew she was in danger, and she was trying to keep us away from Grandma no matter what. Even if Mom should die. I asked Horace if he had any evidence, and he said, 'It's all in my car.'

"'Why there?' I asked him, and he said it was because Mom thought that hidden compartment in the trunk was the safest place. She'd gotten pretty paranoid by that point. She didn't even trust the safe-deposit boxes at the bank. And I got to thinking about the vision you had on the night Mom died, how you just saw me opening the trunk, not what I was supposed to find inside. Of course, I'd naturally assumed the most important thing was the forged adoption papers. I mean, who wouldn't? But it turns out there was something else in that folder, something that we ignored.

"Because I do believe in your gifts, Lee," she told me, her hand on mine as we waited for the doctors to stitch up Horace. "I really truly 100 percent fucking do. I just don't think you always interpret your visions right. Maybe that's my real purpose. Maybe that's what I'm actually good for."

My head was all swirly, my heart broken and numb. Had I really killed Grandma? Had I really lost the Farm, lost Cass, lost everything? But Murphy kept talking, like if she didn't get it all out now I would never believe her, I'd be lost to her forever.

"Anyway, that night I took the keys and went through Horace's trunk again. This would have been at like two A.M. or so, when it was still pitch dark outside. Besides the hundreds of batshit letters from Grandma, there were a lot of files in that trunk, including a whole stack of court records, newspaper clippings, and Mom's own handwritten notes detailing these mysterious deaths that happened in Benign, Louisiana, twenty-five or twenty-six years ago. Suicides and such, real dramatic sad things, like the mayor of the town slitting his wrists with a knife and then handing it to his wife, who did the exact same thing to herself. Or this rich old lawyer who cut his own throat in his bathroom." I remembered my vision, the one I'd had after the party at the tenant house, and it made me sick. "Grisly stuff, and it was only happening to the rich folks in town, according to these old documents of Mom's. And you know who they willed all their money to? You guessed it—right to

Grandma. Turns out Jeremiah wasn't this benevolent sweet-heart of a guy after all. Turns out he was pretty mercenary, prey-ing on the richest in town to fund the growth and development of the Farm.

"The research had been Mom's work, what she was so dis-tracted by, what she was so paranoid about. Because Grandma knew Mom had been reading up on the Farm, on all those deaths that happened around that time. Maybe she had a vision, I don't know. But Grandma sent Sheriff Bearden to fuck with Mom's head, send her a warning to quit poking around, Mafia-style. Remember the murdered hummingbird on our doorstep? Sheriff Bearden. Horace even thinks that it was Sheriff Bearden who messed with Mom's tire and that's why she wrecked her car. It's impossible to prove, but that's what he says, and I believe him. Besides, the night Mom died, she drove off because she saw Sheriff Bearden sneaking around the house. That's what she was trying to end. She saw him hightail it to his car, and she wanted to track him down herself and make him own up to it."

Yeah, that sounded like Mom. I could see her hopping in the car, going after him when she had the chance, whether or not Horace said it was a good idea. She would have chased Sheriff Bearden to the ends of the earth if he'd pissed her off bad enough.

"The first chance I got, I was gonna bust Horace out and grab you and make a run for it, but then I saw you and Grandma sneak off to the shed, so I followed you. And the rest is fucking history. At least I hope it is."

"Was that why Mom married Horace?" I said. "Because she thought he could protect us?"

"I think so," said Murphy. "I think she thought it would help to have the law on her side for once. For what it's worth, I think he really did love her though."

I remembered sneaking around in Horace's head, trying to get him to admit he had killed Mom. He did love her, I knew that.

"It makes sense," said Murphy. "Maybe Mom was sick of Grandma's money, you know? Maybe she was tired of living off what our Uncle Jeremiah basically stole."

I can't even tell you how much I hated hearing that. I hated hearing that almost more than anything.

At first I refused to believe Murphy. I told her that Jeremiah was good, deeply and truly so, that he was probably the greatest person I'd ever known. She cocked an eyebrow up at me about that, and then she went and got all the documents from the car. I sat there in the hospital waiting room, reading every word. And I had to admit it made sense, you know? Why Mom had been the way she was, the reasons she raised us how she did. Everything came together in my mind, and it was all sad and ugly.

Sitting there in the emergency room along with all the moaning sick people, amidst the beeping, whirring, buzzing hospital sounds, the chatter of bored, angry, sad, fighting people, I couldn't help it—I bawled my eyes out. I cried for Mom, and I cried for Grandma, and I cried for Cass, and I cried for the Farm.

But mostly I cried for myself. I cried for my glorious future, the bright and shining hope of my visions. I cried because I knew I would never be great, ever.

I would never be much of anything now.

HORACE SURVIVED, JUST SO YOU KNOW. YOU'D
probably have to run him over with a tank to kill that guy. He
told his colleagues at the sheriff's office what had happened
to him, about how Murphy and I ran off after our Mom died
and he came to find us, how he got held against his will by our
grandmother and tortured and all that. But when the cops
went to investigate, they didn't find any bodies. The house
was in order, like someone had tidied it up and then left on a
trip. Grandma's and Sheriff Bearden's bodies had vanished,
the blood mopped up, the barn chained and shut, everything
all nice and squeaky clean and put away, not a sign of a cult as
far as the eye could see. They did say a family by the name of
Urquhart was squatting in the attic, saying they had a claim
to the land, that it was rightfully theirs and one day they'd
prove it. The cops asked me if I wanted those folks off the property, and I said no, to let them stay, that we'd deal with the
details later.

I could tell the people at the sheriff's department all thought Horace was nuts, even though Murphy and I confirmed his story. They asked if we wanted to go back to Benign and point out people to prosecute in person, but I said no. I think I'd die if I ever had to face those people again. I just don't think I could handle it.

One thing keeps bugging me, and I know it's selfish, but we've pretty much established that I'm a selfish person. Here it is:

When did I become the bad guy?

I mean, I meant well, didn't I, wanting to be a leader, wanting to guide the Farm into becoming something glorious? Didn't I start off right, desiring good things for people, giving everyone a purpose, putting life and hope back into their lives? Didn't I stand opposite the Urquharts and the Gentlemen and the Clock Without Hands, all the evil and corruption that had spoiled Benign, that kept it from becoming the beautiful place it was always intended to be?

Or had I just done it all for myself, really? Had I loved the attention, the adoration from Grandma and the townspeople, from Jeremiah and Cass? Had I loved having my own special purpose, being chosen from the beginning of time, plucked from the great mass of people in this world to be the bearer of visions, the prophet of the Spirit, the leader of my people?

Had it really just been about me all along, wanting to be liked, drunk on power and the affection of strangers?

Was Murphy actually the hero of the story? Same as Mom was the hero of her own tale for letting her brother die, for making the sacrifice that had so thoroughly fucked up her life?

Because let's face it, all that power had gotten to Jeremiah, changed him somehow. I can't believe he was born wrong. I mean, Mom loved him, right? At least at first? They were best friends, same as Murphy and me. And yet something had happened, something had driven them apart. Jeremiah said it was Mom's jealousy and that Murphy was the same way, but something in me doubted that. Was the Spirit corrupt in itself, something evil, or is that just the nature of power? I remembered my vision of the guy slitting his throat, and I thought there was no way I would have ever made someone do something like that.

But what about everything that happened in the toolshed with Horace? I mean, hadn't I tried to break Horace's mind, to make him into another Carl Urquhart—to make him a slave, basically? Was that really so much better?

I'd had power for all of a week, and it had already corrupted me. Maybe the power itself was corrupted because our great-grandfather stole it to begin with. Or maybe it was me who was already corrupted, ruined from the start. Maybe I'm just a bad person, always have been, and I spent my whole life waiting for a chance to show it.

Or maybe people aren't so simple as that, all good or all bad. Maybe those words are insufficient to describe how people really are, how vast and complicated and murky and strange we are in our hearts. How our purest desires become warped and twisted, and even at our best there's something busted in us that wants to rise up and destroy everything. It's like Grandma calling the Urquharts trash when they were just laid low because of what her own father had done. I can't even really think of Grandma as bad, not totally. I mean, she did love me, and she did want the world to be a better place. It's confusing.

Some prophet, right? I wasn't any visionary genius. I wasn't a leader of people. I was just a neglected kid who wanted everyone to love me. And I nearly sacrificed my own fucking sister to get it.

Do you have any idea how humiliating that is? How completely and unbearably pathetic? I'm still so ashamed of myself, most days I can barely look in the mirror.

Murphy seems mostly okay about everything. A week after we got home, she started sneaking out every night, partying again. She even invited me out with her one night. I was so excited I couldn't believe it. We wound up at a party at some senior's house, watching him and a few other guys play FIFA. The music was turned up really loud, and everyone sipped beer and kept going out back to smoke cigarettes. They all seemed to know Murphy and to like her too, though she didn't act much like she did at home. This Murphy was quieter, cooler, and more aloof, not the loud, foulmouthed girl I knew. I took a beer but didn't drink it, just let it get warm in my hands. I was so nervous, so scared I would embarrass Murphy in front of her friends. But they were pretty nice to me, all things considered. I mean, to be honest, none of them seemed to care that much that I was there. Still, I kept looking around, watching all the kids my age or older, seeing them lean against walls and look disinterested, probably texting each other even though they were in the same room. I just kept thinking, *Is this it? Is this what everyone's doing all the time, that secret world of parties and friends and being cool that I've always longed for?* It was kind of a letdown, to be honest, especially after my time at the tenant house, partying with those kids. Sneaking out turned out to be pretty boring by comparison.

When we came back home, crawling in through her bedroom window, Murphy asked me if I'd had any fun.

"It meant a lot to me that you asked me," I said.

"That bad, huh?" she said. "Well, thanks for coming with me anyhow."

She punched me in the arm, and then I went off to my own room. It did mean a lot that she had invited me out, truly, but I probably won't ever go again.

Murphy's changed in other ways too. She's been painting. Not my visions or anything like that, thank god. Her own stuff, landscapes mostly, and they're pretty damn good. She has this thing for houses at night, streetlights, with no people visible at all. They're mysteries, her paintings, like wrapped presents that no one will ever open. They scare me a little bit.

We still live with Horace, though he quit the sheriff's office and we had to move into a smaller place. I think he was forced to resign, his whole crazy story of being locked up by his dead wife's vanished mother a little bit too much for anyone to believe. Horace is running a private security firm now, and you can tell he absolutely hates the shit out of it. But so what? It's not like my life is peachy keen either. Mom's schooling did not even remotely prepare me for the SAT, which I have to take next week, and I'm supposed to start thinking about colleges. How the fuck am I supposed to care about college right now? I was almost an accidental cult leader, you know? College frankly seems like a waste of time after something like that.

For a while I figured Horace held it all against me, how I thought he had murdered Mom, how I nearly killed him myself. I mean, if I were him, I sure as shit would. But the other day I was sitting on the back porch, reading the collected works of Frank Stanford, a poet I found from Arkansas. He's really good. He might be one of the greats, I'm telling you.

Anyway, I was reading outside, the sunset light hitting my book so perfectly it was like the pages were glowing, like they were holy writ handed down from the mountain, and a hummingbird floated over and took a sip out of one of Mom's old feeders. I was just watching it, this little miracle, wondering if it was real or if it was a vision, when Horace walked up. He sat down across from me, and I thought I was about to get it good, that he was finally going to tell me what a piece of shit I was, how I nearly got him killed.

"Can I ask you a question?" he said.

I nodded.

"Is it too much for you to think that your mother actually loved me? That she married me because she wanted to?"

I just stared at him. I didn't know what to say.

A great sadness seemed to swallow Horace then, and it was like he deflated in front of me, like all that tough-guy bullshit faded out of him and he was just a slumped-over middle-aged man, bald and heartbroken.

"Or maybe she thought me being sheriff could protect her from your grandma," he said, "that I'd be tough enough to keep the old bitch away from y'all. Guess I failed at that. Guess I failed at just about everything. But I will tell you this, and you best believe it: I loved your mother with all of my heart. I thought she was the kindest, smartest woman I ever met in my life. I would have gladly died in her place, and that's the truth." He took a deep breath and sighed. "I also wouldn't have adopted you kids if I didn't want to be a daddy to y'all. I know I'm an asshole most of the time, but that's just what I know. If you'd ever met my father, you'd understand. He's dead now, thank god. All I'm saying is, I'll do my best if y'all will have me."

That's when Horace handed me a ratty old paperback book. It was something called *The Postman Always Rings Twice* by a guy named James M. Cain.

"Ever read this?" he said.

"No," I said, "but I've heard good things about the movie."

Horace grinned. He'd lost a tooth back at the Farm, and the gap was like a little black hole in the middle of his mouth.

"The movie's a classic, sure," he said, "but this book is even better. Cain is no fucking joke."

"Are you asking me to read this?" I said.

Horace shrugged. "If you want." And then he got up and left me alone.

Well, I did read it. And you know what? It was great. One of the best books I ever read in my life, and I mean it. I know I'm mostly a poetry guy, but I loved the sparseness of the language, all the danger and thrill and seediness of it. Frankly, I loved everything about the book. I told Horace that one night while he was cooking dinner, and he couldn't believe it.

"No kidding?" he kept saying. "You really liked it?"

"No," I said. "I *loved* it. Like, a lot."

You would have thought I'd just handed him a million bucks.

Also, Horace has been giving me cooking lessons. I'm not half bad either. I make a mean shrimp scampi. I even told him about a vision or two that I had, and he didn't talk shit to me about it. Because I'm still having those visions, let me tell you. They're worse than before, happening daily now, sometimes coming at me so fast I can't tell what's real and what isn't.

I'm still a freak. I'm still a loser with no friends. Even if I have a pretty okay stepdad, all of that shit is still true. I'm terrified of college. What if everybody hates me there as much as they hate me here? I haven't had any visions of college, thank god. But what if that means I'll die before I go to college? What if that means I don't have any future at all?

I get going like that, and it's almost too much. It's like I'm falling down a well and there's no bottom, and if I don't reach out and grab the rope with the bucket on it, I'm just going to tumble forever. Sometimes I hate my visions and I hate my brain and I hate all of it so much I want to gouge my own eyes out. But then I'm afraid that I'd have the visions all the time, just in my mind, and there wouldn't be any reality left to distract me. I barely even know what to do with myself. I miss Mom, and I miss Grandma, and I miss Cass, and I miss our old life before Horace, before the Farm, before all of it.

But I haven't even told you the worst part. I haven't told anyone. You have to promise you won't tell anyone either.

Sometimes, late at night, when everyone in the house is asleep but me, I think about the Farm. I think about the vision I had where I was the leader of everybody, where I was famous and rich and happy, where Cass loved me, where I maybe married her and had a bunch of kids, where I spoke at every Gathering and everyone thought I was the greatest, where I had the voice of a prophet, where every vision I had was received by a multitude as a miracle, a gift straight from God, or something like God.

And just for a moment, I wish it had all happened that way.

I wish Murphy had run out on me, just taken Horace and bailed and not stopped to get me too. I wish she'd grabbed him and the Trans Am and hightailed it to brighter pastures, never giving a thought to me again. I wish I had been left the leader of a congregation, the prophet of the Farm, on TV every weekend, broadcast worldwide, streamed a million times on the internet.

Maybe I wouldn't have been like Jeremiah, you know? Maybe I could have done it right and the power wouldn't have gone to my head, the Spirit wouldn't have infected me like it did him, turning him rotten to the core. Maybe I could have used my visions to help people, not rob them. Maybe I could have been the real prophet, the one to actually bring light to the world.

Because the fact is, I'm pretty sure the sacrifice worked. I spilled Grandma's blood. And I hear the voice of the Spirit at night, whispering things in my ear, telling me what is possible for me, that all of these things can be my reality anytime I choose. Sometimes I catch glimpses when I'm talking to people—the teller at the bank, the lady in line in front of me at the grocery store, Horace, even Murphy—and I see into their lives, and I feel the pull of the Spirit guiding me, telling me exactly what to say to get everything I want from them, what would make them love me and follow me forever.

I think maybe I could go back to the Farm again, do it right this time. And it makes me miss Grandma so bad I can't stand it. I miss the way she loved me and how great she thought I was. I miss Cass and what it felt like to have a whole crew of people want me around. I miss having a grand purpose, knowing I'm part of something bigger than myself, and I want it back again. I want the Farm. I want everything.

Those nights are the worst, nightmares of loneliness and pain and desire and regret the likes of which I've never known before, and I'm never sure I will survive them.

But then the morning comes, and it's like I can breathe again, and I'm okay.

The morning always comes, damn it. And I get to hear Murphy sneak in through her bedroom window like nobody has noticed she's been out all night. I get to listen to Horace slump through the house, each thunderous footfall rattling the pictures on the walls, until he gets to whistling and cooking up his patented jalapeño eggs Benedict for breakfast. I get to remember that I had a mom who loved me, and a grandmother too, even if she was kind of a psycho. I get to remember everything I had and everything I lost. I get to remember that I have a gift, even if I have to keep it quiet, have to keep it in check. I get to remember that there's poetry and there are books and that somewhere out there in the world, there might be a place for me, there might be other people who are like me, who like the same things I like, who will accept me for who I am without any Spirit compelling them to. I haven't found that place yet, but I know it must be out there somewhere. It just has to be. And that's something, I tell you.

It really is something.

ACKNOWLEDGMENTS

I would like to express my love and gratitude for the following people: Mom, Dad, Chris, Jess Regel, Maggie Lehrman, Emily Daluga, Jaya Miceli, Megan Abbott, William Boyle, Jack Pendarvis, Liam Baranauskas, Good Idea Club, Tom Franklin, Len Clark, Mary Marge Locker, P.S. Dean, Phil McCausland, Will Stephenson, and Michael Bible. Thanks be to God. And thank you.

JIMMY CAJOLEAS grew up in Jackson, Mississippi. He spent years traveling the country and playing music before earning his MFA from the University of Mississippi. His debut YA novel, *The Good Demon*, received three starred reviews, from *Booklist, Publishers Weekly,* and *Kirkus Reviews,* which called it "eerie and compelling." He lives in Brooklyn, New York.